Dancing in the rain

caroline Easton

CONTENTS

Chapter 1	1
Chapter 2	21
Chapter 3	39
Chapter 4	59
Chapter 5	77
Chapter 6	97
Chapter 7	113
Chapter 8	127
Chapter 9	141
Chapter 10	155
Chapter 11	165
Chapter 12	179
Chapter 13	193
Chapter 14	207
Chapter 15	221
Chapter 16	239
Chapter 17	259
Chapter 18	273
Chapter 19	295
Epilogue	313
Acknowledgments	331
About the Author	333
Books by Caroline Easton	335

Copyright © 2013 by Caroline Easton
All rights reserved. Published in the United Kingdom.

No part of this book may be used or reproduced in any form or by any means electronic or mechanical, including photocopying, recording or by any information storage and retrieval systems, without prior written permission of the author except where permitted by law.

The characters and events portrayed in this book are fictitious. Any similarity to real persons, living or dead is coincidental and not intended by the author.

Cover Design by J C Clarke, The Graphics Shed
Editing by LH Editing Services.

Chapter one

"How many times, you lazy bitch! Are you completely stupid, or do you just like making me look like an idiot?" Dave Ryan clenched his jaw in anger, his eyes wide open in rage as he shouted at his wife. His hands were clenched into tight fists, balled at this sides and ready to use.

Jane Ryan was not the stereotypical image of a woman you'd expect to be scared of her husband. She wasn't little or waif like, nor was she tall or large framed. Maybe she was carrying a little extra baby weight still but nothing major. She was your typical girl next door; a little over five feet seven and of average build. In fact everything about her was average, from her mousy brown hair to the tip of toes, her peers had made sure she'd known that from a very early age. Growing up in a suburb of Leeds, West Yorkshire, a place where people didn't mince their words, Jane knew her limitations. When her teachers had informed her parents that she was aiming too high with her career aspirations, Jane had simply given up trying. Instead settling for passable exam results which would lead her nowhere specific. The women in her family didn't grow up with aspirations of going to University or having a career, they merely got a job to pay the bills. It was a of way life. Not the best but not the worst. Jane had followed suit; a job that helped to pay the bills and a small but adequate house not far from where her parents lived. No need to spread her wings too far, now was there? Nobody would have guessed the life she led was less than perfect.

Yet here she was backed up into the corner, with her hands held up in defence against her husband. Racking her brains, she desperately tried to think what it could possibly be that she had done to trigger his anger this time. Fear fogged her brain, making it hard to make sense of her thoughts. And then it hit her. The washing. It was still hanging on the washing line as the rain battered down upon it. All of her husband's clothes were dripping wet through and would need to be washed again. That would be Jane's job, but of course that wasn't the issue, as far as the enraged man who now stood nose to nose with the woman he referred to as his wife was concerned. She'd disobeyed him; let him down; failed at being a housewife once more. He was livid, and his whole body shook with anger, so much so that Jane could feel little droplets of his saliva on her face as he furiously spat out his words. She turned her head slightly to avoid the feeling of his hot breath on her face.

She knew there was no point in answering him back or defending her actions, whatever she said it wouldn't make any difference. It didn't matter that she'd been cleaning the rest of the house to his exacting standards and had ensured the rest of the washing was loaded into the machine. If anything, making excuses would enrage him further so she knew it was best just to keep quiet. Over the last few months she'd learnt to take the rough with the smooth. She just needed to distance herself from him when he was like this and block out the angry outburst.

As the door slammed shut, Jane stood still for what seemed like ages; listening intently for any sign of him coming back. A creaking floorboard or the sound of him breathing. She'd fallen for that trick once before, never again. He'd pretended to leave the house following a previous fight, it was only when Jane dared to venture from where he'd left her cowering that she walked straight into him, well straight into his fist, as he waited to pounce outside the kitchen door. No, she needed to know he'd definitely left the house this time before she'd dare to move again.

The crying from upstairs jolted Jane back to the

here and now. The reality being that Freya, her baby girl, was awake and needed her. That she could do, taking care of her daughter was something she knew she was good at. Nobody was going to take that away from her. The housewife stuff would come, whatever it took to perfect that side of her marriage, she'd do it.

Collecting her daughter from her bedroom where she'd been napping for the morning, Jane prepared lunch for her, trying to keep everything normal for the little girl. "There you go, all finished and clean. Shall we go for a walk?" Tucking Freya into her pushchair, Jane kissed the tip of her daughter's nose as they headed out of the door. The need to clear her head of all the earlier tension was strong. She was acutely aware of the injuries she'd sustained this time around, they were becoming more and more pronounced with every volatile argument. Her back was sore from landing against the doorframe as he'd slammed her against it. He had pushed her so hard, Jane had been in danger of falling all the way down the cellar steps had she not managed to turn away from the door in time, grabbing at the door frame at the last minute to steady herself. Walking helped with the pain, it allowed her to stop thinking about it. At least she could take comfort in the knowledge she wouldn't have to explain away any bruising this time.

He had only made that mistake once before, giving

her a black eye; only then he'd insisted on telling everyone that Freya had thrown a toy at her and she'd been too stupid to duck in time. Jane knew better than to disagree with him, laughing with him instead and agreeing that their daughter had a mean throwing arm for a one-year-old. Nobody had thought to question the bruising or the story he had spun. Why would they? To everyone on the periphery of their lives he was the image of a perfect husband and father. Attentive, with very clear goals on the direction their life together was heading. To everyone else, family life was Dave's *thing*.

The couple had met at high school where he'd been the typically mainstream student; popular and a little cocky. He'd been good at sports and generally had a small harem of girls who were more than willing to jump if he asked them to. Jane, on the other hand, was the polar opposite; quiet and insular, keeping to herself most of the time. Dave had singled her out as a bit of a challenge, making sure he took care of her right from the very beginning, always including her in everything he did. He made her feel like her opinion mattered, that she was indeed worthwhile. She'd never expected someone like him, good looking and one of the most popular boys in her year, to even notice she existed. Not only had he noticed her but he'd made her feel special and beautiful, when she hadn't really fit in at school. She had never been popular or one to spend time with the 'in' crowd so to speak. Instead she spent most of her time either alone reading, or with the handful of friends she'd made Being with Dave put paid to all that. The young couple had been inseparable from more or less the very start of their relationship, the transition from friends to dating had come quickly. It hadn't been long before just hanging out together outside school turned into them spending every evening and weekend together. They'd make trips into Leeds on a Saturday afternoon where they'd snack on chips as they walked around the city centre before heading to the cinema to see the latest release. Dave would always treat her to something small those shopping trips, it might be a pair of earrings from a market stall or a bunch of daffodils. Jane didn't care what it was, the little gestures meant so much to her, they made her heart leap around in her chest and her skin tingle with excitement. She didn't need big, overblown acts of affection, the little things were what made her feel loved. Dave's friends became a joint circle of friends which suited Jane fine, after all she really didn't need anyone else.

When they left school and got jobs, buying their first house together had been the obvious next step. Jane loved having their own place, it was only small with two bedrooms and an attic room upstairs, which was now Freya's, but it was home and it was theirs.

They spent months renovating the place, redecorating all the rooms, choosing paint together. They were always refusing the constant offers of help from Dave's father, Thomas. The couple wanted this to be their home, to be able to make it their own, Dave wanted to make it perfect for them, he'd said. He would always steer Jane in the right direction when it came to choosing the furnishings, if it had been up to her, the whole house would have been drowning in pink fluffy cushions and overly sparkly accents. Instead it was beautifully decorated in muted colours with nicely co-ordinating accessories, nothing flashy or over the top. The house was comfortable in nature and appearance. He was much better at co-ordinating stuff than she was, his ideas always seemed to work better. Thinking back, Jane realised that's when it all had started, the controlling behaviour should have been the first red flag, but she hadn't really noticed when or just quite how the balance of power had shifted between them. Well, not at first anyway. It had been a slow but steady twisted journey.

Hindsight is such a wonderful thing and looking back Jane could *now* see where things had perhaps begun to change for the worse. Sitting watching TV one evening Dave said, "Why don't we get rid of your car? We don't need two really." The comments came right out of the blue and Jane was stunned into silence as she tried to process what he was saying. "I can take you to work and back." He shrugged his shoulder nonchalantly. "We could use the money for a holiday then." It seemed like a sensible plan at first. Jane did only use it for work, never really driving it at any other time. If they went anywhere together as a family Dave always drove. He liked his car better, anyway Jane knew she wasn't the best driver in the world. The few times she had driven him it had always ended in a row, he would constantly point out how she didn't plan ahead, or judge the road properly. He fiddled with the controls making the car too hot then too cold, changing radio stations constantly when he knew it irritated her. It was easier, calmer even, if she just let him drive everywhere.

Trying not to portray the shock she felt at his suggestion, Jane reluctantly agreed. "I suppose it makes sense, it'd save us a bit of money too, not running two cars." He seemed to appreciate that Jane had given in gracefully but in reality, she just didn't want the arguments that came with driving or mentioning the fact that she actually liked having her own car; it wasn't worth the hassle.

A hopeful Dave carried on, "Paul at work wants a run-around for his daughter; shall I ask him if he wants it then?"

Jane nodded vaguely, "You could do, I mean if he

needs a car and we're definitely selling mine?" The car was the only thing that was truly hers, she'd saved up for months to buy it while learning to drive, she'd be sad to see it go but she knew Dave only had their best interests at heart. The money would be useful too. "The money would come in handy, I guess…"

And there went her independence two days later. Driven away down the quiet, tree lined lane she lived on by some bloke Dave worked with. As Jane's car disappeared down the street, Dave turned and ushered her inside.

Trying not to appear too sullen Jane turned to Dave and asked, "Have you spoken to your dad, can we use the caravan next week? The money from the car should be enough for us to have a really nice week away," Jane asked, now a touch giddy at the thought of taking Freya to the beach. A little family holiday might just be the antidote they needed. Dave was always more relaxed and easier to be around when he had a few days off work. The stress obviously aggravated his anger issues.

"Are you fucking insane? There's no way we can afford that. How far do you think a hundred quid goes? Anyway I need that cash for some things for the bike," he snapped. Instantly dismissing Jane's idea of a family holiday by the sea.

Somewhat taken aback by his cruel words, Jane

continued. "Well if there's any left over, Freya could use some new clothes. She's getting huge now, growing out of everything." Jane smiled at her husband trying to make light of the situation, no point in worrying about a week in the caravan. Her father-in-law would make sure they got to go later in the year as usual; it was his *gift* to them once a year.

Dave chuckled, somewhat sinisterly before whispering in Jane's ear, "There won't be." Then turned and walked out the door, a large wad of cash in his back pocket.

Jane unlocked the back gate at her parent's house. She hadn't really intended to walk that far. In fact she never usually visited her Mum and Dad after an argument, there was always the worry that she might let something slip; open her big mouth and cause even more hassle. Freya was also fast asleep again in the pushchair. Jane gazed adoringly at her little girl, if she'd got one thing right, if was her baby girl. She was perfect, from the mop of blonde curls to the tip of her tiny toes. Oh well, Jane thought, chance for a cuppa and a natter while her beautiful daughter snoozed.

"Hiya, it's just me. Shall I stick the kettle on?" Her parent's never locked the door to their end terrace house, despite being burgled three times. Would they never learn? The area they lived in had really gone to pot in the last few years. The streets were lined with rubbish and graffiti, with small groups of youths from the local school gathering on every corner. The truancy officer was a regular visitor to her parent's street these days as he rounded up hordes of errant kids. "Dad out, is he?"

"It's Saturday, is the pope Catholic? That pub must have magical powers." Jane's mother, Elaine, chortled. "He'll be back in an hour anyway. Where's my beautiful granddaughter, come here, you." The grey haired, slightly rounded, woman lifted Freya from the pushchair as the toddler struggled to open her eyes. The sleepy daze was soon replaced with glee when Freya realised where she was.

"So much for a quiet cuppa then, eh?" Jane tutted jokingly. Elaine smiled sheepishly as she carried her granddaughter into the front room.

Elaine eyed her daughter worryingly, taking in the dark circles beneath Jane's eyes and her drawn complexion. "You look tired. Everything okay?" Jane hadn't told her mum about how difficult things were. She didn't know where to start; *Jane* didn't understand it, so how on earth could she begin to explain it to anyone else? Jane didn't want the older couple to worry about her, she was an adult now and she'd manage her situation on her own. Anyway, Jane was sure things would calm down soon. Dave's job at the factory was showing signs of being a bit more secure now so there wouldn't be as much stress at home. Things had got worse since his firm had been taken over last year, nobody knew where they stood with the new bosses, quite a few of them had already been given their cards and Jane knew how worried Dave had been, he saw it as his job to provide a roof over their heads and put food in the fridge; he had old fashioned values in that respect.

Jane smiled reassuringly, "Everything's fine, Mum. This one's still not sleeping through the night. She was up at four-thirty this morning, again!" Elaine wasn't listening; she was too busy playing on the floor with Freya. She doted on her first grandchild like you wouldn't believe. Freya was never left alone to entertain herself for a second. Why would she need to when her grandmother would happily play all day long? Jane's parents were a huge support for their daughter, insisting on looking after their grandchild when Jane had gone back to work, Elaine had made her opinion known when the couple had suggested putting her in childcare instead. The result was that Freya adored her grandma.

As she finished her cup of tea and glanced at her watch, Jane gasped, "Oh no, look at the time. I'd better be off, Mum. Dave will be back soon and I haven't even thought about dinner yet." Leaning in, Jane kissed her mum on the cheek before gathering Freya up and bundling her back into the pushchair.

"Well that was a flying visit, you've only just finished your drink. Did you walk down here? Didn't you come in the car?" Elaine looked puzzled, knowing just how much her daughter hated to walk so far with the pushchair.

Jane fussed over Freya, tucking her into the pushchair as she avoided making eye contact with Elaine. "Yeah, didn't I tell you that we sold my car? There wasn't any point in us having two when I only use mine for work. Dave sold it to someone at work; we didn't get much for it though, only about a hundred. At least we won't have the running costs of it though now."

The disbelief showed on her mum's face. "That doesn't seem a lot. I thought it wasn't very old, your car?" Elaine wasn't very good with cars, not being a driver she had no idea; she just knew Jane's was blue. To be fair, Jane hadn't really understood how much cars can depreciate in value so quickly until Dave had explained, apparently Jane's wasn't very desirable either, nobody wanted a blue car that hadn't really been looked after all that well, even though it wasn't that old. Dave had assured her he got the best price he could for it.

Jane laughed at her mother's limited knowledge. "That's all old, small cars are worth at the minute."

"Well, there's a bus due in five minutes, you'll be home in no time." Elaine crumpled her brow, the hurt showing instantly at her daughter making fun of her, Jane suddenly felt guilty. The last thing she wanted to do was upset her mother.

Jane cringed. "I don't think I have enough cash on me, I didn't really intend on a visit today so I didn't bring any money." She dismissed the idea quickly. "We'll walk, it's easier with the pushchair anyway." Not that there was ever any money in the house these days. Dave always seemed to need the small change that was found lying around *and* anything she had left in her purse at the end of the week too for that matter. He blamed the coffee machine at the factory for short changing him constantly.

"Don't be daft; you can't walk in this rain, it's pouring down out there. Here, take this." Elaine shoved some money into Jane's jeans pocket. "I know how much you hate the rain. You and Freya will be drenched by the time you've walked home." She kissed both her daughter and Freya. "See you tomorrow, love."

Jane dashed out of the door and down the garden

path, if she was quick she could just make it in time to catch the bus. After a fifteen minute, bouncy journey along familiar streets, the bus pulled up to the stop and Jane struggled to get off with Freya tucked under one arm and the pushchair under the other. "Come on, sweetie, let's get you home and fed, out of this awful rain, eh?"

Freya giggled at her mum, grinning away. "Teatime," she sang out loudly.

As she pushed open the front door with her backside, Jane overbalanced in the hallway and almost fell sideways into the lounge.

Dave stood, walking the short distance across the room towards his wife and child. "Where have you been?" Was the first thing he said, letting her know he had beaten her home.

Not allowing any eye contact with her husband, Jane fussed over her daughter, unzipping her coat and placing it over the back of the armchair. The familiar feelings of dread began to swirl around her stomach. The anger hung heavy in the atmosphere, Jane knew this could escalate quickly if she didn't handle the situation properly. "We ended up at Grandma's, didn't we, Freya? We went out for a walk when you went left, she was a little unsettled, and I thought the fresh air would do her good."

"Did you walk home?" he growled angrily at Jane, his eyes widening with every breath.

"Nah, we jumped on the bus back, wanted to get dinner sorted for us and get Freya bathed." Her mouth had dried up causing her lips to almost stick to her teeth as she spoke. Again, Jane tried to damp down the fear that gripped her.

"Where did you get the bus fare from? Where's the bus ticket?" Dave quizzed his wife with the quick fire questions.

Jane tried to remain calm and upbeat, not allowing her pounding heart to give her away. "Oh, Mum insisted on giving me the fare when she saw how bad the weather was. It made sense so I could get back in time to feed Freya, think I must have dropped the ticket getting off the bus, and we wanted to get home to see Daddy, didn't we Freya?"

With a quick surge forwards, Dave pushed Jane with such force that she bounced off the wall, which in turn propelled her forwards again, ensuring she landed sprawled across the pushchair. Dave gripped his wife by the arms, pulling her upright. "I want the ticket when you use the bus in future, do you understand?" he hissed in her ear.

Jane tried to release herself from his grip as she pulled backwards. "Okay…" She stammered. She knew he liked her to tell him where she was going when she went out, but he wasn't usually this bad when she visited her parents. She regularly dropped in on them and it hadn't been an issue up until now. Quite why it had changed suddenly, Jane didn't know.

"Things are gonna change around here. Dad thinks I'm too soft for my own good." Too stunned to respond, Jane kept quiet and scooped Freya into her arms for a cuddle but Dave grabbed for the infant. "Give her here, you can make dinner, I'll bath her and get her ready for bed." Dave loved his daughter to bits, worshipped her even. He believed that having kids was the best thing he had ever done and couldn't wait to have more. He made sure he told anyone who would listen. Knowing better than to argue, Jane reluctantly handed over their daughter and headed into the kitchen. At least he'd have time to calm down while she cooked tea.

As she stood blankly staring into a pot of chicken curry, watching it bubble as she stirred, she began to wonder how things had got this bad. Was it wrong that she'd gone out without telling him? She couldn't really remember when it stopped being the occasional argument and started being something else. To make matters worse she didn't know how to stop it escalating. She tried to stick to the rules; never went anywhere without asking his permission; never spent any money unless he knew about it first. The fridge was always well-stocked with all the food he liked, just as he requested—she even made sure she bought the right brand of beer for him but still it wasn't enough. He still got angry. Jane still made him angry.

And each time she paid the price for her so called stupidity.

Dave looked over his wife's shoulder. "What you making me to eat then?" he asked as she stirred the pan on the hob. The tone of his voice remained even, not an ounce of the anger he'd shown earlier broke through.

She continued to absentmindedly push the chicken around in the sauce. "Chicken curry, okay? It's nearly ready." Jane smiled warily at him. She wanted to put some distance between them but if she flinched it would enrage him again. So to keep the peace she stood stock still.

Dave turned his nose up. "Don't fancy that, it stinks. Makes the whole house stink too, why don't you cook that sausage?" he muttered, peering into the fridge now.

It wasn't a question.

Trying to cover the anger she felt towards him, Jane smiled a little too sweetly in Dave's direction. "Erm...okay, I can put this in the freezer for another night this week. It'll be about half an hour then. That okay?" He had already gone back to playing with Freya and was no longer interested in the food or anything else she had to say. Jane let out a long breath, praying the worst was over for today. She just had to get through dinner and get Freya off to bed, then all she needed to do was focus on watching the clock tick towards a reasonable hour, when she could make her excuses and disappear off to bed.

Chapter two

Dave dangled the car keys in front of Jane, his face expressionless.

"Here, you take the car. I'll go to work on my bike today. It makes more sense when you've gotta drop her at your mother's."

"Are you sure? I could walk if you want. It's just twenty minutes to Mum's and then ten minutes from there. I don't mind." Dave glared at her with wide eyes as his lip curled into a snarl. The familiar feeling of fear welled up inside Jane's stomach, the butterflies seemed to be trying to tie her intestines in knots. She had no idea why she'd even opened her mouth, what she should have done was just smile and take the keys from him. That would have been the sensible, rule-following thing to do.

Dave leaned in closer as he spoke "Is that what you think of me? That I'd let my daughter walk, in all weathers, to your mother's? Take the fucking car and stop arguing with me. Do you like to wind me up?" his spit hit Jane's cheek; he was so close to her face as he ground out his words.

Jane busied herself putting Freya's coat on and making sure she had her bag all packed. She didn't dare look at him. "No, no not at all. I just thought it's much further for you to get to work, that's all."

Dave threw the keys at his wife without even a backward glance. He kissed Freya, grinning at her. "See you later, Pookey, Daddy loves you." The door clicked shut as he left for work. Finally Jane and her gorgeous baby girl were alone and the calm that ensued whenever he left the house was a welcome relief. The peace she felt whenever it was just her and her baby was the kind of feeling she craved permanently. Sadly, she knew it wouldn't last. Glancing up at the clock on the wall, Jane considered calling in sick at work just so she could spend the day at home with Freya. The worry of what effect this whole domestic situation was having on her daughter weighed heavy on her mind. She knew the shouting and all the angst wasn't good for the sweet little girl, a toddler shouldn't witness her parents being angry with each other.

Forty minutes later Jane had dropped Freya off at her parents and was turning into the car park at work. Tiredness overwhelmed her, the sleepless nights and early mornings, not to mention the stress of walking on egg shells all the time, were really taking their toll on the young working mum. Staring in the rear view mirror, Jane ran her fingertips over the dark circles that surrounded her eyes. Her skin was starting to sallow too she realised as she peered even closer at the reflection. She turned the engine off and leaned forward to rest her head on the steering wheel but seconds later she almost leapt out of her skin at the banging on the window.

Her best friend and colleague, Lindsey was grinning at her through the car window. "Come on, sleepyhead!" Lindsey Barkley was the life and sole of everyone's party. Invited or not. Her bubbly personality rubbed off on all around her. Her big green eyes sparkled when she laughed. You couldn't help but smile when she near.

Jane unclipped her seatbelt as she laughed heartily and climbed out to join Lindsey. "Just you wait until you've got kids! I'm going to laugh my backside off when it's you looking knackered and old." She playfully shoved her hysterical friend in the arm, knocking her off balance ever so slightly.

The mere mention of kids caused Lindsey's eyes to cloud with fear. "Not happening anytime soon, that I can promise you. Come on, it's my turn to make the tea." The two girls had become best friends, almost as soon as Lindsey had come to work in the office and began sharing a workstation. They did nothing but giggle and sing along to the radio for most of the day. Lindsey made the day go much faster, even making the boring, mundane work seem like fun. Lindsey was the younger of the two but only by a few months and had just got married a few months ago. Jane envied her easy-going nature; the tall, slender, flame haired girl never worried about anything, she was rock solid in her own skin. Everyone that came into contact with her was instantly a little in awe of her. She was in command of any room the moment she entered it. It was a trait that Jane was a little jealous of; self-confidence was not her forte.

Their arms linked and laughing at each other's quirky nature, they waltzed through the doors ready to tackle the working day.

As she finished off her morning cuppa, Lindsey turned to Jane. "So, how do you fancy a day Christmas shopping, not next Saturday but the one after then? Sam's away for the weekend and I thought we could hit town early and make a whole day of it. We could have a nice lunch with a few cocktails too, what do you think?"

Lindsey had been going on for weeks about how much fun it would be, to do all of their shopping together, getting everything done in one day. Jane still hadn't had managed to work up the nerve to mention it to Dave. She wasn't sure how he would feel about it, although things had been a lot better over the last few months. There hadn't been as many occasions when he'd physically hurt her. He still flew off the handle at the slightest thing, but Jane hadn't suffered any bruises for a good few weeks now. It seemed like her husband was really trying to rein his temper in lately. She pondered the idea of broaching the subject later that night, perhaps now might be a good time to test the water.

"Oh sorry, I completely forgot about that. I'll mention it to Dave tonight; see if he can take care of Freya that day. Is that okay?" Jane didn't want to sound too hopeful but she really could do with a girly day shopping with Lindsey. A little escapism might be nice.

"Yeah, course it is, bet your mum would have her anyway. Oh, I saw these really cute pyjamas for her the other day. I'm going to wrap them up for her, to go with her Christmas present." Lindsey was always buying things for Jane's daughter, and for Jane for that matter. Although the presents she bought Jane weren't usually as cute as Freya's. The last she'd bought her had been a book all about Elvis, last week, and she could not contain her giggles as Jane peeked inside the bag.

Jane had laughed, actually she kind of snorted back at her. Not quite sure why she was receiving the joke present. "Is this payback for something horrible that I did to you?" She lifted the book up to exam it closer.

Lindsey looked hurt, after the number of times she'd suffered through the same CD Jane insisted on playing. "NO! You love Elvis; that CD is always on in your car."

Guilt flooded through Jane, the last thing she wanted to do was offend her friend. Listening to and enjoying someone's music was one thing but a whole book on them, well that was a different ball game. Yes, Jane liked the music but a book on him, really?

"It's great, thank you. Just what I always wanted. Really it is!" Jane grinned as Lindsey looked a little less offended by her original comment.

Later that night, the conversation about the shopping trip went much better than Jane had dared to hope it would. "I think it's a great idea, you could do with a bit of time to yourself," Dave agreed. "You're always at work or with Freya, then there's all the housework you do. Yeah, don't see why we can't sort something out."

Taken aback slightly, Jane wanted to make certain he wasn't going to change his mind at the last minute. "You're sure you don't mind? I don't have to go, we can do the shopping together if you prefer?" Dave dismissed her concerns with a quick shake of his head as he went back to watching the TV.

Dave promised to ring her parents to ask them to look after Freya for the morning as he would be at work and knew he couldn't take the day off. He would collect her after work and spend the afternoon with her while Jane was out with Lindsey. He actually seemed relieved that he wouldn't have to get involved in the present buying this year. *See*, Jane thought to herself *I can do this marriage thing*. If she could ease the pressure on him just a little, she hoped it might make life easier for both of them. Who knows, she may even have a little fun on the day too.

Jane slept really well for the first time in weeks that night, secure in her thoughts that things were finally on the mend. Maybe they had finally turned the proverbially corner, and there would be no more bruises or marks to hide.

As they walked up to the huge glass fronted store, Lindsey turned to her friend. "Right, Jane, this is a really posh store. When we go through the door, do not touch anything!" Giggling and flicking her long titian coloured hair over her shoulder, Lindsey watched the doorman pull open the heavy door that led into Harvey Nicholls, allowing the girls to enter.

Jane was a little upset by the comment but knew

her friend was only joking. "You cheeky devil! I'm not three, you know. I can walk through a department store without causing a disaster." Jane pushed Lindsey through the door first just in case, though.

"Yeah, yeah, that wasn't you then that knocked the coffee pot over in the café? Oh, and what happened to that small child who got hit in the head with your bag, was that his fault he got too close? You can be a nightmare! I don't know about you but I cannot afford to replace some of the stuff in here, so just be careful." Jane stood open mouthed, a little upset by her friend's comments, Jane admitted to being a little accident prone at times but it wasn't so bad.

Jane pouted a little as she called after her friend. "Shall I just go home now then? I mean, if I'm such an embarrassment to be around, that is."

With a contrite look on her face, Lindsey held out her hand to her friend. "I was joking! What's happened to your sense of humour lately? C'mon, let's shop 'til we drop."

Jane scurried to catch up with her shopping partner. "Can we go to the men's bit first? I want to see if I can get something for Dave today. What are you getting Sam?"

Lindsey's face filled with glee, her eyes widened as she spoke. "We're not doing the present thing this year; Sam's booked us a mini-break instead. We're off to

Venice on the sixth of January for a long weekend." Lindsey was obviously very excited about the holiday.

The prospect gave Jane food for thought; maybe she could suggest something on a much smaller scale to Dave, maybe a night in a B&B at the coast would be more in their reach. "You lucky thing! Has he got a brother? He's always whisking you off somewhere or other." It wasn't jealousy, well not really, but Jane was envious of the easy going nature of her friend's marriage. They didn't seem to have to work at it, everything always seemed to fit into place for them. They seemed so in love and it was obvious that Sam worshipped her friend. All the fleeting glances that passed between them, the constant hand holding and little kisses were all the things Jane yearned for.

The lift door opened onto the men's accessories department and Lindsey was off on a mission to help her friend find the perfect present for her husband—regardless of the cost. Watches and cufflinks were all on show in shiny, immaculate glass cases. Racks of ties and other clothing hung neatly in colour co-ordinated rows. Jane didn't know where to start, it all felt overwhelming. Perhaps this wasn't the right place to shop for Dave's Christmas gift after all. She couldn't picture him in anything she'd seen on display here. He wasn't a designer clothes kind of person, instead he preferred his regular fit jeans from a chain store, paired with an equally generic shirt. Nothing that made him stand out from the crowd or drew attention to him. Dave didn't see the point of wasting silly money on something he could get from twenty quid elsewhere.

"Here, why don't you try this on?" Lindsey held aloft a beautiful teal coloured sleeveless wrap dress. "This colour would look fabulous on you."

Jane adored the dress but there was no way she was trying it on, firstly she couldn't afford it and secondly that would mean exposing the healing bruises on her arms. They were obviously hand print marks which meant Lindsey would ask questions Jane wasn't sure she was ready to answer. Things at home had settled down again leaving Jane hopeful that there'd be no further marks to explain. "Nah, I think it's more you. Sam would pop a vein if he saw you in that." Jane turned to find the changing rooms. "Go on, I'll wait here." Lindsey didn't need asking twice.

Exhausted and many shopping bags later the girls sat in a very swanky restaurant, it was beautifully decorated in tasteful black and gold, very art deco in feel. The ambient lighting created a more intimate dining experience meaning that the tables were mostly occupied with couples enjoying leisurely lunches or girlfriends who'd popped in for a mid-shop cocktail sitting at the bar. Lindsey fit right in as she sat confident flipping her hair over her shoulder as she looked around the room, but Jane felt a little bit uncomfortable. She and Dave rarely went out to eat, and if they *did* it was more of a bar meal occasion; somewhere they could take Freya and go without getting dressed up. This place was on another level entirely.

Lindsey perused the drinks menu. "Shall we just order a bottle of wine then, or do you want a cocktail?" Jane's ladies-who-lunch mentor muttered from behind the very extensive drinks menu.

"I don't know. I don't really drink that much, do I? You pick, I'll just have whatever you end up having." To be truthful Jane didn't have a clue, the cheap bottle of wine she was used to from the corner shop probably wasn't on the menu here. One glance at the price list told her that. She wasn't sure what the difference was between the house white and the next bottle on the menu, apart from the price tag.

Lindsey addressed the very handsome waiter who stood beside their table dressed in all black, Jane was certain he'd winked at Lindsey as he spoke which only served to make Jane feel more uncomfortable. "We'll have two mojitos please, and I'll have the sea bass. Thanks." Pen poised at his pad, he turned his attention towards Jane, with a twitch of his head he asked, "And for you, madam?"

Jane had no idea what half the things listed before her were or if she'd like them. It wasn't the burger and chips menu she was used to. The room seemed hotter as she ran her finger along the list of pasta dishes. She could feel the waiter becoming impatient, not to mention the heat of Lindsey's eyes boring into her from across the table. Dave always ordered the food when they were out, she wasn't even sure how to pronounce half of the menu. "Erm.... yeah can I have the....erm....the linguine, please?" Jane shoved the menu towards the waiter and quickly busied herself looking through the bags of shopping they'd accumulated so far, trying to avoid any further decisions which would need to be made about her lunch order.

As her gaze settled on the watch she'd selected especially for Dave, panic crept in. She really hoped he liked it; she'd just wanted to spoil him a bit this year. They'd both been making a really big effort recently, and slowly Jane was beginning to remember all the things about him, that she'd fallen in love with. His ability to make her laugh for one thing, the little lopsided grin, which he saved just for her when nobody was looking. The way his eyes lit up when he told her how beautiful she had looked on their wedding day, two years ago, still made her heart skip a beat or two. If they could rescue all those feelings, then she was positive they could come out of the other side smiling.

As they stood outside in the rapidly decreasing temperature Lindsey struggled with her bags. The air was filled with the smell of roasting chestnuts from the vendors scattered around the city centre. The Christmas lights lit up the dusk filled evening, spreading a soft glow along the street. "Right, are you calling Dave to pick us up, or shall I ring Sam? He should be back now." She busily shoved smaller bags into the larger ones, to make it easier to carry her huge haul.

"I tell you what, I'll ring Dave and you can have a coffee at mine before Sam comes to get you. Would you mind taking Dave's present home with you, he'll only end up rooting through the bags and find it if I take it home today?" Jane didn't want him to discover his gift, she wanted to wrap it up with some nice fancy paper and stick it under the tree, but being the big kid he was, she knew he couldn't wait for Christmas; he was like a child when it came to secrets.

It was dark when Lindsey finally got around to calling her husband to come and pick her up. The girls had the best day shopping, and had managed to get all the gifts that they'd set off to buy for their family and friends. Jane had only Lindsey's gift left to buy and she knew exactly what she was going to get; the beautiful silk scarf she'd seeing her admiring in Harvey Nicks earlier, she'd just need to nip back into town to pick it up. Dave and Jane stood at the door, and waved as Lindsey climbed into Sam's car. With his arm casually strung around Jane's shoulders, Dave laughed at Sam trying to get his car out of its very tight parking space. The neighbours had obviously not been happy that he had left it outside their house, not leaving enough space for them to get out. After three attempts he got out, throwing the keys to Lindsey to drive; who, with one quick motion, and missing the neighbour's car by a hair's breadth, was out into the road and waving back at her friends before they shut the door and went inside.

Dave pulled his wife in towards his chest and planted a kiss on her forehead. "Looks like you had fun today. You should try and arrange something again soon, just the two of you. Me and Freya had a great time today, it was nice just being the two of us, she loved the park. Kept running back to the biggest slide. God, it frightens me, just how fearless she is. She's definitely your daughter." He cupped her cheek in his palm and smiled. "I like seeing you happy. You look lovely today. Shall I make us something to eat, or are you still stuffed from your posh luncheon date?"

Jane smiled broadly. "It was definitely posh, I felt a little out of place but it was nice. The food was lovely but all the shopping has given me an appetite." Together they ventured into the kitchen, still joined together by Dave's arm.

Half an hour later Freya was fast asleep and they

were tucked up together on the sofa, glass of wine in hand and the stereo on. They had spent a lot of time talking recently, well Dave had, and Jane mainly listened. Work was going well for him, the changes all seemed to have settled down leaving him feeling more stable, and there was even talk of him applying for a supervisor's role in the near future. Jane too was happier at work now. Having struggled leaving Freya when her maternity leave had finished, her baby had seemed so little and of course she felt nobody would look after her properly. It didn't matter that she was leaving her child with her parents for just five hours a day; Jane had still wanted to be the one to look after her full time. Money was tight though, and the mortgage wouldn't pay itself, so having altered her hours to part time she'd reluctantly gone back to work. They were doing alright financially. They would never be rich but they got by each month.

Dave confided in her, telling her that he didn't want to be like his dad, who had made life difficult for his mum because money was in short supply when he was growing up. He confessed he just got frustrated when it appeared nobody was listening to him, or people didn't do as he asked. Jane knew he was referring to her and the situation they'd found themselves in recently. He begged her to see that if, she could just stick to the ground rules he was certain they would be okay, that they could make it through whatever had thrown them off course and get back to the happy go lucky couple they used to be. He swore he didn't mean to upset Jane, that he loved her dearly, and he didn't want her to be frightened of him at all.

He also, for the first time, told Jane all about the day his mother threw his dad out.

"I was seven when my dad left. I remember coming home from school and finding Dad sat on the front lawn with my brother and sister, Dad pulled me down into his lap and told me he was leaving. I thought he meant on a work trip at first, I didn't really understand, I never noticed the suitcases behind him." Dave ran his hands over his face, trying to rub away the anguish. "He kept talking about someone called Rita, and that she was going to let him live with her now." Shaking his head, Dave struggled as he tried to continue. It came to light that Thomas, Dave's father had been having an affair with Rita for years before he left Dave's mum. They were married now and seemed happy enough, but that didn't make up for the cheating. "He told us that our mum didn't love him anymore, so he had to go, no other explanation or reasoning. I remember telling him that I loved him, so that didn't matter, he could stay and we'd be happy again. My dad just shook his head, said he couldn't do that." Dave's eyes glassed over with unshed tears causing him to blink wildly as he tried to clear them.

Dave reached out to grasp Jane's hand. "My dad's old school; a quick slap now again was how you kept your wife in line in those days. Friday and Saturdays, down the pub with your mates, the rest of the week screwing the different women he met on the long haul HGV trips that made up his working week. I'm not like him, I don't want to be like my dad. I want to be a better husband to you than he was to my mum."

Marie, Dave's mum, told a very different version of events. She'd been the victim, losing a baby at the hands of her husband. She'd been five months pregnant, when a very drunken Thomas had lunged at her and pushed her down the stairs. That had been the deciding factor for her. Marie had seen a lawyer as soon as she had been discharged from the hospital. Her family had been with her the day she gave Thomas the good news and finally sent him packing.

Rita had turned out to be The One, she wouldn't hear a bad word said against Thomas. He had been the victim in her eyes, and had never had the love of a good woman to keep him on the straight and narrow. They had married as soon as his divorce came through. Dave's brother Mike had refused to speak to him since that day on the lawn, but Dave and his sister, Julie kept in regular contact with them. As far as Jane knew, Thomas had never laid a finger on Rita.

Jane placed her hand on Dave's arm and squeezed gently. "I'm not your mum and you're not your dad, I'm pretty sure we can work this out. If you want to try, we can. We have to keep moving forward, that's all. Things have been better recently, haven't they?"

Dave swiped his fingertips under his eye and along his cheek as he nodded. "Can we really try? I mean, actually both put the extra effort in and make this work again, for Freya's sake?"

"Of course, that's all I want, and not just for Freya, for us. I want to make you happy. We can do that, I'm sure we can." For the first time in what felt like ages, Jane seemed to be able to breathe a little easier again.

Chapter three

Jane loved Christmas, it always made her excitable, but this one was special, Freya understood what was happening this year. Her excited little squeals as they dressed the tree warmed Jane's soul. The fairy lights hanging from the mantle sparkled, holding the little girls attention as she helped to carefully place all the ornaments. Freya giddily awaited Santa's arrival, as much as Jane anticipated Dave's reaction to his gift. Sitting around the tree early on Christmas morning, they watched their daughter jump in excitement at the sight of the mountain of gifts that awaited her. The shrieks of glee filled the house with each present Freya opened, the wrapping paper being ripped hastily to reveal the toys inside. To Jane's delight, Dave loved the new watch, she'd lovingly picked out for him—it wasn't anything too expensive, but more than she would normally spend on him. It had taken a lot of persuading on Lindsey's behalf for Jane to buy the watch but after seeing his reaction, she was over the moon with her choice.

Of course, Dave complained that she'd spent too much. He said it made what he described as 'the few bits he'd bought' her look like meagre offerings in comparison. For a moment the knotted stomach and sweaty palms, along with the familiar feeling of fear, crept in as Jane waited for him to fly off the handle at her overly lavish gift. When it didn't happen, the relief was immense. Dave had bought Jane a beautiful, blue beaded bracelet from Freya, which she adored and couldn't stop gazing at.

With a cheeky grin, Dave made a little confession. "I didn't get you a gift yet, sorry."

Her shoulders slumped as Jane tried to hide the disappointment from her face. "Oh I don't need any presents, I have everything I need right here." The smile spread across her face as she looked up at her husband.

Dave's little plan had worked, Jane believed he hadn't got her anything. "I said I didn't have anything *yet*. That's because I thought we could go to the car dealership tomorrow and look at upgrading the car?"

Jane's eyes sparkled, the skin around them wrinkled a little as her smile broadened. "Really? Can we afford it?"

"I've saved up a little money and we can trade the old one in. I thought we could get something you'd like to drive a bit more?"

The excitement built inside Jane, causing her breathing to quicken, "So it'll be for me to drive?"

Dave leaned in and kissed her forehead. "Well, during the week, yes. You can use it for work." Not only was he going to allow Jane to drive it, but he revealed he was registering the new one in Jane's name; it would technically be *her* car. He insisted it made more sense, as she was the one who would drive it each weekday. Dave planned to use his bike on good days, or his friend could pick him up if the weather was too bad. Buying the car together had been a new experience, Jane wasn't used to being asked her opinion on things like a new car. Big decisions were normally left to Dave to make. Jane had been so excited when he let her narrow the choice down to two cars.

Dave studied the two cars Jane kept coming back to, a white Ford and a silver Vauxhall. "That means then, that you like either of these, yeah?"

Jane wanted to do a little happy dance, he'd actually listened to her and taken her needs into consideration. "Yes, neither are too big for me, I feel comfortable in them both. The Ford's cheaper though."

It didn't matter to her that Dave made the final decision, or that he chose the Vauxhall, it made more sense that he chose, as he had a better understanding of what they needed as a family. Even so, Jane felt like they'd made a massive step forward because he'd let her bring it down to the final choices.

She loved the new car, it made her feel as though he really did understand how she'd felt over the last few months. She felt like they'd had a grown up discussion, weighing up the pros and cons of both vehicles. She was happy in the knowledge that he was trying really hard with this fresh, new start.

The Christmas holidays meant a full two weeks off work for both Dave and Jane. It was an old Leeds tradition that a lot of the older companies closed for the full duration, giving their staff a much needed rest. The time at home had been surprisingly relaxing, not the usual running around spending every waking minute visiting distant relatives like most other years. Their parents graciously accepted that they were a family now and Freya wanted to spend time with her mummy and daddy, never mind all the new toys that Santa had delivered.

The second gift Dave had kept a secret from his wife was that he'd arranged a night away for them. After much secret planning with Jane's parents they were ready to drop one very over-excited toddler off with her grandparents. In a few more minutes they would be free to enjoy their first night out together in a very long time. They didn't have to pick Freya up until the following day and to say Jane was a little apprehensive was an understatement. They'd never left her overnight so this was a huge step for all involved. But, with a few gentle words of persuasion they were child free and heading off to enjoy the night.

An hour later, Dave guided the car into the car park of the Rainsmere Hotel and restaurant.

Jane's heart began to race, her cheeks flushed with excitement as she took in the large Gothic style building with its Gargoyles sitting proudly on each corner, guarding their kingdom. "Oh my God! I can't believe you brought me back here! I love this place, thank you." She leaned over and kissed him as she bounced giddily in her seat.

Dave seemed nervous, almost shy as he spoke his next words. "I tried to book us a room too but they were full, sorry, we can come back again and stay for a long weekend if you like? We can bring Freya too, if you like."

Jane sat and stared at the lovely old building and its overly ornate windows and its meticulously manicure grounds. "That'd be lovely, you know I love it here, thank you so much, this is perfect." It was the place Dave had booked them in to with his very first wage years ago. She could remember every single detail of that night; how she'd felt like a grown up for the first time ever, dressed up in her favourite dress and heels. They had talked often about coming back, but had never done anything about it. The hotel wasn't too far from the east coast either, maybe twenty minutes or so at the most. That was another place they'd spent many a day out together, wandering aimlessly along the beaches or piling pennies into the slot machines, before eating fish and chips out of the paper.

Dave held his hand out for Jane to hold, "Come on then, let's go eat eh?"

The restaurant buzzed with small talk from the other diners as Jane and Dave sat opposite each other. The crisp white table cloths glowed white in the dimly lit dining room and the glassware glistened in the candle light. All through dinner they laughed at silly memories, and just enjoyed each other's company again. There were no awkward silences or strained conversation, just an easy companionship. "I don't want to go home yet," Dave sighed as they headed back to the car arm in arm.

Jane glanced up at him through her eyelashes, smiling sweetly. "Well...we don't have to just yet; you know we could go for a walk on the beach."

Dave stared at his wife as though she'd grown another head or something even more peculiar. "Are you serious? It's January in case you hadn't realised.

It'll be freezing, bloody brass monkeys in fact." He added in an over exaggerated shudder for effect.

She didn't want to go back yet either but Dave was right, it was freezing and dark. Neither of them had brought hats or scarves with them, it was a stupid idea. She tried to hide the disappointment she felt behind a bright smile. "It was just a thought, and the tide's probably in now anyway, never mind it doesn't matter. Let's go home." Jane wrapped her arms around herself, trying to trap in a little warmth.

"No, you're right, come on; the coats are in the car. I'll buy you a coffee from that little café you like, the one that never shuts and your feet stick to the floor." He laughed loudly, clutching Jane's hand tightly as he broke into a sprint dragging her along behind him towards the parked car. Euphoria filled Jane, it'd been a long time since she felt this happy. Not since the early days of their relationship had she felt this giddy. They were acting like a pair of loved up teenagers on a first date, and that was blissful.

They arrived home a little after one in the morning, they were tired but happy. Their cheeks ached from all the laughing they had done. Jane couldn't remember the last time they'd had so much fun together.

Dave wrapped his arms around his wife's waist tightly, pulling her in closer to him. "Thanks for tonight, Jane. I really enjoyed it. I know it's going to take time, but I'm going to fix us, I promise. It might not be all plain sailing but I *will* try."

Jane slid her hands up around his neck, drawing him in for a kiss. "I know and thank you. I had fun too, now come on, let's go to bed." She felt him grin against her mouth.

"Now I like the sound of that!" Jane giggled as he slapped her backside, as she shot off out of the room, heading upstairs to their bedroom.

After strapping Freya into the car seat on Monday afternoon, Jane climbed into the driver's seat. It had been nearly three months since Dave's last outburst and they had even managed a few more nights out together, quiz night at the local pub had been a good night. Their life together seemed to be on more of an even keel these days. Both of them were actually looking forward to coming home from work again, however, Jane made sure she continued to stick to the little rules. Dinner on the table, Freya ready for bed. That sort of stuff helped to make the days easier for Dave. They had worked out a nice safe routine together and as long as she didn't deviate from it too much, they were good.

Jane had been home an hour when Dave walked through the front door. "Hi, where's my little Pookey?" Freya ran to her daddy as he took his work boots off, arms held high begging him to pick her up. He swung her round and around in the air while she giggled uncontrollably.

"She'll be sick! She's just eaten," Jane warned him to no avail, they were now rolling on the floor having a tickle fight. It filled Jane's heart with joy watching him with their daughter. The delight he brought to their little girl's life was precious beyond words.

With his face screwed up tight, Dave almost gagged as the stench wafted up from his daughter's behind. "Oh my God! I think someone needs a nappy change. Come on, stinky, let's sort you out."

Jane reached down to pick up Freya's changing bag, handing it to Dave. "If you're okay with this, I'll just go finish our dinner off. It's just about ready," Jane made a move to head off into the kitchen. "Lasagne okay?" She yelled back over her shoulder.

Once his daughter was all cleaned up, Dave made his way down the hall towards the kitchen and his wife. "I love your lasagne. What time you heading out with Lindsey tonight? Do you need me to run you into town, or is Sam taking you both?" Dave asked as he slipped his arm around his wife's shoulder and stole a piece of garlic bread.

Jane slapped his hand away and laughed, "Hungry are we? Lindsey's picking me up at seven-thirty, if that's okay? Sam has to meet his brother in Leeds anyway, and then Lindsey is staying here tonight, so we'll grab a taxi home. Shouldn't be too late, I don't think." It was the works night out, they happened at least once month, but this was the first time Jane had joined them. In the three years she had worked there, she hadn't socialised with them once. There'd always been somewhere to go with Dave, or she'd been too busy. Then she fell pregnant and subsequently Freya had come along. Lindsey had been begging for the last six months, *at least*, for Jane to go with her; apparently they would have a great night with everyone. Work nights out had a reputation for getting messy; Jane knew this from all the canteen gossip that usually followed on a Monday lunchtime. She had every intention of distancing herself from any shenanigans at all costs.

After making sure that Freya had eaten enough and that there wasn't anything stuck to the walls, Jane began to clear away the dishes into the dishwasher.

As he moved up behind her, Dave grabbed the plate from Jane's hand, ushering her out of the kitchen. "Right, shower now, or you won't be ready when she gets here. I will tidy up when I get this little lump of trouble settled into bed." Dave scooped Freya out of the highchair and headed off upstairs but not before planting a big, noisy, wet kiss on Jane's cheek, making their daughter laugh hysterically.

The nerves kicked in as Jane began getting ready; putting on nice clothes and make-up wasn't the norm for her. It was something she only did when Dave was with her. There wasn't any need for 'that muck' he'd tell her if she suggested wearing a little make up on a daily basis. He assured her she looked great without any assistance from fancy clothes and lipstick.

Popping his head around the door frame, Dave checked to see if she was nearly ready. "Lindsey will be here in a minute, you look nice."

Jane took a second look in the mirror, checking out her reflection for the hundredth time. Was the black dress too short? Was it too low in the front? Her head swam with all the indecision. "I don't know, maybe I should just cancel, stay home with you instead?" Jane questioned.

Dave chuckled and shook his head, "You'll have fun and you look amazing, that dress is perfect for you. Stop worrying and go enjoy yourself." He moved closer towards Jane, "Freya's going to bed, I've got a couple of beers in the fridge chilling and I'm going to watch the footy. You'll only be bored if you stay home with us."

As she checked out her reflection one more time,

she gave the hem of her dress one final tug downwards, Jane turned and kissed him. "I love you,"

Dave kissed her back. "I know, love you too."

Of course Dave had been right, he always was. Jane had a brilliant night laughing with all the other members of staff from her department, people she didn't really associate with at work, but now she realised that most of them were pretty easy-going. Lindsey took care of her all evening, hardly leaving Jane's side for more than a few seconds at a time. She dealt with ordering at the bar, because she knew how much Jane hated to be the centre of attention. Or maybe she just realised they'd be waiting hours as Jane wouldn't push her way to the front, meaning they would have longer to wait for their next drink. Which wasn't an option, as far as Lindsey was concerned. After dancing the night away with her colleagues, Jane's feet were sore as they stood in the taxi rank waiting for the next cab to roll up and take them home.

"Sshh! It's late, don't wake them up." Lindsey was drunk and doing the whole, louder-than-talking whisper thing.

Jane handed her a glass of water and two painkillers. "Here, take these and perhaps you'll get away with only a mild hangover, instead of a raging one, in four hours when Freya wakes us both up."

It was two in the morning and her child was an

early riser, they'd be lucky if they managed three hours sleep before Freya was up and ready for the day. Jane had spent the last couple of hours of their night out trying to convince Lindsey to leave, but she'd kept insisting on one more dance or one more drink, then she wanted to say good night to Dennis or Mark or whatever his name was from accounts. But Lindsey was right, they'd had a really good night. Her feet may hurt from dancing and her face may be sore from all the laughing they'd had done but she'd had fun.

Jane was beyond tired, as she crept into the bedroom and slid under the covers trying not to wake Dave. He turned over sleepily and threw his arm across her stomach pulling her in close to his body. Jane entwined her fingers with his, holding his hand as he slept. She closed her eyes and drifted off to sleep snuggled in safely, with her husband cuddled up behind her.

No sooner had Jane fallen asleep than she was been awaken by her own little ray of sunshine. "Mummy! Mummy! Morning time." Freya's little fingers lifted up Jane's reluctant eyelids. The little girl loved the freedom her new 'big girl's' bed gave her. Jane, however wasn't convinced.

As she glanced at her watch on the bedside table, Jane groaned as the numbers indicated six-thirty, a lie-in as far as her little bundle of joy was concerned. She didn't care it was Saturday and her mummy didn't have to go to work, Freya just wanted to get up.

Jane rolled over to find the bed next to her empty and cold. Dave must have already left for work. Saturdays were part of his normal working week, but at least he would be back at lunchtime, giving the family the rest of the weekend together. Given the headache Jane was now acutely aware of, she doubted very much if anything could persuade her to move from the sofa for the rest of the day.

She clambered from the bed and waited for the room to stop its rotation before she risked standing up and pushing her feet into the slippers that awaited her. "Come on, you, let's go make Auntie Lindsey a nice cup of tea. You want some cereal?"

Freya threw her arms and legs around her mum allowing her to be carried her downstairs. "Hungry tummy."

Jane had just settled her daughter into her highchair, cereal in front of her, and flicked on the kettle, when Lindsey appeared at the kitchen door looking less than pretty.

Lindsey winced at the light from the window. Jane smirked at the sight of her friends screwed up face. "Oh my God, you look like I feel. Do want tea or coffee, Mrs Caine?"

Lindsey muttered "Tea, please." As she dropped

onto the chair next to Freya. Holding her head in her hands.

Jane set a hot cup of tea in front of her friend; Lindsey dropped her head to the table and groaned.

As she cradled her tea in her hands, Lindsey turned her attention to Freya. "Do you not know that this time should not exist at the weekend, Freya?" She teased the little girl, lifting her head a fraction as she tickled the child's little foot, which was sticking out from underneath her highchair tray.

"Auntie Linny, you funny!" Freya said, chuckling as she stuffed more milk and coco pops into her mouth.

"Sam's going to pick me up at eleven, if that's okay with you?" Lindsey spoke as she watched Jane move around the kitchen.

"Yeah sure. Dave won't be back until lunchtime anyway."

The two young women spent the next hour sitting eating bacon sandwiches that Jane had made them and drinking lots of tea as they chatted amiably. "So, who's that fella you were all over last night, Linds? I think he thought all his birthdays had come at once, when you were shimmying up and down his leg!"

Lindsey almost choked on her breakfast. "God, Jane, you make it sound way worse than it was. I was just messing about, having fun, letting my hair down. You remember that, don't you?" she scoffed at Jane and then cringed. "Sorry, I didn't mean that. Mouth's in action, but my brain's still not functioning yet, you know how grumpy I am when I am tired," she instantly added, after seeing the look of horror on her friend's face.

She was right though, Jane thought, she had forgotten how to enjoy herself of late. Life had just kind of taken over. Growing up, she didn't have a life plan, or anything like that. Jane had been content to see where life led her, she wasn't a go-getting but more of a wait-and-see kind of girl. She'd always been content to follow the crowd. Her Saturday job, in a local fashion boutique, had led to her first full time job. After years of working in the boutique, Jane decided it wasn't for her anymore, and had landed her current job without too much trouble, working in the call centre of the large retail company, where she had met Lindsey.

Lindsey tried to justify her previous comment, albeit not very well. "You tell me all these stories, about how much fun you used to have on nights out with your mates when you were sixteen. Sneaking into bars with fake ID, getting chatted up. I guess getting married and having Freya really made a difference." Lindsey pondered over her coffee cup. "You know, you can still be you, and have a little fun now again; it's not a crime to have a life outside of this house and your marriage. It doesn't have to be all doom and gloom. All work and no play makes Jane a dull girl you know." She glanced over at Jane, pulling her eyebrows into a frown. "Dave doesn't mind you having a night out with me, does he? God, you need some time to yourself too...lecture over. Sorry, honey." Lindsey pushed her chair away from the table, stood up and hugged her friend tightly from behind. "Can I grab first dibs on the shower?" She laughed, as she ran up the stairs. Leaving Jane to ponder over that little pep talk she was sure Lindsey had just given her.

The urge to tell her best friend everything was strong, even though Jane felt they were over the nightmare now and coming out the other side, maybe Lindsey would be a bit more understanding of why Jane was reluctant to *let her hair down* too much. Maybe talking it over with Lindsey would help Jane to make sense of it all? But then if Dave ever found out she'd let slip the things that had happened he would never forgive her. He was trying so hard now, she didn't want to jeopardise his efforts, their relationship was back on track and moving in the right direction. Why would she rock the boat now?

"Don't take me for a fucking idiot! What time did you get in? It was after midnight, you really expect me to believe that you didn't *do* anything?" The hand around Jane's arm grew tighter still, his other hand, fiercely gripped her cheeks and squeezed. A cold sweat broke across Jane's forehead, her stomach rolled as it tried to push its contents back up and out. She pulled in air through her nostrils in a vain attempt to quell the nausea. Her eyelids blinked rapidly as Jane tried to stop the tears from falling. Her spine hurt from being pushed against the wall in the bedroom, his face so close to hers she could feel his breath hitting her cheek. "The lads from work were in that dive of a club you decided to go to last night too; you didn't factor *that* into your little plans, did you? I've heard all about your little antics last night."

The words stuttered up her throat and out of Jane's mouth quietly. "Honestly, it wasn't me. Lindsey was dancing with some guy from work, but I wasn't doing anything wrong. I was just dancing with the rest of them, that's all." With one swift movement Dave brought her head forward with his hand, and slammed it back into the wall, for a second time. It hurt like hell, the sharp pain flew through her head and neck, causing Jane's stomach to flip and send a wave of nausea up through her body.

A look of mania broke across Dave's face. "Try again, darlin'. Greg saw you both, all over the guy; he even showed me the photo he took on his phone, for

Christ sake. Do you have any idea how humiliating it was, having to listen to him go on and on about how you knew how to have a good time?"

Bang. Jane's head thumped against the wall again.

Jane tried to fight the dizziness that was beginning to overpower her. "Dave, please listen to me. I wasn't doing anything, just dancing. I had a few too many to drink and was having fun. I talked to Lindsey, this morning about that man, I told her she was being too friendly. I dragged her into the taxi and we came home. We just got a little drunk, that's all." Jane was aware of his grip loosening on her face now; allowing herself to think the worst was over, and placing her hands on his arms she tried to straighten up. He pushed her hands away swiftly as though they were poison, and he turned his back on her as she continued to plead with him, "It was just a night out, we were drunk, yes. But I didn't do anything wrong, don't be mad." Reaching out, Jane tentatively put a hand on his arm again.

Dave growled a guttural sound that seemed to emanate from deep inside. "I am way beyond mad and don't you dare fucking touch me!" He swung around with his hand balled into a tight fist, landing a solid punch in Jane's ribs. Her legs gave way underneath her; she slid to the floor in what felt like slow motion clutching her side. The breath rushed out of her lungs and she gasped to fill them again as stars danced before her eyes, clouding her vision.

Dave walked out of the room and slammed the door behind him, when she heard the sound of the TV downstairs, Jane finally gave in to the tears.

Chapter four

"What's the matter, love?" Jane's Dad sounded concerned, as he watched his daughter wince in pain, while reaching into the top cupboard for teabags. It was a week since the last fight and her ribs still hurt when she stretched. The bruising was now a glorious green and yellow in colour, another couple of days and she was sure it would begin to fade.

Jane smiled broadly, trying to make light of the pain she was suffering. "Nothing, I'm fine, just this new exercise DVD I'm doing. I didn't realise how unfit I am." The sound of forced laughter left Jane's mouth. "The woman is a sadist, but I keep thinking of the end goal!" It was getting easier and easier to lie to them. They had no reason to suspect anything was wrong with their daughter's marriage; Dave made sure that he didn't let anyone see his temper, only Jane was privy to that. The bruising never visible or too severe. He always made a big effort to ensure he was overly affectionate whenever Jane's parent's where around, making sure he portrayed a perfect family unit at all times.

The sound of her father tutting filled the air. "God, if it's that bad, don't do it! You look fine anyway, love. You're just like your mum, and I wouldn't have her any other way, sweetheart."

Jane smiled at him. Her parents had a great relationship, the kind of marriage she had once hoped to have. Jane couldn't remember a single incident during her childhood where she'd ever seen her dad lose his temper with her mum—sure they'd had cross words, but never anything more than that. Jane's dad had worked during the day and her mum had gone out to clean at the local doctor's surgery on a night, when he returned. This meant there was always one parent at home to take care of her, she wasn't farmed out to family or friends for them to look after. There had never been a lot of money around but Jane had been surrounded by love and affection. Her father worshipped her mother and she looked after him in return. In Jane's eyes they had the perfect marriage, they laughed together and had fun together. It would break their hearts if their daughter told them her marriage was less than happy. That's all they had wanted for Jane since she was little, to be happy no matter what choices she made in life. Her parents were firm believers that marriage was for life, you had to work at your problems and come out the other side better for it. If only it were that simple. If only working at it made it all better.

Jane watched fondly as her father played with Freya at the table; she was making him cups of tea with the new tea set they had bought her.

Freya's grandfather pretended to gag on the drink she had made him. "Urgh! That's not tea, that's horrible!"

"Grandpa, I make another one for you." She started again with her little ritual, pretending to put milk and sugar in the cups. Her grandfather gagged again, Freya giggled once more, at him. "You make it, Grandpa." She handed him the teapot and a new cup.

A loud snort of laughter came from the doorway. Jane's mum was back from the shop. Elaine teased her granddaughter. "Grandpa can't make tea, sweetie, he doesn't know where the kettle is, or how it works. That applies to the vacuum, too. Well, most of the appliances actually." Leaning over she kissed Jane's dad on the forehead and he slipped his arm around her waist and hugged her to him.

The old man winked at his granddaughter. "Now that's not true, your grandma is just better at that kind of thing than I am." He pushed himself up from the table, smiling at his wife, and went off to watch the football, leaving Freya and her Grandma to make pretend tea.

Jane knew she had to get a handle on this marriage thing. If only for her little girl's sake. Later that night, Jane sat on the floor beside her daughter's bed watching her sleep. Her little chest rose and fell softly in time with her breathing, her little blonde eyelashes fluttered occasionally on her cheeks. *So peaceful.* She had been there an hour, unable to drag herself away. Dave was downstairs, watching some rubbish television programme she wasn't interested in. They'd hardly said two words to each other since the punch. It was clear that he knew he had overstepped the mark, but there had been no word of apology or begging for forgiveness; no promise of it never happening again. He had just withdrawn into himself, shutting her out completely. He'd been leaving earlier for work, and spending the evenings renovating that bloody old wreck of a bike he adored, so they didn't have to spend any real time with each other. Jane knew what they had now wasn't a marriage; they were just sharing the same house. She wanted, more than anything, to talk to him about what had happened that night. Just to hear him say he regretted it, to acknowledge that what he had done was not right. She just needed him to see that they could work through it, whatever it was that made him mad; she could help to sort it out. Make him see that his problems could be shared with her, and she would do her utmost to make it better. In Jane's mind they belonged together, and she wasn't about to run out on that. After kissing Freya again so softly on her perfect little forehead, she got up from the bedroom floor and went to find him; this had gone on long enough.

As she stood behind the living room door, Jane breathed in a steadying breath, trying to gather her nerves before she pushed the door open. "We need to sort this out, if you want to stay married to me." Where the bravado came from in that moment, she had no idea. Her hands clenched and unclenched at her sides, the nervous sign showing through her bravery giving her away yet again. Worry clouded her thoughts, what if she'd made the situation worse by confronting him? What if he leapt out of the chair and attacked her again? Jane tried to shake the doubts from her head before she continued. "I mean, I can't do... this anymore. Are you listening, Dave? Look at me, please." She was still standing in the doorway, rooted to the spot, her legs unable to carry her any further into the room. The fear of triggering his anger still lurked in the pit of her stomach.

Without turning his head Dave said "I can't look at you, I'm too ashamed." His eyes remained fixed on the stupid car programme which blared out of the box in the corner.

A strangled noise left Jane's throat in frustration. "I told you the truth. I didn't do anything wrong. I was just dancing and having a bit of fun. I would never risk what we have for some stupid bloody drunken bloke on a night out!" She managed to force the words out, her voice breaking as she tried to hold back yet more tears. God, she didn't know where they were coming from anymore. She should have looked like a prune, with the amount of crying she'd done over the last few days.

Still he didn't face her. "That's not what I meant." His voice came out in a despondent whisper. "I mean after what I did to you, I shouldn't have hit you like that, but I was just so mad." Still, his eyes were glued to the TV, he hadn't moved an inch. "You make me so fucking mad, Jane. I don't know what to do anymore. Every time I think we're going to be okay, you do something so fucking stupid and I see red." Dave turned to face her now. "I actually see red, like a mist, do you get that? How could you get it? I mean, if you did, you wouldn't give me all this shit to deal with, would you? *Would* you?" The tone of his voice had changed from despair and pessimism to one filled with emotion.

Was that a tear running down his cheek? Jane had

never seen him cry, except for when Freya was born. She knew she needed to go to him, maybe hold him and tell him it was okay, but it was far from okay. Nothing was okay right now.

With her emotions running high, Jane's voice cracked giving way to a cry. "I didn't do anything to make you mad. I am trying my hardest here to ensure I don't make you mad. I feel like I'm walking on eggshells every day, to make sure I don't make you angry. You hurt me, Dave, and this can't go on any longer. Do you see that? I had a night out with some friends from work and I came home to *you*, nothing else." Rooted to her spot in the doorway, Jane held out her arms in an almost surrender like gesture before letting them drop again and bump against her hips. "I can't live like this, we're supposed to be a team and right now I don't know what to do to make this right and I really *want* to make everything alright again. I want us to be back to normal, having fun together." Hot tears ran down Jane's face now, as her husband studied her. He rose out of the chair, and Jane lowered her gaze to the floor, not wanting to let him see how torn up she was. She tried desperately to pull herself together; she'd sworn not to cry again today.

As Dave reached her, he held out his arms only to watch Jane flinch instinctively as she stepped back.

The hands that were meant to embrace Jane,

instead reached up to run through his hair in despair. "See what I did? You're scared of me." Glassy eyes stared at Jane, imploring her to see his remorse. I don't want you to be scared, Jane. I love you, believe it or not." He pushed past her roughly and walked up the stairs, with his shoulders hunched over he looked broken.

As Jane heard the bedroom door click shut, she let out a cleansing breath, trying to calm her emotions. This was not happening; there was no way she was giving in now. Not after she's managed to pluck up courage from God knows where. She wasn't letting him walk away from her now.

Determined to make some kind of headway Jane marched up the stairs. When she opened the bedroom door Dave was sitting on the edge of the bed looking out of the window. "Can I come in?" she asked cautiously.

Dave laughed without a shred of humour. "You sure you want to risk being in here, alone with me? I saw how you reacted just now. I'm not a wife beater, you know. It was a stupid, *stupid* mistake. One that I wish I could take back." His tears flowed freely now too, his eyes red rimmed and puffy. "The lads at work had gone on and on and on all day about seeing you in that club. I laughed with them, trying to brush it off, trying to stay calm. But they wouldn't let it drop, all day long, and the more I thought about what they were saying, the angrier I got." Snot dripped from the end of his nose, he wiped it with the back of his hand before carrying on. "When I came home and you were here I just...I just, I don't know, I was angry. How could you make me feel like that? Why couldn't you just stay away from them?" he cried out.

Determined to show she wasn't afraid, Jane moved towards him. Yes he had hurt her, but she loved him and this was going to be okay. She was going to make it alright again. "I just had a night out, just *one* night out. If it upsets you, I won't go on any more of them. I just want things to go back to how we used to be. Don't you see how messed up we are?" Cautiously, she placed a hand on his arm, urging him to look up at her. "We can work this out, Dave. Please, just let's try and make this work."

He shrugged. "Would you really want to? I mean, I get that what happened is wrong, *so* wrong, but I do love you." Dave reached over and took hold of her hands, squeezing them gently. "I love you so much, you and Freya are my world. I just get so angry when I'm not in control of what's going on around me. Do you really want to try, sort this mess out?" He was almost pleading with her now.

Jane smiled and nodded in spite of the myriad tears trailing down her already damp cheeks. "Of course I want to try to fix this. I love you too. But what happened the other day, the punch, that can't happen again, you know that, right?"

He wiped his hand across his cheek and then reached out and ran his thumbs underneath Jane's eyes, to wipe her tears away. It was a tender gesture, the likes of which had been missing from their relationship for too long.

He leaned forward and rested his forehead on hers. "You know, I did something today. I looked on the internet for some anger management information. I know I have a problem and I know I have to sort this shit out. I don't ever want you to be scared of me and I don't want us to live like this anymore, but I don't know if I can do this on my own, sweetheart."

Dave's honesty hit her hard making her insides clench. *Oh my God. Is he serious? If he is, I'll back him all the way.* Of course she would. He was her husband and she loved him, despite the recent rough times.

Jane looked longingly into his eyes, desperate to make him see she still cared.

"I'll come with you. I'll ring them, see if they do a couples thing, if you want? Would you want that, would it help, if I came too?"

It was one-thirty in the afternoon and Jane sat alone, in a tiny waiting room with two other sofas, flicking through yet another magazine. They'd been lucky to get an appointment with Marriage Guidance so soon. It normally took months but they'd had a few cancellations, so here they were. Or should that be here *Jane* was. Quite where Dave was at that minute was anybody's guess. He'd only nipped to the toilet while Jane went into reception to tell them they'd arrived.. *How long does it take to go to the toilet?* The receptionist, had rung through to the counsellor once already to say that Dave was in the men's room, and Jane could tell she was getting a little het up now.

Jane gathered up her bag and coat. "I'll just go hurry him up," she mumbled as she headed in the direction of the toilet he had disappeared into fifteen minutes before. She was going to kill him, they'd been damn lucky to get this appointment. Jane had even lied to her boss about why she needed the time off and now her husband was hiding in the loo of all places.

As she rounded the corner, the door to the one and only toilet was open, and Dave was certainly not in there. *Shit, he must have got a bit spooked and gone for some fresh air.* She knew she shouldn't have left him on his own, especially considering how nervous he'd been about how this would work. *Well*, she thought, *I'll just go outside and get him and we can get on with it.* Sure, it was going to be uncomfortable talking about their relationship, but *he'd* wanted to do this after all, it was *his* idea. Jane was all in. As she stepped out onto the street, Dave was nowhere to be seen. She looked up and down the busy road, but he wasn't there and then the realisation hit her.

He'd left her there on her own. He had gone. Where, Jane had no idea but he wasn't here, that was for sure.

Reluctantly, she headed back towards the reception desk. "I'm so sorry, something's come up at home, how much do we owe you for today?" She began scrambling around in the bottom of her bag looking for her purse. She couldn't look into the eyes of the contrite young woman behind the desk. She knew she could see straight through her lie. The perfectly made up blonde knew as well as Jane did that there was no emergency at home. Dave had simply run out on her.

After paying the bill, Jane apologised yet again. "Sorry, I'll give you a ring tomorrow and arrange another appointment." With her head down, she walked out of the building and headed back to the car. At least she knew he hadn't taken it, she had the keys in her pocket.

Seven frantic, worry filled hours after Jane got home the phone finally rang. It was Dave's dad. "I'm sorry, Jane; he turned up at ours an hour ago. He said something about going out for a drink with the lads from work. Looking at him, I guess it was more than one drink. Me and Rita have put him to bed, darling. I didn't want to risk bringing him back in that state, there's no way I'm cleaning vomit out of my car for the next week." Thomas laughed, as he explained that his son was so drunk he hadn't been able to stand up alone when the taxi dropped him at their house.

Jane sighed with a mixture of relief and despondency. "Thanks, Thomas, I've been going out of my mind, he wouldn't answer his phone. Is Rita okay with him staying there? I can come and get him, if you like?" Jane knew her voice lacked the conviction of her words. She didn't want to see Dave at all. Sure, she was glad she knew where he was at least, and that he was safe, but now Jane was suddenly really angry. Her whole body ached from the worry he'd put her through and her eyes stung from all the tears she'd constantly wiped away. She'd spent the last few hours thinking that maybe he had left earlier to get a drink or something, and ended up having some horrific accident and was lying in hospital somewhere. Every possible scenario where Dave ended up dead, had run through her mind at some point as she'd sat at home waiting to hear from him. Now she knew beyond any doubt that he really *had* run out on her, and left her alone in the counsellor's waiting room to make their excuses, while he got wasted in some bar.

He was a coward.

Thomas continued, "Look, it's fine, he's out for the count, passed out cold. I'll bring him home tomorrow, when he's sober and has the world's worst hangover, no doubt. Hey, don't be too mad at him, love; everyone needs to let their hair down now and again. You have nights out without him, don't you?" Her father in law questioned "Anyway, I'll see you tomorrow, give Freya a kiss from her grandpa."

Dave didn't come home the next day. In fact, he stayed away for a week, telling his father that he thought they needed some space, time apart, because they hadn't been getting on very well lately, and that was why he had got so drunk that night. Thomas had willingly agreed to let him stay, hoping it would help sort out the 'petty fallout' he thought they were going through.

Dave called Jane every day during that week. They shouted, cried and ignored each other. He wasn't listening to her anymore. He'd said he was sorry, he couldn't face telling someone else what he'd put his wife through. He tried to explain how he just found himself in a bar, it wasn't planned, he'd gone for some fresh air to try to calm his nerves before the appointment and once he reached the door, he couldn't stop himself leaving; walking down the street and away from where Jane waited patiently, hoping to finally start piecing their life back together.

Dave poured his heart out, "It wasn't intentional, me leaving you there. I almost turned around and came back for you but my legs wouldn't do it." Jane heard him swallow hard. "When I saw the pub, I thought I'd have a quick pint and then come back...but one pint turned into another and before I knew it, it was dark outside and I was hungry."

She couldn't believe what she was hearing. Did he honestly think she'd forgive him for abandoning her? Pat him on the back and tell him it didn't matter? Well, it did matter, a whole bloody lot. "But you didn't come home though, you could have come home."

Dave groaned. "No, I couldn't. You'd have been mad, shouting at me and then who knows what I'd have done in the heat of the moment? Christ, I punched you in the ribs the last time I got mad. I didn't want to risk hurting you again, that's why I went to Dad's." The line between them went silent as she pondered over his confession. Of course he'd be worried about how he'd have reacted to her, he was trying to put things right after all. She hadn't considered that. Jane had merely thought he'd taken the easy way out and avoided coming home to face her in case he hurt her again.

Now she felt guilty. "I just thought you'd had enough of me, that you didn't want to stay married to me anymore. I even thought you were lying dead in a bloody ditch at one point. Do you realise all the pain you put me through simply because you didn't answer your phone?"

A small, humble voice drifted down the phone line. "I am sorry."

Frustrated, Jane almost shouted down the phone at her husband. "Sorry isn't going to cut it anymore now, Dave. You have to show me you want to get help, to put our marriage first now. Above everything else, I need to know you still love me." It was easy to be strong when he wasn't in the same room or even the same house. If he was here, Jane knew it wouldn't be that easy to stand up for what she wanted.

Jane pushed to make a new appointment but Dave didn't see the point, he was sure he couldn't 'wash their dirty laundry in public' as he put it. Jane was left not knowing what to do for the best. Was there anything left of their relationship to fix now? Surely the last few years hadn't been for nothing? Surely having Freya was enough of a reason to try to put things right?

Dave was convinced he had a handle on his temper now, the last blip had frightened him, made him realise he had to change how he reacted to his wife and the situations that arose. After days of soul-searching and pleading, Jane finally agreed that he could come home, that they would make a real effort to make their marriage work because they had to, for Freya's sake, didn't they?

The last thing Jane wanted was for her little girl to suffer, she didn't bring her into the world for her not to have two parents who loved her, and she knew Dave loved his daughter dearly.

He came home Saturday evening, with his dirty washing in one hand, a bottle of wine and a takeaway in the other—his idea of making things up to her. They sat together at the table in an awkward silence, neither one of them daring to look at the other, worrying about saying the wrong thing. They were polite with each other but nothing more as they each pushed the food around their plates.

The atmosphere became easier in the days that followed, slowly slipping back into their routine. After a week of insisting he slept on the couch, to give Jane some space and time to get used to him being back at home, he asked if he could share their bed again. Jane reluctantly let him move back upstairs with her, but she made sure that the minute Freya whimpered overnight, she put the little girl in bed between them. Subconsciously, Jane was making sure that the amount of time they spent alone together was as little as possible.

Chapter five

"Tell me to mind my own business if you like, but are you alright?" Lindsey asked as she ran her hand up Jane's arm. "You don't seem to be yourself lately; you seem tired and a bit withdrawn, is Freya okay?"

Jane, too preoccupied with making sure that she didn't do anything wrong in the last few weeks that she hadn't realised how quiet she'd had become. "No, there's nothing wrong, sorry, I'm fine, just a lot going on at the minute. It's nothing for me to bore you to death with," Jane said, smiling at her best friend trying to look like she was truly alright and not the mess she felt inside.

With her eyebrows pulled in, the concern showed on Lindsey's face. "Well you know you can tell me anything, right? I'll always listen. Hey, I'm pretty good at providing a shoulder to cry on, if you need one that is."

Jane wasn't sure what she wanted her to say. That

her husband had hit her so hard she regularly had to hide the bruises, that he made her feel useless? That she had just about given up trying to make him happy? No, she was certain Lindsey didn't need to hear that, Jane didn't need nor did she want to burden anyone else with her problems.

With a brisk one armed hug Jane smiled. "I don't need a shoulder to cry on, but I'll bear that in mind should I ever need one. I'm fine. Anyway, tell me all about the antics you got up to on Friday night. I heard a few tales in the canteen this morning that I'm hoping you're going to dispute madly."

Lindsey groaned but began to relay all the details of the latest works night out where she had, apparently, gotten into a drinking game with Toby, one of their work colleagues who had become a firm friend, matching him shot for shot with tequila. Jane's distraction technique had worked, Lindsey had forgotten all about her quest to gain any information from Jane.

Lindsey put her coffee cup down on the bench in front of them. "So, I ended up throwing up all of the bloody tequila I'd drunk, into a doorway outside the club with Toby holding my hair out of the way. To make matters worse, Sam turned up just as he was wiping the vomit off my face with a tissue. He wasn't happy."

The canteen door swung open and in walked Toby Parker, his body almost filling the space the door left open. His personality matched his frame, he chortled as he walked towards the girls. His chocolate brown eyes glinted in the light. "Yeah, I knew you couldn't hold your drink. That's fifty quid you owe me, lightweight! Sam needs to get a life. I was only looking after you until he got there." He tutted as he sat down next to Jane.

Jane couldn't help but grin at the huge bear of a man sitting next to her, he was larger than life and didn't give a damn what anyone thought of him.

"Is that coffee for me, Janey?" Before she could react, Toby had stolen the cup and was greedily drinking from it before handing it back to her, allowing her to take a drink. He had a nickname for everyone, it was just the way he rolled.

Jane playfully slapped his arm, "It's a good job I like you, Toby. No-one else gets away with stealing my coffee, you know."

He laughed loudly as he slung his free arm around her shoulders, kissing her cheek, as he always did these days. Not long after he'd lost his wife tragically in a car accident, Toby had relocated to Leeds and joined the company soon after Lindsey had; he was a regular on the girl's tea breaks and a frequent visitor in their section whenever he wanted to avoid the boss. He always made Jane laugh out loud whenever he was around.

Toby and Jane had developed a really good friendship, it had happened quite quickly. Something between them had just clicked, they were on the same wavelength most of the time. Although, he was a complete loon, but she had come to think the world of him. Lindsey had some weird idea that they would end up more than friends in years to come, something that Jane scoffed at. Lindsey didn't buy into the whole one partner for life, idealistic view that Jane had. Instead, she believed that God had lined up several so-called life partners for everyone and that they would come into someone's life at different times over the years, as they evolved and matured through their destiny. Jane didn't buy into this mumbo jumbo view at all. Sure, she and Toby had become good friends but that was all, besides she intended to work at her marriage so it lasted for life.

A voice came over the tannoy announcing that Toby was needed at the other end of the building. With a groan, he left the canteen cursing about how useless everyone was.

Jane nudged Lindsey's shoulder, making her spill her drink down her chin.

"So, when's the next big night out then? I think you need *me* to come along and keep an eye on you. Your husband can't complain if it's me holding your hair back whilst you puke." Jane smiled as she watched the shock wash over Lindsey's face.

Lindsey scoffed. "Seriously? You're voluntarily going to join me on a night out? Without my begging, pleading and trying to convince you what a good time you will have?"

Jane smiled. "Sure, I think I can manage the odd night out with my best friend, that's if you want me to come."

Incredulous, Lindsey squealed. "Hell, yes! They're organising one in about two weeks, I think. Cool, I like having a partner in crime and you're right, my uptight husband can't complain if I'm with you. He thinks you're a nun or something!" Giggling, they headed back to work for the afternoon. Two weeks would give Jane plenty of time to work on Dave. Although he was being so damned nice to her recently, she honestly didn't think it would be a problem.

Six months later and Jane had managed to negotiate the occasional night out with her work colleagues. They tended to be every five or six weeks, which was fine as long as it was just Lindsey and a few others that Dave knew. He had reluctantly given in to her slow, but steady persistent argument that it would be good for them; it would give them something else to talk about together, other than their daughter.

Dave clearly didn't like it though; Jane still had a list of instructions to follow. She had to stick to the same bar, be home at an agreed time *and* he preferred it if Lindsey came to their house first, so that he could be sure his wife wasn't off with someone he didn't know. He was right in the respect that Jane wasn't very streetwise; she was all too trusting of everyone and severely lacking in self-awareness. He knew Jane couldn't look after herself, she always seemed to end up in situations that she struggled to get out of.

Although most of the workmates started out together in one place at the beginning of the night, they rapidly separated off into smaller groups and Jane felt like she had some good friends now, for the first time since leaving school. She no longer felt like she was tagging along with Lindsey anymore; she was one of them. Life at home was better than it had been for a long time; the pain of being on the receiving end of a nasty left hook was thankfully a distant memory.

Dave had been going to anger management classes that he'd found on the internet, he went every Monday night, they were really helping him understand why he felt the way he did. The couple hadn't argued at all the whole time he had been attending the classes. Jane finally felt like she could breathe again. Her confidence was growing daily, she was beginning to feel more and more like her old, self as every day passed.

The lights were on when Jane got home from work, signalling that Dave had finished early. More frequently he was arriving home before her. His company had hit a rough patch and there had been yet more redundancies over the last week. He assured Jane his job was safe, but was keeping his eye on the job section in the paper every week, just to be safe. She liked him finishing early though, it meant he could collect Freya and make a start on the evening meal. He wasn't a great cook, but he was trying, and definitely improving slowly. Jane had increased her hours at work to try to bring in a little bit of extra cash, taking the pressure off him slightly. Every bit helped.

Dave looked surprised when Lindsey entered the room before his wife. "Oh hi, I didn't know you were coming over, Lindsey. Do you want some dinner?"

Jane had forgotten to tell him that Lindsey would be coming home with her for a few hours. Sam had a meeting so couldn't pick her up straight after work, he planned on picking her up in a couple of hours.

Dave looked a little put out, he did his best to make his wife's friend feel at home. They all sat at the table tucking into the curry he had heated up from the freezer, while making small talk about their day. Once they had eaten Dave put Freya to bed and stayed upstairs, giving the two women a bit of space for some *girly time*, as he put it. A short while later a car pulled up outside and the horn sounded, letting Lindsey and Jane know that Sam had arrived. Lindsey grabbed her belongings, kissed Jane on the cheek and disappeared out of the front door.

"She's gone then."

Startled, Jane jumped slightly and spun around. Jane laughed. "You scared me then, idiot! I didn't hear you come downstairs." She turned and pushed past him to make her way to the kitchen and Dave followed behind her. Her heart was still racing from being surprised as she flicked on the kettle while reaching for two cups and Dave was busy tidying the table and pushing the chairs underneath.

As she walked past him, he picked one of the chairs up, and before Jane could move out of the way, he pushed her against the wall, holding her in place with the chair legs. "Why was she here tonight?" He spat his words out venomously. "What's going on? You know I don't like anyone here during the week, or did you forget that?"

Fear gripped Jane's stomach causing it to roll and almost vomit. "Sorry...Sorry, Dave, you're scaring me, put the chair down." His face screwed into a tight ball, nostrils flaring as he glared at her. *God, this isn't good.*

She tried to reason with him. "Dave, come on! Put the chair down. I can't breathe properly. Put it down and we can talk okay?" Jane tried desperately to push back on the legs of the chair to no avail.

As he shook with anger the chair vibrated against Jane's throat. "No, you need to *listen* to me, not talk *at* me. I do *not* want to hear your whiney voice moaning in my ears again today. You need to shut the fuck up and let me speak. *She* does not come to *my* home during the week, do you understand? This is *my* house and I *do not* want her here, is that clear? I'm fucking fed up of hearing her name mentioned in my house." The words roared from his mouth.

Jane closed her eyes, trying to draw in some air to her lungs; the wooden rung that ran between the chair legs was digging into her throat, making it harder to take a full breath. She managed to nod her head just enough for him to see and he moved backwards with the chair, placing back on the floor and tucking it under the table with the others calmly as if nothing had happened. He took a deep breath and turned to face Jane again, in one swift movement his hand connected with her cheek, forcing her head to smack against the wall as a resounding crack echoed around the room. Her surroundings began to swim in front of her eyes as she tried frantically to focus on him, but all she could see was the strange black spots that danced in front of her.

He jabbed a pointed finger towards her. "You see what you did again? All the work I put into fixing things, you just fucking ruined it again." He was only a few inches away from her now, allowing her to feel his breath on her cheek. As she closed her eyes, Jane prayed that the worse was over with. He moved his mouth closer to her ear menacingly, gripping her face tightly. "I hate you for making me like this," he snarled, as he pushed Jane's head back into the wall with huge force. Shit, Jane knew this wasn't good, panic gripped her as she tried to breathe through the pain, she couldn't get her eyes to focus. Her head was pounding and she felt like she was going to throw up, all over the kitchen floor. Her thoughts went to Freya asleep upstairs, if she blacked out that would leave her daughter alone. Jane slumped down the wall, stopping only when her bottom hit the kitchen floor.

Breathe, Jane, breathe. Inhale, exhale, inhale, exhale Dave stormed out of the kitchen. The nausea began to pass as she heard the front door slam shut. Jane wasn't sure how long she sat there for, but it seemed like hours before she could manage to crawl over to the sink and pull herself up. After levering herself up, Jane turned on the tap, splashing cold water on to her face as she bent down to drink from the stream that poured from the faucet. Somehow she managed to get herself upstairs to the bedroom, crawling on her hands and knees and as she lay down on the bed, the tears began to fall while she lay listening to the rain pounding against the window. *'Bloody rain, I hate the rain, it seems like it's always raining lately.'* Jane allowed her thoughts to wash over her, hoping they'd take away the intense pain in her head. Sleep evaded her, the worry that she may not wake if Freya needed her prayed on her mind. When she heard Dave return the dread that he may come find her was overwhelming, it was only as the sun began to rise did she feel a tiny amount of relief.

It was seven-thirty the following morning. Dave had left for work and Jane sat on the bathroom floor, surrounded by shards of glass from the mirror she'd smashed with her hairbrush. She no longer wanted to see the mess that had once been her face; the reflection made her sick to the stomach. If she didn't have the mirror she couldn't see the bruises, and seeing them made what happened yesterday real. His temper was getting worse, and Jane was so ashamed that she couldn't get a handle on the new, revised set of rules that were now in place.

Phoning in sick wasn't something Jane did lightly but this was an occasion that left her no choice so once she had calmed down and splashed cold water on her sore and bruised skin she picked up the phone. "I should be fine in a few days. I think it's just that bug that's going around. I'll call you in a couple of days and let you know when I'll back. Thanks." Ending the call, Jane stared into the hallway mirror. She couldn't go to work, not until the bruises around her neck and face had gone, they were too prominent to cover with make-up. She couldn't face the questions that were bound to come as soon as she set foot through the door. Not to mention the fact that she would have to explain how she got them to her parents.

With a smile reserved only for her daughter, Jane tickled her daughter. "Looks like it's just me and you for a couple of days, kiddo, you up for spending time with mummy?" Freya didn't care where she was or who looked after her, as long as they played with her she was happy. The phone rang on and off all morning, it wasn't Dave checking his wife was okay; the caller ID informed Jane it was Lindsey, obviously worried, as she knew Jane didn't take the day off work for any old thing. In fact in the five years she had worked there, Jane could remember three times when she had taken sick leave. She didn't answer the phone, because she didn't want to lie to her but she couldn't tell Lindsey the truth either. Picking up her mobile phone, Jane sent a quick text to Lindsey informing her that she didn't need to worry, just a bout of man flu that would pass in a few days.

'Text if you need anything' was the reply that came seconds later.

Jane slid down onto the floor and carried on putting jigsaw pieces into place, while Freya whipped them out again, chuckling at how good she thought her little game was. Jane had just cleared away the lunch things when someone knocked at the door. Jane peered cautiously out through the dining room window. SHIT. Toby stood on the other side of her front door. Panic hit her, forcing her to hide behind the curtain, *shit, shit, shit.*

He knocked again and again. "Janey, it's just me, open up." The noise was relentless.

She faked a cough as she replied, "Toby, you don't want to come in here, I'll give you my germs, go back to work. I'm fine, honest."

"Just open the door, will you? I brought you some lunch, you can get the kettle on. Come on, I haven't got long," Toby replied.

It was clear he wasn't about to give up and walk away so she cracked the door open a little way and popped her head around, just enough to make eye contact with her visitor. "Hiya, look, thanks for popping over, but now's not a good time really. I feel terrible, I just want to go to bed." Quickly, she attempted to close the door again before Toby had a chance to contest.

He gasped. "Holy shit! Janey, open the door now or I'm going to force it open." He stepped closer to the door, ready to gain access, he was getting in there no matter what it took.

She tried to hide her face. "What do you mean? I told Lindsey it's just flu, go back to work," she pleaded.

"Please let me in, just for a few minutes, I want to make sure you're okay." Toby pushed on the door lightly so as not to hurt Jane, but giving him just enough space to step through the doorway. "Oh my fucking God, what happened? Have you seen a doctor?" Toby's words come out in one long rush.

Think Jane, think. Her mind raced, trying to come up with some plausible story that would satisfy him, putting an end to his questioning. "I...I erm...I was ...mugged yesterday. Outside the chippy down the road. They managed to get my bag." Jane's gaze fell to the floor, flitting everywhere but to Toby's face. If she looked him in the eyes she knew she'd break her silence.

Toby pulled Jane into a huge bear hug and just held her. "Are you okay? I mean you're obviously *not*, but you know what I mean. You're alright though, aren't you?" He held Jane away from his chest now, scrutinising her face intently, running his hands up and down her arms. "Did you ring the police? What did they say? Did anyone see what happened? God, you look like shit, Janey." He pulled out his phone. "I'm texting LJ to tell her you've been mugged, she'll kill me if I don't. I hope you're ready for her to shout at you too." He was right, Lindsey would give her hell if she found out she'd been attacked and not told her or anyone else.

Jane wiped the tears from her cheeks. "Gee, thanks, that's exactly what I need. No-one saw anything, what's the point of ringing the police? It happens all the time around here and no-one ever notices anything." She shrugged.

Astonished, Toby continued. "Are you for real?" He dialled the number as Jane tried desperately to beg him not to report the made up crime. What the hell had she done now? Ten minutes later, right on cue, Dave walked through the door, closely followed by Lindsey just as Toby finished his call to the station.

Lindsey scolded Jane's husband. "Dave, why didn't you tell me she was mugged? I'm her best friend, don't you think I would want to know?"

Dave looked over at Jane allowing her to see the ice glaze over his eyes. "You know what she's like, Lindsey, she made me promise not to tell anyone about it. Some crap about being embarrassed about it and she felt stupid." He shrugged his shoulders as he looked

Lindsey straight in the eyes. God, he was a damn good liar. "Anyway I'm here to look after her now, I told her not to go to that bloody off licence on her own, there's always loads of idiots hanging around down there on a night, but she sneaked out for a bottle of wine while I put Freya to bed. I told her I would go when Freya was settled, but no, she had to go, didn't she. How are you feeling, sweetheart?" He pulled Jane into his arms, holding her a little too tightly for comfort. She immediately sensed his anger.

Seemingly satisfied with his answer, Lindsey scolded her friend for being so stupid, "Why didn't you listen to him? I can't believe you went on your own. What were you thinking?"

Jane tried to down play the situation. "I don't know," simply shrugging as she spoke. "I thought it'd be okay."

Lindsey assured Jane it was not her fault she had been attacked, telling her she should listen to her husband more often. It was the said husband that let the two police officers in, shooting a warning glare at Jane as he did.

Jane couldn't look Dave in the eyes, preferring instead to study the pattern on the lounge carpet intently. "Toby rang them when he saw my face. Sorry, I tried to stop him, told him there was no point ringing but he wouldn't listen."

Dave nodded. "No, he's probably right, isn't he. It needs reporting, then maybe some other stupid woman won't get hurt, eh?"

Jane was relieved he was playing along for now; amazed he hadn't fobbed them off at the door with some story about calling them being a mistake.

Instead he told the P.Cs, "She's alright really, aren't you, babe? She didn't want to make a fuss, officer, but come on, I'll tell you what happened." Dave directed them to the lounge, motioning for the uniformed officers to take a seat. "Why don't you go put the kettle on, Jane, make your friends and these gentlemen a drink." He signalled for Jane to leave the room.

"Sir, why don't *you* put the kettle on instead? It's Mrs Ryan we've come to see anyway," the taller officer countered as he indicated for Jane to take a seat. "Mrs Ryan?"

Without taking his eyes off Jane, Dave informed him, "Well, she isn't really up to talking about the attack, to be honest; she gets upset if we go over it, so I can tell you what happened." The Constable wasn't taking no for an answer. "I understand that, but I need to get *Mrs Ryan* to tell me exactly what happened. Not you, now what about that tea?" He dismissed Dave along with Jane's friends, while motioning for her to sit down. Panic ran through Jane as her pulse raced, the room felt as though it was closing in on her with every second; what did she do now? Staring at the door that led to the kitchen, Jane watched as the second officer closed it firmly behind the retreating trio, leaving her alone with the taller one, who had dismissed her husband's presence.

Then in a gentle voice he said, "Now, Mrs Ryan, shall we start at the beginning?" He smiled softly at Jane while she struggled to make up a half decent story, rambling through mismatched, made up facts. The questions just kept on coming as she tried desperately not to tie herself in knots with the web of lies she'd created as a cover story for her disastrous marriage. Had she got a good look at them? Did anyone else see the attack? What time did it happen? The nightmare couldn't end soon enough. Jane sat wringing her hands in her lap as she tried frantically to keep to the same details she's initially given.

Once she had finished talking the officer slipped his notepad back in his pocket. "Well, if it happened outside the fish and chip shop we should have them in no time. The owner had CCTV put in a month or two ago, fed up of all the lads hanging around outside causing him grief. It's a really good system too, so looks like you might be in luck; makes our job a little easier. I'll go there now and seize the footage and then we can take it from there." He stared at Jane with a concerned expression waiting for her to respond, but she couldn't.

"What's wrong, Mrs Ryan? Do you want to add anything to your statement?" he asked.

"Did I, erm...It wasn't *right* outside the shop it was a...erm, it was quite a way up the street really, surely that won't be on the tapes, will it?" *Please let him say no.* Making eye contact with the officer now, Jane searched his expression looking for some kind of nonverbal answer.

He sighed and shook his head despondently. "Well I'll have a look, no harm in looking. Are you sure you don't want to tell me anything else? I mean your bruises aren't really typical of someone who has been mugged." He waited patiently again while Jane struggled to find something to say. "You know, it sometimes helps just to say it really quick." He smiled gently at the young woman before him.

With her arms folded across her chest in defence, Jane shook her head. "No. I didn't want to ring you in the first place, it was my friend's idea. I know you can't really do anything. I'll be fine, I just feel like I wasted your time, sorry I wasn't more helpful with a description and everything." She stood, indicating she was done with this charade.

After showing the police out, Lindsey hugged Jane tightly. "Oh Jane, look at you, why the hell did you not tell me?"

Jane's tears started to flow, only this time she was

crying because she'd lied to her friends. The bruises would heal, but how she was ever going to look them in the eye again, she didn't know. Perhaps she could just leave her job, then she wouldn't have to deal with them she thought, but then her job was the one thing in Jane's life that was keeping her going right now

Lindsey stood. "Well, seeing as Dave is back, we'll get off. I told the boss what happened, he isn't expecting you back till next week, honey. I'll call you tomorrow, okay?"

Jane nodded, unable to form words. She watched Lindsey and Toby head out the door, silently wishing they would stay here with her, at least for a little while longer. Maybe then it would delay the inevitable.

Chapter Six

When Jane returned to work the next week the bruising on her neck had gone. The marks on her cheeks had faded to a lovely greenish yellow colour, which she had done her best to cover with make-up. The fresh bruising around her arms were, however, covered with a long-sleeved T shirt. They'd appeared not long after her friends had left the house, following the supposed attack. It hadn't been that bad actually, just a threatening shake to make sure she knew that, yet again, she had screwed up.

Right on cue, Toby walked through the door at ten o'clock. Mug in hand, ready for a catch up. "Is that kettle on, Janey?" he asked planting the usual kiss on his friend's cheek, whilst giving Jane the obligatory one-armed hug.

With a smile, Jane flicked the kettle on. "Give me your cup, it's filthy, I'm not making you coffee in that unless it's clean." She headed over to the sink, absentmindedly pushing up her sleeves whilst the sink filled with water. As he handed Jane his cup, she saw Toby glance down at her arm. She hastily pulled the sleeve back down, covering the large bruise that was now on show. After making the drinks, she sat down next to Toby. "There you go, one cup of coffee, just how you like it." She busied herself with the paperwork she'd been working on when he had entered the room, trying to avoid his eyes and the questioning gaze that rested there.

Toby turned his attention to his coffee cup, trying to make light of the words he was about to say. "You know, you can tell me anything, Janey, and I won't say a word to anyone. I won't judge you, I'll only listen, if that's what you want," Toby stated gently as he stirred his coffee.

Jane swung her head around so quickly she felt a little dizzy. "What are you on about? T-tell you *what*?" She stuttered as she struggled to think straight.

A look of benevolence flooded Toby's face, mindful of not scaring her into a corner he continued. "I know you weren't mugged, darling, and I'm hoping we're good friends, that you trust me enough to be able to tell me the truth. I understand if you can't yet, but I need you to know that I'm here, when you can. When you find the strength, I'll be right here waiting." Jane opened her mouth to speak but he interrupted before she could say anything more. "I know you lied to me, you said it happened outside that chippy but your freaky hubby said you went to the off licence for wine. I don't get why you lied to me. I can help sort this shit out for you, if that's what you need me to do. Just tell me what you need me to do." Toby paused, giving Jane a moment to digest exactly what he was saying. "I watched my mum go through this sort of shit and I saw the tell-tale marks on your arm too. So please don't try to deny that they are there." He took a deep breath and a large drink of his now lukewarm coffee. Jane knew he was waiting for her to say something but she didn't know what *to* say. *Did he just call Dave freaky?* That surprised her. Everyone usually thought he was a great bloke, salt of the earth, great dad, no-one had ever referred to him as *freaky* before.

Toby placed something on the desk. "Here, I picked this up for you yesterday, if you don't want to talk to me, then maybe you could give them a ring and you know, they can help you. If you want them to, that is."

Jane glanced down at the card he had pushed along the desk towards her. *Leeds Women's Aid, helping to protect women and children from domestic violence*, it stated, nice and neatly. She read the card twice, just to make sure. *Oh shit, he knows, he really knows.*

She had to think fast. "Toby...I don't need..." What

didn't she need? Him? The card? The phone number? "You don't understand...honestly, it's okay. I'm okay, it's really nothing to worry about." She reached out to touch his arm but he'd stood up.

A pained look graced his chocolate brown eyes. "You're right, I don't understand. Not at all, but I do know it's not okay, darling. It's *really not okay* and I mean it, you should talk to someone, talk to me or them. I'm here for you when you're ready." He turned and headed out the door, leaving Jane clutching the small business card like her life depended on it. Her heart raced as it pushed the blood around her body. The distant noise echoed in her ears as she tried to make sense of everything Toby had said.

Jane had just about decided to go after him when Lindsey walked through the door. "What's up with Toby, he just blanked me and walked right past as though I didn't exist, you two had a lovers tiff?" she asked, half joking.

Horrified at the insinuation, Jane gasped. "Lindsey! Quit saying things like that, he's just a mate. If someone overheard you they might get the wrong idea. I don't know what's wrong with him, he wasn't very talkative with me either, perhaps it's work or something, I don't know." Jane babbled while trying to hide the card Toby had given her. She wasn't just hiding it from Lindsey, she also needed to make sure Dave didn't find it.

Lindsey stared at Jane quizzically. "Mmm, I don't think so. He's been off with me for the last week. I thought he was just missing you being at work, but now I think there's definitely something going on with him. I'll have to do my best Miss Marple impression and get to the bottom of it." She giggled to herself, before she headed off to file the papers that had been left in her tray. Jane spent the rest of the afternoon not knowing whether she should seek out Toby or bury the whole conversation in hope it would die a natural death. If she did find him, she knew she'd only fabricate more nonsense to cover up her abusive relationship. What was the point in that? It was another web of lies she didn't need to spin.

A trip to the supermarket at three o'clock in the afternoon with a grouchy, tired child was not Jane's idea of fun, but because she'd forgotten to order milk and a few other things on the internet shop that had been delivered two days ago, she didn't really have a choice. She just wanted to get home, run the bath and chill out before Dave got home from work. If she was quick, she could maybe do a bit of cleaning too, which would make for an easier night. Dave hated when the house was untidy, said he couldn't relax properly which in turn aggravated his anger issues. Jane rushed through the shopping list, which Freya was now happily chewing up, and headed back to the car.

When Dave got home three hours later his dinner was not only ready, but it was actually waiting on the table for him. The house was tidy, Freya was ready for bed and playing happily in front of the television.

He eyed Jane suspiciously. "What's going on? It's not normally this calm when I get in, you're not off out again are you?" Jane laughed lightly. "No, no I'm not going anywhere, just seemed to get everything sorted when I got in that's all. Thought it might be nice to be able to sit down together with nothing to do once she's in bed. Here, sit down and eat before it gets cold, I made your favourite for you." She sat at the table, pouring two glasses of wine and began dishing out the dinner onto his plate. They ate in silence while watching their daughter play.

Once all the dinner things were cleared away, Jane put Freya to bed and headed back down the two flights of stairs from Freya's attic room. She had just closed the door at the bottom of the second stairway, when her head was yanked back sharply, the pain shot down her neck as she cried out instinctively.

Dave growled in Jane's ear, "Where have you been?" She couldn't answer him, her voice just wouldn't work so he repeated the question more aggressively. "I said, where the fuck have you been, bitch? And don't say nowhere, I just checked the mileage on the car and you haven't just been to work and back, there's an extra five miles on the clock. Where did you go?"

Jane could feel him shaking as he spoke, the vibrations coming from him were making her already tender scalp even more sore, from where his vice-like grip held her hair.

Terror washed over her, he'd never checked the mileage before. Her eyes blinked rapidly trying to wash away the tears before they fell. "I had to get milk and a few bits on the way home. Sorry, I should have let you know this morning but I forgot, sorry...I'm really sorry, Dave." She reached up to try and release his grip on her hair but he twisted his hand more, intensifying the pain as he did.

Her apology only made Dave yank harder on her hair. "Don't fucking touch me! You're lying to me again. You stupid, stupid bitch." He refused to let go of Jane's hair. Her hands were now desperately clutching at her scalp, trying to ease the pressure, as he pulled harder down the stairs.

Jane bumped down the first few steps on her back before giving up the struggle against him. As he turned the corner, dragging her behind him, she felt an almighty pain in her back, it took her breath away instantly. Jane fought to fill her lungs with air but it took a good few gasps before she could finally breathe again.

Dave kicked open the door at the bottom of the stairs and in one smooth movement, slid Jane past him and shoved her through the doorway, into the lounge. She landed in a crumpled heap on the floor in front of the sofa. He loomed over her, pulled back his leg and kicked her in the back. Hard. Fear and nausea took over as she emptied the contents of her stomach all over the lounge carpet. He spat, "Maybe next time you won't lie to me, and you can get up and clean that fucking shit up before I get home." Without a backward glance, Dave walked out of the house, slamming the door behind him.

Three days later Dave moved out of the house and into his father's spare room again. This time his dad knew that he had hit Jane. He didn't understand why Dave was the one who had to leave though, he made it very clear he thought they were both overreacting to the situation. It was just a slap after all. According to Thomas it was nothing major and it happened in all the best marriages, apparently. The couple had talked and talked about Dave leaving for a short time, to give them both some space. He knew he was in the wrong and Jane was now too screwed up to even think for herself. So screwed up that the day he left with his father, she cried and actually begged him to stay. Dave had kissed her tenderly and promised it was just for a few days and he would ring every day so they could sort it out. The anger management counsellor Dave had been seeing agreed with Dave and said he thought it was a good idea to spend some time apart, maybe then he could reassess how he managed his outbursts and be better equipped mentally to deal with the challenges that married life presented. Jane wasn't so sure; she'd never really been on her own, let alone had to take care of a child by herself. She seriously began to worry how she would cope without him.

Dave's promised phone calls came at the same time every night, he gave Jane enough time to get Freya settled into bed, sort everything out for the next day and then they would chat on the phone for as long as they needed. The conversations had been short initially, ten minutes maximum, and very strained, consisting mainly of how Freya had been or what new things she was doing, but they had gradually turned into the epic hour-long chats that now took place nightly. They reminded Jane of how things used to be, when they were first dating. Spending hours talking or texting, forgetting everything else but what existed in their own little bubble. Jane could once again see the man that she'd fallen in love with, years ago. The funny, caring, gentle man that actually did love her deep down underneath all of the crap. The few days that Dave intended to spend at his dad's turned into weeks, and Jane was missing him.

"Hiya, how you been today? How was work?" It was the usual opening line to their nightly chats. Jane asked cheerily.

"Not good, baby, I don't feel good." Dave's voice sounded weird, not his usual jovial self, his speech was slow and very precise. It was almost as if he was having to concentrate on forming each and every word he spoke.

Jane's stomach flipped with nervous tension. The sense that something bad had happened loomed large in heart. "Dave, what's wrong?" The concern showing in Jane's voice now.

"It's nothing, just taken care of something I should have done a long time ago. I don't want you to worry anymore, everything's going to be okay now. I talked to the counsellor this morning and he knows it's my entire fault. I made sure he knows it's all my fault. He knows what I am and what I did to you. I've taken care of everything. I've taken care of it for you, Jane." His speech became more slurred as muttered out his words.

"Dave. You are seriously worrying me now, what have you taken care of, what's happened, Dave?" Panic clutched at Jane's throat, gripping hard. Her heart raced, sending her blood rushing around her body. She could hear her own heartbeat in her ears as she waited for him to answer.

"I don't deserve you or Freya. I have to sort this out. I should have walked away ages ago, but I was too much of a coward. I can't keep hurting you like this. I don't want to hurt you anymore but I can't walk away. Do you understand, I had to do this and I don't want you to worry? I left a note downstairs explaining everything and it's all going to be just fine, now." Jane could hear the drowsiness in her husband's voice. He wasn't okay, something was very wrong.

Shit! Shit! Shit! What had he done? "Talk to me, honey, what happened? Are you on your own? Where's your dad?" Terror evident in her voice, the fear seizing at her body as she tried to get him to tell her what was wrong. "Dave, please listen to me, tell me what happened." Jane shouted.

"I have to make it right, Jane. I won't hurt you anymore now. Baby, I took some pills and I'm scared, really scared. I need you and Freya, baby. I just needed to talk to you before…" *Oh my God! Oh my God, oh my God, think, Jane, think, Jane.* "Dave, I'm going to put the phone down, alright? Listen to me; I'm going to phone an ambulance, okay? It's going to be fine, darling. Just hang on for me." She heard the click of the line going dead. Fumbling with the phone, she dialled the emergency services and then his dad, sobbing, as she relayed what had just happened.

Thomas almost roared at his daughter in law. "You bitch! This is your fault; I promise, I will never forgive you if he dies." Thomas, almost screamed down the phone at her but she didn't care, she had to get to the hospital. She had to be there when he arrived, she needed him to be alright.

The twenty minute journey to the hospital felt like hours as Jane fought to drive through the tears that wouldn't stop filling her eyes. Every traffic light turned to red as she approached, slowing her down even more. She cursed each set of lights as she sat waiting for them to turn to green. The guilt that she'd driven him to this was overwhelming her now. After struggling to park the car, Jane raced through the hospital grounds in search of the A&E department. She tried to ignore the fact that her father in law was hot on heals and trying to beat her inside the building.

"Mrs Ryan? I'm the consultant on call today. I've been taking care of David this evening. Shall we sit down?" He led Jane from the waiting room into the relatives' room down the corridor. A feeling of dread hit her, they only took people to this room when they were expecting seriously bad news. *He's not going to make it. He's going to die.* The thoughts rushed around her brain as she entered the all too quiet room with

Thomas close behind her. She was sure the doctor had picked up on the thick tension between them. He'd have been stupid not to.

Jane clutched at the doctor's green scrubs. "How is he, is he alive, he isn't dead, is he? Please, tell me he's not dead!"

The doctor smiled sympathetically at Jane as he gestured for her to take a seat.

"No, Mrs Ryan, he isn't dead. We ran some bloods on him, treated him for the overdose but to be honest the toxin levels in his bloodstream weren't that high, not high enough to cause any lasting damage anyway. He's feeling a bit sorry for himself right now but you can see him in a minute."

Air rushed from Jane's lungs, her shoulders sagged in relief. "Oh thank God. Thank you, thank you so much." Tears streamed down Jane's face as she slumped in her chair, her hands now shaking uncontrollably. She was no longer aware of her father-in-law sitting beside her, glaring at her.

"This is all your fault; don't even think about going in there to see him," Thomas growled at Jane.

The doctor glared across at Dave's dad with a stare that obviously said not to mess with him. "Actually, he is asking for *you*, Mrs Ryan, he said he didn't want to see anyone else tonight. Before you go in though, I should tell you that David will have to see the psychiatrist tomorrow. We need to assess him and decide on a course of action or treatment to make sure this doesn't happen again. Does he have a history of mental illness or any other episodes of a similar nature?"

Dave's father walked out of the room and slammed the door shut behind him making Jane almost jump out of her skin. A heartbeat later she turned her attention back to the doctor. "No, no he hasn't done anything like this before. We've had a few problems recently and are separated at the minute but I'll be taking him home with me as soon as he can leave. I'll take care of him." Jane knew this was all her fault; it was because of her that this had happened, she would make sure he was okay, that they were okay.

Dave spent two days in the hospital before leaving and moving back home with Jane. Thomas refused to speak to her, he even avoided visiting the hospital when he knew Jane would be there; instead, he would ring Dave's mobile to check on him. But Jane didn't care; she was going to make everything better, eventually.

Jane prompted Dave. "Have you taken your Citalopram today? You know you have to take it every day." She was scared if he missed one day of his medication they'd be right back to square one.

Without looking at her Dave sighed as he shook his head in irritation. "Jane, I took it, alright? Don't nag me, that's what got me into this mess." He stomped out of the house and went back to working on his bike. The doctor had signed him off work for a month after the overdose. He was just a week into the time off work and had devoted his time to seeing the counsellor and doing up the shit heap of a bike that had sat outside on their driveway for the last two years.

Jane had told Lindsey about what Dave had done, but had sworn her to secrecy; she had of course lied about *why* he did it; stating instead that the pressure of his job not being secure anymore and a dispute with his family were the things that had tipped him over the edge. How could she tell her best friend that it had been her that had caused him to take an overdose? Jane was too ashamed to admit to anyone, that *she* could be the reason someone would consider taking their own life, as an option to get away from her and her ability to screw things up. No, she wasn't going to tell anyone about the shambles that her life had become. Dave had taken the tablets as a cry for help, and what could Jane do but help him?

Chapter Seven

After almost two months off work, Dave had finally been given the go ahead to return. To the outside world he appeared fine, only Jane knew different. She was the one who saw the little spikes in his behaviour, the subtle changes in his speech not to mention the moodiness that had taken up permanent residence now. They weren't really living together as a married couple anymore, more like co-existing, roommates. Jane was sleeping in their bedroom, with Dave preferring to spend every night on the sofa. It hadn't been a conscious decision they'd made really; he just stayed up watching TV until late at night, falling asleep downstairs and not bothering to come to bed at first. But after a week or two he had started to keep a pillow and blanket behind the sofa, so he didn't have to sleep upstairs with Jane. She wasn't about to argue, it made her life far simpler if he stayed away from her.

They put on a united front together for Jane's

parents, keeping up the routine visits to see them for Sunday lunch, but Thomas had made it clear that Jane wasn't welcome at his house anymore. So Dave took Freya to visit him and Rita on his own, leaving Jane with a regular weekend afternoon to herself. After spending the first few times worried sick that he wouldn't bring Freya home, she actually looked forward to it now. She often spent time alone reading, which had become a new passion for her, or catching up on household chores, sometimes it was lunch dates with Lindsey. Jane felt like she was making herself a priority for a change, which had been difficult to begin with, but was rapidly becoming much easier. Freya would always be her number one priority but Jane also realised that her daughter benefited more from a relaxed and happy mum. The time they spent together was better, less fraught.

"We're back, you in?" Dave shouted through the house.

"Yep, in the cellar, just clearing out some rubbish, won't be a minute." Shoving the rest of the stuff for the charity shop into the fourth bag of the afternoon, Jane headed up the stairs to give Freya a cuddle.

Dave's eyes widened at the sight of his wife, his eyebrows almost reaching his hairline. "Tea? God, you look a state, you're filthy! I would have done that if you asked, you know." Dave hated the fact that his wife was just getting on with things these days, not really waiting for his permission to throw stuff out anymore or reorganise the house. Tidy house, tidy mind, her mum always said and it was fast becoming Jane's mantra.

Jane walked over to the sink. "Yeah, please, how was your dad?" She washed her hands, scrubbing away at the dirt caught around her nails. Things hadn't improved any between her and Thomas but she was trying to be the better person and not let his anger rub off on her.

Dave busied himself making tea for both of them.

"Good, he's asked if we want to go the caravan with them next weekend."

Jane was shocked that she'd been included, but pleased all the same, maybe her father in law was coming around a little. "Oh, that would be great, we could do with a break away from here, don't you think?" Already, Jane was mentally planning what washing and ironing she would need to get on with, so she could pack after work before they left on Friday.

"Erm... Well actually, he erm, kind of meant just me and Freya to go with him and Rita. I said you wouldn't mind. You don't mind, do you? I mean I just thought that well, I thought we could do with a break away from each other and it would be great for Freya. You could have a weekend to yourself, maybe have

Lindsey over to stay, make it a girls' weekend." He paused and scratched his head thoughtfully. "If you don't want me to go..." He was stirring his tea so hard, Jane thought the bottom was going to wear out of the cup.

She had to turn away quickly, so he didn't see the tears that had just started to roll down her cheek. "No... I mean, no, it's fine, of course you two should go. I'll ring Lindsey and see what she's up to." Why was she crying again? Her stomach knotted in apprehension, she'd never spent a night away from Freya since the day she'd been born. She realised he'd only suggested two days away with their daughter. He wasn't leaving her, *just a weekend break that's all, Jane, get a grip, woman!* Jane tried to push back the worry of being separated from her little girl for the first time ever. She forced herself to think of the lazy mornings, two full night's sleep and a night out too, without having to worry about what Freya needed. No, this was going to be good. She mentally gave herself a good talking to.

The dreaded day arrived and Jane watched as they left. Dave had taken a day off work, when his father had suggested they miss the weekend traffic, going a day early, giving them three days at the caravan instead of two. Jane didn't mind, instead she was really quite looking forward to the time alone now. She too had taken the day off, meaning she had a lazy morning, after she had waved them off at the door. Freya had insisted she took her bucket and spade in the back of the car with her, refusing to pack it into the boot with her other toys she had picked out.

Dave rolled his eyes as he smiled at his daughter. "Anything for a quiet life," he muttered as he strapped her in, while she tried to bash him on the head with the spade.

Jane closed the door and breathed out deeply; now if she got her act together, she could tidy up and maybe even take her mum out for lunch before her girls' night out with Lindsey.

An hour later Jane and her mum sat at the table in the bistro window, each perusing the menu. Zac's was a small café come bistro in the evenings where Jane had fond memories of spending Saturday mornings eating breakfast with her parents when she was little.

Elaine sat across the table from her daughter. "Oh this is nice, love, we haven't spent much time together recently, what with you virtually chucking my granddaughter through the door in a morning and rushing off at night. We haven't had a catch up in ages."

She was right, Jane knew that since Dave's overdose she'd kind of shut herself off from them, preferring to keep busy at home, making sure he didn't do anything stupid again. She hadn't even told them he had tried to kill himself. They wouldn't understand

and she couldn't face trying to make up a story or explain; they just wouldn't get it. It was much easier just to keep them in the dark about it all.

The sigh that left Jane's body was long and slow. "I know, but you understand what it's like with a little one to look after, she doesn't sleep very well either so I'm constantly tired. What with Freya, Dave and the house to look after, I don't seem to have any time to myself these days, Mum. Sorry." Jane found it quite upsetting how easy she could lie to her parents these days. There was never a scramble for words anymore, they just rolled off the tongue now. It was strange how something like deceit became the norm.

With a swift shake of her head, Elaine dismissed her daughter's apology. "Don't be daft; no need to be sorry, we were just worried about you. Anyway, it's lovely that the two of them are spending some time alone this weekend. I wish your dad had been more like that when you were younger. You're lucky having him, you know. He's so good with that little one; you don't know you're born. Your dad didn't know your backside from your elbow when you were Freya's age! So tell me, what have you got planned for the next few days, love?" Elaine sipped at her coffee as she waited for Jane to answer.

Over lunch Jane told her mum about her plans for a night out with Lindsey. She was coming over for a take away, no doubt a few vodka tonics would be involved too while they got ready. Then there would be a lazy Saturday morning, followed by a bit of retail therapy before heading over to Lindsey's house for dinner and a film they planned on renting. Sam was going to drive Jane home Sunday morning so she could get a nice meal organised for when Dave got back.

"Oh that sounds lovely, just what you need, eh? I know you don't like staying at home alone, you never did." Elaine couldn't understand her daughter's fear of being alone; she loved her time alone when Jane's dad disappeared off to the pub or worked night shifts, said it did them good not to spend every spare minute together, but Jane hated it. Daytime was fine but nights were a different matter, it gave her time to think. She always left the TV on when she was completely alone, even if the sound was turned down, it made her feel like she had company. Silly as it sounds, it made her feel better. Even Lindsey thought she was mad, she had even laughed when Jane asked if she could stay over.

"Alright, scaredy cat, I'll babysit you, don't you worry." had been her exact words but Jane knew she didn't mind. She loved the idea of having a weekend together, instead of just a few hours on their rare nights out.

Lunch with her mum was over too quickly and

Jane made a mental note to make time for more days like this, she was acutely aware there would be a time when her mum would no longer be there but thinking about that made her feel way too emotional. She wanted to enjoy the time she had with her parents in their twilight years.

After dropping Elaine off at home, Jane headed home so she could get ready for Lindsey's arrival. If she was lucky, she'd be able to sneak in a hot bubble bath before her friend appeared for the night.

One Chinese takeaway later and the girls were dancing around Jane's bedroom, getting ready for a night on the town. They'd already downed one bottle of wine, leaving Jane well on her way to being tipsy. Tipping her glass to her lips, she finished the last drop of wine as Lindsey sang along loudly to Pink's 'Don't Let me Get Me' badly.

"Come on Jane, dance with me." Lindsey held out her hand to grab Jane's as she danced past. It was a sign of things to come for the night ahead, Jane was sure of that. Nothing but fun to be had for the next 48 hours. If she could count on Lindsey for anything it was brightening up her day. Jane took the offered hand, and together they danced around the room, wiggling their hips in time to the beat.

As they entered the heaving bar, Lindsey grabbed

Jane's hand, making sure they weren't separated. The place was buzzing with people all gathered and ready to start their weekend. The atmosphere was warm and welcoming with the sound of laugher filling the air. The music spilled from the speakers causing the floor to vibrate ever so slightly. A feeling of giddiness washed over Jane. It felt good to be out having fun with Lindsey.

Lindsey caught the barman's attention. "Two white wine, please."

With a wink in their direction he bent to collect the bottle from the fridge. "Coming right up, beautiful."

The girls settled on bar stools, people watching was one of Jane's favourite pastimes, and there was no better place to do it than in a packed pub in the centre of Leeds. The crowd was eclectic, from business men to students, they all mingled around the pub making small talk. Jane felt relaxed.

It wasn't that long ago that Jane would have had a panic attack at the mere thought of being at a bar without Dave, she still felt a little anxious but as long as Lindsey was with her, she was happy.

Jane was too busy giggling with Lindsey to notice the two men that had taken up residence beside them. "Evening ladies, can we buy you a drink?"

Jane held up her hand, "No, we're fine, thanks."

She answered at the same time as Lindsey held her glass aloft, gesturing for another white wine.

With a nudge to her friend's ribs, Lindsey accepted their offer. "We'd like white wine, please."

Jane huffed. Worried that maybe one of Dave's colleagues were somewhere amongst the throng of people, ready to report back all of her misdemeanours. She placed a hand over the top of her glass. "No, seriously, I don't want another. Thanks." The smile on her face was a little tight but polite.

The taller of the two men, stood directly next to Jane, smiled. "It's just a drink, you can watch the bar tender pour it too so you know it's safe, if that's what you're worried about?"

Shaking the worries from her head, Jane lifted her hand from the glass and grinned. "Okay, sorry. I'll have a drink, thank you." *What harm would one drink do?*

The guy waved a twenty over the bar trying to get the barman's attention. "Good girl," he winked slowly at Jane. Jane wasn't expecting the warm glow that rushed through her with that wink. Before Jane got to the bottom of her glass of wine, Lindsey was up and dancing with the second guy.

She swivelled around on her chair to watch Lindsey dance flirtatiously with the stranger. "She's having a good time," Jane's admirer stated. "I'm Mark, by the way."

"Jane. That's Lindsey, and yes, she likes to party," Jane giggled as she watched Lindsey shimmy up and down her suitor's body in time to the music. "Oh dear, I think you should rescue your friend before she scares him off!"

Mark threw his head back and laughed. "He can handle himself. So, is this where you spend all your Friday nights?"

Jane shook her head. "No, this is a first. Honestly, I don't come into Leeds very often at all."

With a small nod, Mark frowned. "That's a shame, was hoping I might bump into you again sometime."

Jane's cheeks flushed. "Oh," she fiddled with her hair, tucking the errant strands behind her ear only to immediately untuck it again so she could hide behind the veil it created. Her cheeks stained pink. She turned her attention back to Lindsey in order to avoid any further embarrassment.

Lindsey squealed as she beckoned to Jane, begging her to join her on the dance floor as Maroon 5's Moves like Jagger filled the room. "That's our song, sorry," Jane hopped off the stool and headed onto the dance floor. Immersing herself in the music, she danced with Lindsey, intent on having a good time with her friend. Lindsey turned her back on Mark's friend, focussing on Jane instead as they immersed themselves in the atmosphere.

As they sat at the table on Saturday morning laughing about their antics of the previous night and discussing the planned retail therapy they would embark on after lunch, Lindsey's phone rang at the bottom of her bag.

Scrambling through all the rubbish she kept in there, it took her a good few seconds to locate the ringing phone as it continued to scream at her to be answered. "Hello," Lindsey answered in a sing-song voice. Jane watched as Lindsey's expression went from one of happiness to worry. "Oh God, I'll get a taxi now. No, don't leave her on her own, I will be there in about thirty minutes, okay?" Lindsey's face was now ashen, and she was obviously on the verge of tears. Whatever it was, it wasn't good news.

Before Jane had a chance to ask what the problem was, Lindsey was up and out of her chair, the words coming out of her mouth in a hurried garble. "Sam's mums in hospital, they think she had a heart attack. I have to go, Jane, sorry. Can you ring me a taxi while I grab my stuff? Oh God, he's in tears, it's bad, Jane." Silent tears were flowing down Lindsey's face now as she tried to organise herself. The more she hurried the less she seemed to be achieving.

Jane nodded. "Of course, do you need me to come with you? Or do anything?" she offered.

Hurriedly Lindsey began shoving everything in her

overnight bag. "No, it's fine, just the taxi, thanks. No point in you sitting at the hospital being bored, is there?"

Jane tried her best to console her friend. "Okay, just ring me later when you know what's happened. I'm sure she'll be fine, honey." Unfortunately this wasn't Lindsey's mother-in-law's first heart attack. She'd had one about six months ago, when they were all on holiday together. The doctors had told her she had been lucky to survive it, giving her a load of medication to take, but Lindsey was convinced she hadn't been taking them as she should have done.

With her best friend heading off to be with her family, Jane was left to her own devices. Most normal people would embrace this—not Jane. With Lindsey no longer in the picture for the weekend, the fear of the questions and possible repercussions it could lead to if Dave found out she'd been alone all weekend began to wash over her. It didn't matter how long they went between fights or bouts of violence, the anxiety of it happening again never left her. Jane knew just how selfish she was being, worrying about herself rather than Lindsey's situation but her fear was real and justified. She wasn't sure she'd ever get past that feeling or the dread that still hung over her head daily.

Trying to keep herself occupied and her mind off the possibility that Dave would ring or somehow know she was alone, she busied herself tidying up the house, making sure the few bits that were out of place were now firmly back where they belonged. She contemplated changing the bed sheets but knew that would spark Dave's suspicion, it didn't matter that they weren't sharing a bed, he'd still check the room when he came back. Just in case.

Exhausted from not only the cleaning but mentally worn out from all the worrying, Jane decided to try a little relaxation with her book. A nice long soak in the tub with a glass of wine might just be the antidote she needed.

She had just slipped into a lovely hot bath, when there was a knock on the door. Pushing herself up and out of the bath, Jane headed over to the window with a towel tightly wrapped around her body. Peering out of the window she looked down to see Toby, standing on the doorstep.

"I'm in the bath! Down in a minute," Jane shouted down at him. Quickly, she threw on some clothes and then ran down to let him in.

Chapter eight

Toby stepped through the open door, into the kitchen. "Hello, darlin'! LJ just texted me, told me you were on your own. Crap news about the mother-in-law, eh? She said you hate being alone in the house, so here I am. Where's Freaky anyway?" Toby refused to use Dave's name ever since he had seen the bruises and put two and two together. There had been a bit of tension between the two friends for a while after that incident, but thankfully they were back to their usual banter. He hadn't mentioned it again and Jane certainly wasn't going to.

Jane bumped shoulders with her friend, teasing him for calling her husband names. "Don't call him that! He's taken Freya away for the weekend. I told you the other day they were going to the caravan for the weekend."

"Oh, yeah you did. LJ had invited me out with you

two last night, but I had plans, sorry, Janey. You got that kettle on yet? Probably best I didn't go out anyway, I know he doesn't like you spending time with me. We don't want to upset Freaky, now do we?"

Jane slapped him hard on his arm, laughing at Toby making himself at home in her kitchen, as he searched the cupboards for cups and teabags. They spent the afternoon texting Lindsey, whilst chatting about everything and nothing. Putting the world to rights, as Jane's mum would say. Toby knew all the gossip from work, he revelled in relaying all the gory details of the latest office affairs that he was privy to, making Jane laugh out loud so much that her cheeks were aching.

Toby glanced at his watch. "Janey, my stomach is rumbling. Shall I rustle up some dinner? In fact don't answer that, grab your coat. We'll go grab some alcohol from the off licence, then I'll rustle up my famous jerk chicken for my best mate. No arguments."

The idea of being alone in the house with Toby made her nervous and a little twitchy. She knew Dave would find out he'd been there, one of the neighbours were bound to mention it in conversation, giving her away. The thoughts of any repercussion weighed heavy on her mind but Toby was here now offering to keep her company for a while, like any good friend would. How could she resist an offer like that? Grabbing her bag, they headed out of the house pulling the door shut behind them.

"Jeez, that was good. You've been hiding that talent from me." Jane pushed her plate away, full from the delicious food Toby had insisted on cooking for them, Jane filled up his glass with the wine they'd bought earlier before topping up her own.

Toby looked smug. "Well, let's just keep my cooking skills a secret between me and you, shall we? My mum taught me how to cook, but I only do it on special occasions. Don't you dare tell my flatmate. He thinks I don't know where our kitchen is." His larger than life laugh echoed around the kitchen. "Come on then, let's go watch that chick flick rubbish you rented."

It wasn't rubbish, Thelma and Louise was one of Jane's favourite movies. As far as she was concerned it wasn't too much of a chick flick, as Toby called it, more life affirming in nature.

Jane was aware it was getting late. "Don't you have a home to go to? You don't have to babysit me, despite what Lyndsey told you. God, she's going to pay for that!" Jane giggled, maybe there'd been one too many glasses of wine consumed.

"Nah, I'm going to sleep on your couch and keep the scary men away. Oh yeah, I forgot he's away already, isn't he?" Toby guffawed at his own joke.

Jane gasped at the thought of Toby spending the night. "Toby! You can't, don't be daft, I'll be fine." Dave would go mental if he knew Toby was even here, let alone if he found out he had stayed on the sofa. With sweaty palms, she felt slightly nauseous as the familiar feeling of anxiety crept through her body, she couldn't let Toby stay overnight. That had disaster written all over it. "Seriously, I'll be fine. You really should go."

"I've had too much to drink to drive home, Janey." Jane looked crestfallen. "I can try get a taxi if you want, but that means leaving my car parked outside your house all night. Up to you." Jane knew she could call him a taxi, but what was the point? He had already taken his socks off and settled himself in front of the TV. "If you're worried about him finding out, then leaving my car here wouldn't be a good idea either, would it?" Toby pointed out. "But, if you really want me to go, I will. I understand."

Jane sighed, she knew he was right. "No, it's fine. Stay." She said with a small smile.

Sinking down next to him, Jane gave in gracefully, pressing the button to switch on the film. What Dave didn't know wouldn't hurt him. Toby would be long gone before Dave got home on Sunday afternoon, she had no intention of telling anyone that Toby had stayed the night and she was pretty sure Toby wouldn't say anything either. Settling down, Jane tried to push the unease she felt aside and enjoy the rest of her evening.

As the movie played, Jane could almost hear the cogs whirring in Toby's mind. She knew he wanted to say something and she thought she knew what the topic was. But she wasn't going to encourage the conversation so she tried to concentrate on the movie.

Toby turned to her and took the remote, hitting the pause button he finally spoke. "Speaking of scary men, you know we are going to have to talk about the elephant in the room at some point." He held up his hands to halt her interruption. "And before you go off on one of your *'it's not what you think'* rants, just hear me out. Okay?" His gaze softened along with his tone. "I know he's hit you. I don't know if it was a one off or if it's a regular thing. If it was a first, then believe me, there *will* be a second time. But, you need to understand that I know." His deep brown eyes were filled with sincerity and concern. Jane opened her mouth to interrupt him but he placed a finger gently over her lips to silence the words before they came. "Let me finish, okay, Janey? I know you're scared, because my mum was too. But I can't sit here and watch you go through what she did with my dad. I told her about you, about the bruises. She was the one who gave me the card for the refuge place. She said if you ring them they can help you and Freya move out to a safe house. He wouldn't even know where you'd gone. I'd help too. Please, Janey; let me get you out of here."

He paused to gather his thoughts, the pain of his childhood present in his eyes. "Mum went to one, when she finally found the guts to leave my dad. Mum also said I had to understand how hard it was bound to be for you, going through all this shit. She told me to back off, because it had to be *your* decision, but I'm seriously done with backing off, standing by and watching while he continues to hurt you, one of my best friends, isn't an option for me anymore. I need to know you and Freya are safe." He reached out to wipe the tears from Jane's cheeks, leaving nothing but silence between them. She didn't know what to say. Here he was, trying to look after her, and all she'd done was lie to him. Could Jane trust him with the truth? It suddenly dawned on her that she had to tell someone, so why not Toby? If she had to confide in someone, it may as well be someone that seemed to understand the predicament she was in.

Taking a deep breath, she finally found the courage she needed. "You're right. He did hit me. He *does* hit me, I mean, well it's not always hitting, he doesn't beat me up, if you know what I mean. Sometimes it's just a push or a shake. It wasn't a one off but... I don't know, it's not always that bad. More of a warning sometimes when I step out of line." Jane's head bowed, looking anywhere but at Toby.

Toby bobbed his head down allowing him to make eye contact with Jane. "You know that it's not alright, don't you, darlin'? You do know that you don't have to put up with it, Janey? Look at me, sweetie." He put his hand under Jane's chin, guiding her head up to look him in the eyes.

This wasn't the man she knew, he was normally full of banter, so carefree and easy-going but with a crumpled brow the look on his face was anything but carefree now.

Jane averted her gaze again. "It wasn't always like this you know. I wasn't always like this. A mess, I mean." The words came out in a sniffly state as her emotions got the better of her. Now she'd opened up the can of worms, there didn't seem any way of stopping the words that appeared intent on spilling forth.

Toby gritted his teeth and closed his eyes briefly. "You're only a mess because *he* made you a mess. This is *his* fault, Janey, not yours." It was clear he was trying to control the anger he felt but to her it was evident in his gaze. Jane felt guilty for involving him now. It really wasn't his problem to solve.

Jane shook her head vehemently. "Is it, though? He wasn't like this before we married. Everything was great. I just make him angry. I do stupid stuff.... I do things I know he hates but...I...well I just forget to stick to the rules, you know?" She twisted her hands in her lap as she made the excuses that had become second nature to her now. She'd spouted them off to all and sundry God knows how many times in the last year, that she almost believed them herself.

"Oh my God! Are you being serious? Rules? RULES! For God's sake Janey, there shouldn't *be* rules to stick to! You're his *wife*. Not his bloody servant. This is not *your* fault." He stood up and paced the room. "You haven't done anything wrong and even if you *did* make him mad, it doesn't give him the right to hit you. I could kill him!" He spat out the words, running his hands through his hair in what seemed like exasperation, he was scaring Jane a little. It didn't take much, the thin line between her projected fear and reality was becoming blurred. A cold sweat began to creep across her back as she worried that she'd triggered the same reaction in Toby as she did in Dave. The inability to see that all men were not assholes clouding her judgement of the current situation.

"Look, I've annoyed you now. See how easy it is to lose it with me, I told you it's my fault, this is all my fault." Jane's voice was now barely above a whisper, she didn't want to wind him up anymore. Acutely aware of how volatile a situation could become in the blink of an eye, Jane backed up slightly, folding her arms around herself in protective mode.

Picking up on Jane's actions instantly, Toby lowered his voice, moving so he was beside her again. "Honey, no, *you* haven't made me mad. I'm not mad *at* you, I'm mad *for* you, don't you see?" He reached out, taking Jane's hands in his, circling his thumbs across the back of her hands, it felt good, calming in a way. "Come on, sit here with me. What do I have to say to make you understand you don't deserve this? There isn't just you to think about, is there? I mean think about what this is doing to Freya. Do you want her to grow up thinking this is normal, that men hurt women?" It was a low blow, Toby knew that but he wasn't above using whatever he had to in order to make his friend see sense.

There it was, his trump card played right to Jane's face. "You see that's what's happening here, Janey. Freya is getting a screwed up view of how life should be, and she's seeing you covered in bruises even if she doesn't see him hit you." A look of horror flashed across Jane's face, she'd not thought about Freya noticing the marks. In all honestly she believed she'd protected her from seeing the violence between them but Toby was right, she had seen her bruised and swollen face. "Oh no, she hasn't seen him hit you, has she? Please tell me she hasn't seen that." Toby shook his head, hopeful Jane hadn't let it get that far. "Do you know why I always call you Janey, and never Jane? Because if you don't do anything about this, I'm terrified that one day, I'm going to have to identify your body, laid on some mortuary table, with a Jane Doe tag around your toe. I can't bear the thought of that. Don't you dare accuse me of being over-dramatic, it happens all the time. Loads of women die because of their screwed up partners. One thing leads to another, and before you know it, they're gone. That could happen to you, darling, you see that, don't you? He could go too far one day and all this would be over."

Toby's thumbs continued the slow, steady circles on her hands but she couldn't speak, she could only shake her head. He had just shocked the life out of her. Jane never knew why he used the nickname, she'd always just thought it was his thing. He never called anyone by their proper name. He was right of course, why hadn't she seen it like that, would Dave go too far next time and what was all this doing to her daughter? She was certain she didn't want Freya to grow up in this environment, but she knew she needed two parents, parents that loved her. And Dave did love Freya, she knew he did, she could see it in his eyes, every day. Jane was still sure she could fix this broken thing, masquerading as a marriage.

Toby's voice brought her back to the present. "Talk to me, Janey. I need you to talk to me," he pleaded, trying to get her to look him in the eyes.

She stared at a dirty mark on the carpet and made a mental note to clean it up before Dave saw. Keeping her focus on the stain she spoke. "I can't leave him, Freya needs her dad, don't you see that? She needs him and he would never hurt her, never in a million years. He's brilliant with her, you haven't seen them together. Freya adores him. If I leave him, he'll make me leave Freya with him because I can't support her on my own. I can't be on my own, what would I do? I couldn't run the house, keep a job going and look after Freya all on my own! This is my world, Toby, nobody else's. Mine. I'm fixing this mess, it's going to be fine." The words came out in one long breath now and she felt more hot tears trail down her cheeks. "I made him go to his parents for a while, you know, we were working it out. I told him I didn't want him to come home just yet, that maybe we were better off apart for a while, but then he took the pills and phoned me to tell me what he'd done. I phoned the ambulance, dashed to the hospital but the doctor said he hadn't taken that many and maybe it was just a cry for help. Well, there wasn't much else I could do, was there? I had to let him come home, I had to look after him, make him better again and maybe then, when he saw that I can look after him properly, it would all just stop. It's getting better now; you don't see how he looks at me sometimes. Since the pills incident, well, he's different. He loves me and that's all I ever wanted." Jane wasn't sure who she was trying to convince.

"Pills? Pills. You mean to tell me he overdosed? Can't you see that wasn't a cry for help, honey, that's controlling a situation? If he wanted to die, he would have taken enough to make sure he did it properly and he wouldn't have called to tell you either. He did it when you said you didn't want him to come home, that you wanted out of the marriage. Can you see that now, Janey?" Toby now held Jane's face in his hands to stop her looking away from him; he was trying to make her concentrate on what he was saying.

She focused on his dark eyes, staring intently at him, he just didn't get it, how could he? "No, he did it because I drove him to it! You're sitting there, telling me I should leave him," she shouted. "ME LEAVE HIM? Are you insane? I can't leave him. What would I do, why should I leave this house, Freya's home? Why me, Toby? Go on, tell me! 'Cos I sure as hell don't know anymore, you have me down as this completely different person, I'm not that girl. I'm not that strong."

She screamed, trying to make him see the bigger picture.

Realising he'd pushed her too far, Toby tried to rescue the situation. "Calm down, okay? I understand, I really do, okay. Just please, calm down, I didn't mean to upset you. I'm just scared for you. I just wanted you to know you have someone fighting your corner with you. But I get it, I can back off if that's what you want, but just know I'll always be here when you're ready."

Toby let go of Jane but remained at her side, she could see the confusion, despair even, on his face but knew she had made her point. She wasn't going to give up on her marriage just yet, not when she knew she could fix it, if she just tried that little bit harder.

Jane wiped the tears from her cheeks. "Toby, all I need you to do is be my friend, if I need you to fix something, I'll ask you. I'm an adult, I got myself into this mess and I can get me and Freya out of it if I need to, but I don't. I love that you're here supporting me, that you're my friend, but can we please stop all this soul-searching rubbish? It's finished, nothing bad has happened for a while now. I think he scared himself out of it and well, you know, it's going to be fine." Jane was well aware that it seemed like she was trying to convince herself, just as much as she was Toby.

Toby looked crestfallen "Look, I *am* your friend; I'll always be here for you, no matter what happens, or what decisions you make about your future. I promise you that. Now, shall we watch the end of this crappy film or are you going to drag out that duvet for me, 'cos I ain't going nowhere tonight, darling." With that it was over, they were back to ignoring the elephant in the room, as he had so eloquently put it.

Chapter nine

"Jesus! The little sod just bit me!"

Jane could hear Freya screaming hysterically, as she rushed in from the kitchen. Dave was pacing the room rubbing his forearm. She quickly glanced over at her daughter, her attention was automatically drawn to the large, angry red hand print, which was glowing on her leg. He'd smacked her, he'd physically harmed their daughter. Bile rose in her throat as nausea swept throughout her body. They'd never lifted a finger to their daughter ever, they'd never even needed to tell her off. Now Dave had hit her.

Jane rushed over to Freya "Did you smack her?" She scooped up the crying infant to try and ease the little girl's hysteria and discomfort at the same time. "God, Dave, she's a baby, you can't hit her. Look at her leg!" Jane turned to take Freya into the kitchen, trying to think what was in the medicine box that would maybe ease her pain quickly, when Dave yanked the child out of Jane's arms, making the little girl cry out again, only this time it was fear and not pain, Jane could see it on her little face.

Dave's mouth screwed into a tight ball as he snarled. "Give her to me, she needs to learn she can't bite me and get away with it." His voice was chillingly calm. He was angry, no matter what she said or did, it wouldn't be enough to stop him now.

But no way was Jane going to give up that easily. "Dave, give her back to me, please! Please, let me put something on her leg, look, she's scared. Dave, give her to me, please," Jane begged him as she tried to grab her daughter out of his grasp, but it was too late, he was already heading upstairs, with Freya screaming for her mum.

With her heart beating out of her chest, Jane ran up the stairs after him. "Dave, what are you doing? Please, give her to me, you've hurt her leg, Dave. Please!" But the plea fell on deaf ears, as he opened her door and placed her in her room. He calmly turned around to Jane, pulling the child's bedroom door shut behind him.

He held the door closed with one hand, while the other grasped Jane around the throat. "She stays in there, until I say she comes out."

Freya pounded on the other side of the bedroom door, screaming to be let out over and over again. He hadn't turned her light on, just left her in there in the dark, he knew she hated the dark.

Jane knew her daughter was terrified. "I'm here, baby, it's okay, Mummy's right here, Freya, shush now." She tried desperately to calm the little girl down somehow, but Freya's pounding on the door continued. Jane pleaded with her husband. "Dave, she's scared, come on, let me get her, please." Her heart hammered against her ribs. Jane needed to get her out of there, but she couldn't do anything for fear that the situation would escalate even further, resulting in yet more violence at the very least. At least she knew her daughter was safe in her room, with him on the same side of the door as Jane. If he flipped, he'd take it out on her not Freya, that was knowledge enough to keep her by his side. She just had to figure out a way to calm him down. Tears were running silently down her cheeks as she stared at his face, not really seeing him, just wanting to get to her little girl, now more than anything.

A voice floated up from the lounge. "Hello? Where you hiding at?"

As Thomas's voice drifted up the first flight of stairs, Dave's grip on Jane's throat released and he opened the bedroom door. "Shut her up. Now," he growled. "Just a minute, Dad, just sorting Freya out, I won't be long, go get a beer from the fridge," he called down the stairs. He turned to address Jane once more, a mask of angry disdain falling once again as he hissed, "Shut her up now and sort yourself out. I want her in bed in the next ten minutes, do you understand me?" Unable to form words for fear of stoking the fire raging beneath his skin, Jane just nodded as she pushed her way past him to cradle Freya in her arms.

Jane picked up her daughter holding her close against her chest as she tried to calm the toddler. The screaming settled to sobbing as the little girl fell asleep in her mother's arms. Jane had cuddled her to sleep not wanting to let her go, with every fibre of her being wanting to protect her little girl. Once Freya's hiccupping sobs had settled into gentle snores, Jane carefully laid her in her bed and covered her up. She sat for another ten minutes, just watching Freya sleep, not really wanting to let her daughter out of her sight, knowing that she was safe while she slept. She knew Dave had gone out for the night with his father. They were off to the car auctions with some hair-brained scheme about buying, fixing and selling cars, to make a bit of extra cash. She honestly didn't care where he went as long as he wasn't anywhere near her or their daughter. She prayed he would end up staying with his parents for the night instead of coming home.

Jane lay in bed with her eyes closed tightly to keep at bay the tears that threatened to fall. Her child had been hurt by the man she loved unconditionally. The man she was supposed to be able to trust. Jane had no idea how to fix this now or if she even wanted to any more. It was one thing hitting her but for him to harm their daughter was beyond even Jane's comprehension.

She thought she'd only been asleep for a matter of minutes when she opened her eyes and glanced at the clock, it was after eleven, which meant she'd been in bed a few hours. Something must have startled her awake so she lay there holding her breath, listening to the stairs creak as Dave made his way up to their room. Jane screwed her eyes tight shut, regulating her breathing to a steady pace, she wanted him to believe that she was sound asleep. She lay very still while she listened to him undress, dropping his clothes onto the bedroom floor. He walked around the end of the bed, sliding in under the duvet. Still, Jane tried to keep her breathing slow, regular. Her jaw ached from clenching it tightly shut. As his arm slid over her and under the nightgown she wore nausea rose throughout her. Her body tensed as his hand moved up to cover her breast. She froze, not wanting to let him know she was awake. He continued kneading her breast, rubbing his thumb over her nipple. The smell of alcohol repulsed her as his breath felt hot on the back of her neck. Still pretending to sleep, Jane rolled onto her stomach, hoping to stop his amorous but unwanted groping. Dave sniggered as he pulled the hem of his wife's nightgown up and threw his leg over her, parting her legs as he did. He moved so he was positioned directly over her back, with his legs firmly planted between Jane's, he began to softly bite at her shoulder.

Jane wriggled and tried to move out from under him "Dave, stop it, it's late. Go to sleep."

But instead he held her in place with the full weight of his body. "You're awake then, sweetheart." He laughed darkly. "Come on, let's get this thing off you." He was yanking up the hem of the nightgown that separated them.

Pushing harder now, Jane twisted her body out from under him, managing to roll him to his side of the bed again. "No, Dave, don't, I don't want to. Get off me. Just go to sleep." He sat up as Jane tried to settle back down, pulling the duvet up over her shoulder, gripping it tightly in her clenched fist.

Dave leaned over and kissed her cheek as he grabbed her wrist, positioning it above her head, effectively stopping her from moving anywhere. He pulled Jane's other arm up, joining them, holding them together in his fierce grip. All the time Jane struggled against him, protesting. He moved over her, his legs parting hers again.

She didn't want this. "No, Dave, stop it, get off of me, now!"

He clamped his free hand over Jane's mouth to

silence her. Thrashing her head from side, Jane tried to release her head away from his grip, struggling against his hands.

He growled, "Just shut up. I'll be quick," The smell of alcohol worse now as he lowered his face to her neck. Nudging her legs further apart, he pushed inside her roughly. The burning pain was just bearable, as he began to thrust quickly in and out of her. The tears spilled from Jane's eyes, running down past her ears and onto the pillow, beneath her head. "Oh fuck, you feel good, sweetheart. Nice and tight, just how I like it." He muttered into Jane's neck, as she managed to finally turn her head away from him, desperately trying to block out what she was being subjected to, she tried to concentrate on listening to the rain hitting the windows. Hearing the distant rumble of the thunder, anything to distance herself from what he was doing to her. His pace quickened, as Jane lay there numbly accepting she couldn't stop him, yet too frightened to scream out in case Freya came in or he hit her again.

Dave grunted and sunk his teeth into Jane's shoulder, biting hard enough to draw blood. He rolled off, turned his back on her and soon drifted off to sleep with gentle snores. Jane crept out of bed, desperate not to wake him and slipped out of the room into the bathroom, where she sat curled in a ball on the floor, sobbing until the sun began to rise; only then did she dare switch on the shower. She stepped underneath the scorching hot water, and began to scrub away at her skin over and over again, not content until her alabaster skin glowed red from the force at which she washed. Trying to get clean, whilst washing away all traces of what had happened last night.

Dave didn't speak to Jane before he left the house, not even to tell her where he was going. The only indication that he had gone out, was the gate rattling shut as he walked towards the car. Jane breathed a huge sigh of relief, knowing that she had a little while now before she would have to face him again. She had no idea what she was going to say or how he would react towards her, but at least for now she could relax. Looking around the kitchen, Jane searched for something to clear her mind, cleaning, that's what she needed to do now to take her mind off everything. Spending the next few hours tidying, clearing the mess, would do her good.

Later that day as Dave walked in through the door Freya happily ran towards him. "Daddy! Daddy! Look at my picture!" She was so excited to show him her creation. "Look, Mummy helped me," she proudly stated. All memories of the smacked leg now gone from her mind.

Jane heard him respond from where she sat, heart pounding and holding her breath. Thankfully he sounded happier. "Wow, Pookey! That's lovely, look at all those pretty colours too. Where's Mummy now, baby?" he asked.

"Kitchen," Jane heard the little girl state. Her pulse quickened, knowing she'd now have to face him.

Jane watched with trepidation as Dave walked into the kitchen smiling at her. He crossed the room, heading straight for the table where she sat with her hands wrapped tightly around her coffee cup, trying to gain a little comfort from the heat it radiated. He had a huge grin plastered across his face when he bent to kiss her. Jane moved her head to the side, making him miss completely.

He huffed. "Okay. That's how it is then? What's up with you?" He sauntered over to the sink, leaning against it, crossing his arms over his chest. "Come on then. Let's hear it."

Jane scrunched her brow. "What's wrong with *me*? Are you for real? Dave, you *raped* me last night..." She tried to keep her voice steady and strong even though she was feeling anything but.

He scoffed. "Raped you? Are you serious? We're married or had you forgotten, with all those nights out on the pull with your slapper mate?" He shook his head and curled his lip. "That's what adults do, you know. They have sex occasionally, sometimes they even do it weekly, but I suppose that concept is lost on you." Sarcasm dripped from his voice as he kept his arms crossed, holding his wife's gaze, taunting her. Refusing to let her look away from him.

With an inner strength that bubbled up from somewhere Jane replied, "That wasn't sex, I can assure you of that. What happened last night was rape. Non consensual sex. I said no over and over again. I can still say no, even though we are married," she informed him defiantly. "I don't have to agree to have sex with you just because a scrap of paper says we're married." She stated her case as calmly as she could, in spite of the way her stomach knotted with fear. If she stuck to the facts he couldn't really argue, could he?

Dave pushed himself away from the sink and made his way back to his wife's side. Jane's whole body stiffened in the chair, holding her breath, not daring to move. As the cold sweat covered her back, a tight lump formed and lodged in her throat. She had no idea how she was managing to speak, let alone trying to make her point. Jane closed her eyes as she waited for the pain she knew was sure to come.

He leaned in behind her, over her shoulder as he spoke quietly but menacingly into Jane's ear. "Perhaps you need to give it up a little more often, then I might not need to wake you up in future. Get a grip, Jane." It was clear Dave didn't think he had done anything wrong.

Gathering all the strength she could, Jane stood up from the table, pushing her chair back firmly into his legs, without a backward glance she made her way towards the kitchen door. Mentally high fiving herself for how she'd handled the whole situation. She'd survived relatively unscathed, sure her nerves were in tatters and her brain felt as though it had been fried twice over, but she was in one piece.

She stopped and turned to face him. "No Dave, not anymore. I moved my things into Freya's room this afternoon. I'll be sleeping in there from now on." She sounded braver than she felt as she walked away from her husband, leaving him to think that over. If he came after her now, then so be it. She knew she would readily take a punch over what happened last night, any day. Her sanity and Freya were all that mattered now; somehow she was going to survive this whole shambles of a so called life.

Days passed without event, Dave spent most of his time outside tinkering with the wreck of a car he had bought at the auction, while Jane busied herself looking after Freya. She had stopped making his meals but then again he was never around at meal times. If she was in the lounge, Dave stayed in the kitchen. Each night when Jane went to bed, she would hear the lounge door open and the television switch on. She wouldn't allow her body to give in and go to sleep until she heard him make his way to what used to be their bedroom. It was only once she knew, beyond doubt, that he was asleep that Jane could relax enough to close her eyes. It was over these days that realisation hit home. She had to get out; there was no marriage left to save. She couldn't fix things now and more importantly she didn't *want* to.

Their fourth wedding anniversary loomed next month and Jane was determined it would be their last. As soon as Dave left for work the next morning she fired up the internet, searching for the number of the advice place Toby had told her about, wishing desperately she had kept the card he had given to her. Once she found the contact details, it took her another hour to pluck up the courage to make the call, but when she did the words just flowed out of her mouth.

Jane relayed everything as quickly as she could, hardly stopping for breath. Thirty minutes later, and after Jane had been made aware of all the options available to her, they had arranged an appointment for her the next day, it would be with a local solicitor who specialised in domestic violence cases. The girl on the phone assured Jane that it would be a female lawyer she would meet with, the young girl also arranged for a support worker to be there with her. Apparently the support worker would go over her options in person, help with Freya during the meeting and even hold

Jane's hand if she needed it. After replacing the handset in the cradle, Jane let out a huge breath, along with a few tears; tears she vowed would be the last she cried over her husband.

She had to stay strong now.

Chapter ten

After waking with the larks—well not really *waking* because that would infer that she had actually slept—Jane went through the usual mundane motions of getting ready for work as she tried to keep her anxiety at bay. Only she wasn't going to work today, she was going to see the lawyer and the lady from the Women's refuge place. It was D-day, or day one as she was preferring to call it.

Jane dropped Freya at her parents' house, trying to keep the atmosphere normal and light, despite the fear and panic she felt rising within her as each minute ticked by. Continuing with the normal routine with her parents, sticking to her usual work day schedule, she didn't want to give anything away. She still felt she couldn't tell them yet, instead she wanted to get everything sorted out in her head first. She needed to know exactly what her options were before she told anyone what had been happening for the last three years. The last thing she needed right now was to have to deal with her parents' feelings on top of everything else. They'd blame themselves, they'd blame Dave and his parents. She knew exactly how the conversation would pan out, she could see it plain as day in her mind's eye. No, she couldn't cope with their emotions as well as her own. If the last few months had taught her anything, it was to put her own needs first, to protect herself first and foremost.

As she handed over Freya's things, Jane avoided her mum's gaze. "Right, everything's in Freya's bag. I've put her one of those pudding things in she likes...oh and there is a bun each, for you and Grandpa that Freya made yesterday." Jane was terrified her mum would guess that she wasn't going to work today; she'd managed to book a day's leave at short notice, thankfully. Instead of sitting at her desk, in just two hours she would be sitting in some office, relaying the horrific details of her life to a total stranger. Doubt started to creep in, chipping away at her. *Perhaps I should just go to work instead?* She wondered. *No, it's just a talk this time, nothing major, nothing to worry about*, she batted down the uncertainty, trying to keep on top of it. It was nothing to worry about unless Dave found out. Shaking that thought from her head, Jane focused on her daughter again.

Elaine smiled broadly at her granddaughter. "Oh,

lovely! Shall we have them after our lunch, Freya, before Grandpa goes to play golf?" She turned her attention to Jane. "You okay, love? You look really pale this morning, you not feeling well?" She gently touched her daughter's forehead as if she were a small child again.

Jane brushed her mum's hand away and forced a laugh. "Mum! I'm fine, just tired. Look, I have to go. See you later, Freya." She kissed her daughter goodbye, hugged her mum and left.

She had two hours to kill until her appointment. Once she was out of sight of her parents' she pulled the car over and fished around in her bag for her mobile phone. She tapped in the number she'd memorised and hit the call button but once it connected the line rang and rang with no answer. *Come on, pick it up, will you!* She chanted to herself.

Just as she was about to give up, a familiar voice spoke at the other end. She breathed a sigh of relief. "Oh thank God! I was just going to hang up. What took you so long?"

Toby laughed out loud. "What's the matter, darlin'? Shouldn't you be enjoying your day off, lounging in bed or whatever it is you lot do when you've got free time? Hang on a minute, Janey." Toby was speaking to someone else in the background, she couldn't catch who it was but they sounded in a rush, it sounded urgent.

Jane tried to end the call, knowing that it was the nerves that he forced her to ring Toby. "Tobes, it's fine, you're busy, I'll talk to you later, okay?"

"No, no, it's sorted, what's up? You don't sound like your normal cheery self...oh God, Janey, what's happened?" She could hear the panic is his voice now. "Janey, where are you? I'm guessing you're at home. I'm on my way now. Janey?" His words were hurried and Jane could hear him scrambling around for keys and the scraping of his chair against the floor as he obviously rushed to stand.

"Tobes, I'm fine. Stop panicking." Jane laughed at the irony of her trying to calm him down, how the tables had turned. "Listen, I've done something stupid...I've, well I called that number you gave me a while back. They've made me an initial thirty minute appointment with a solicitor this morning, only now it doesn't seem like such a good idea, Toby." The silence on the line was deafening. Jane moved the phone from her ear, checking she hadn't accidently cut her friend off or lost signal. No, the call was still connected. "TOBY! Are you still there?" she almost yelled down the line.

"Yeah, I'm still here. I'm just waiting for you to tell me about the something stupid thing you think you did." Toby's voice had returned to its usual calm, reassuring tone. The drama and panic that had been there moments ago had now vanished.

"What? I just told you I called that number, I have an appointment at ten-fifteen, Toby. Why aren't you listening to me? I'm all confused and you're not listening!" Jane was going to lose it with him if he didn't start paying attention to her. Had he really not heard her?

"Janey, that's not stupid, that's the most sensible thing you've done or said in months. Is Freya with you?" Toby questioned.

Frustration ran rife through Jane, she didn't need Toby being smart with her now, she just needed, well she wasn't actually sure *what* she needed from him but she knew the sound of his voice calmed her.

She could feel her resolve waning rapidly now. "No, she isn't. Look, I've just lied to my parents; they think I'm on my way to work. I dropped Freya off as normal and virtually ran out. I can't do this, Tobes." With every minute that passed and the appointment grew nearer, she wasn't at all sure she was doing the right thing. Once she'd seen the solicitor there would be no going back. Dave would know what she'd done and there would be a price to pay. Jane knew that the price would be high; the highest yet, probably.

Toby's voice interrupted her fears. "Yes you *can*, because I'm coming with you. I told you I'd be there for you, no matter what. Look, meet me at that little café, the place near the ring road, you know the one with the big tree things outside, pretending to be something it's not. I'll be there in twenty minutes, okay, Janey?" His calm voice levelled out the anxiety in Jane's. She knew that if he could do anything to ensure she saw this solicitor, he'd do it, whatever it took. The relief she felt knowing he wanted to come with her was immense. Jane knew he wasn't going to let her take the next step alone.

Even so, Jane protested. "You can't leave work, Toby. I can't ask you to do that. That's not why I called. Look, I'll just cancel it and head home. It's fine." She couldn't think of any reason why going to the solicitor would be good now. Her mind was swimming with all the possibilities of what Dave would do to her, she was certain he'd find out what he'd had done behind his back.

Toby's voice raised an octave or two. "Don't you dare cancel that appointment! Stick your phone on hands free and just drive to the café. I'll ring you back when I'm in the car... Janey, *please* don't cancel the appointment. I need you to go see the solicitor, okay? Are you listening to me?" Toby pleaded. Jane could hear him moving through the building they worked in, no doubt making his way to where his car was parked.

So not only had she messed up her day, but she'd messed up his day too.

"Yeah, I'm listening. Okay, I'll meet you at the café but I'm not promising anything, Tobes. I can't make you any promises, not until I have it all straight in my head." With that, Jane stuck her phone in the hands free cradle and set off to meet her friend at the little café as instructed.

The café was busier than usual, but wouldn't that be that case when all Jane needed was a little peace and quiet to calm her nerves and think through her actions? There was never usually more than a handful of customers throughout the day. It was clear that the new owners had tried to improve its appeal to the growing early evening clientele. Gone were the tired old tables and covers and shiny new bistro style furniture stood in their place. The menu had been updated from that of a greasy spoon to offer food more befitting its new revamped interior. Jane missed the old style café even though the revamp was much needed. It used to be the kind of place you'd pop into before embarking on your Saturday morning shopping trip. Somewhere you could be invisible and at peace. The new owners wanted rid of that image, preferring to entice the up and coming early thirty year olds instead.

Jane watched the door of Zac's Café intently for thirty minutes, waiting for the great big bear of a man that was Toby to walk in. She knew he wouldn't let her down, if he said he'd be there, he would be, but as the minutes ticked by Jane had found it harder to stay seated and not run like the wind.

The door swung open and in walked Toby. Grinning widely at Jane, he made his way through the morning coffee drinkers, towards the table where she was seated. "Hey, lovely. You okay?" Toby filled the chair next to Jane as he planted the usual kiss on her cheek, and as he did her face crumpled, and the tears that she had managed to hold at bay for the last few days finally spilled over. Toby didn't speak; he just leaned over, taking her in his arms, holding her tightly while she cried into his chest. She no longer cared that the other customers around them would be staring at the pathetic person she felt she had become.

Toby let her cry until she was exhausted, then he carefully held her shoulders to right her posture. When he was certain she wasn't going to sob again he released his grip on her. He wiped the tears clear from her cheeks before taking her face in his hands. "Better?" he gently asked. Jane only nodded once. "Good, 'cos this lot think I'm the bad guy that made you cry." He motioned with his chin to the staff behind the counter, who were now busily trying not to look in their direction.

Regret was running through Jane even more now. "Oh no, sorry, Toby, I didn't think. Sorry."

Toby chuckled. "Hey, stop that. I'm a big boy, I can handle them. Where's this appointment at? Do we need to go yet? I'll drive, you can't drive in that state. God knows how you got here in one piece." He took Jane's hand in his as he made to stand up, pulling Jane behind him.

Jane remained seated. "I don't think I can, Toby," she said quietly.

"We'll go together; it's a half-hour appointment. You can survive half an hour. You don't have to do anything else today. Then I'll bring you back for your car and we can go for a drink after, okay? It's just thirty minutes, Janey. Thirty minutes, come on." He gently pulled on her hand, willing her to stand beside him.

Thirty minutes, could she get through that length of time? Jane wasn't so sure she could do it alone. "Will you come in with me? Please, Toby."

He nodded as he led Jane out the door. "I wouldn't have it any other way. I said I'd be there for you and I meant it." With Toby by her side it seemed to give her permission to allow all her fears to manifest at once. Her world seemed to spin on its axis, as her knees felt weak. Jane linked arms with Toby in a bid to keep herself upright. As the spots began to fill her field of vision, Jane realised it was all getting a little real now. She was really doing this.

When they reached his car he opened the passenger door and helped Jane inside. Toby pulled out the seatbelt, passing it to Jane to fasten, only when he heard it click into place did he gently closed the door. Jane knew he was making sure she couldn't make a run for it before he made it to the other side of the car.

Once he had started the engine and pulled the car out into the stream of traffic Toby gently placed his hand over Jane's, squeezing slightly in solidarity. She just about managed to turn her head in his general direction and offer a faint hint of a smile. He never took his eyes off the road or his hand away from Jane's; evidently desperate to convey that he was with her in this, no matter. Jane thought that maybe he was gripping her hand so tightly because he was also terrified she'd get there and refuse to go in but that was a bridge they'd have to cross when they got there. Jane wasn't a religious woman but she offered up a silent prayer to whoever may be listening, asking them to give her all the courage she needed to get through the next hour of her life.

Chapter eleven

"Mrs Ryan, Ms McCarthy's ready for you now. Just follow me this way." The young girl in the smart black trouser suit smiled sweetly at Jane. Toby had managed to entice her out his car but only after another five minute pep talk and a promise that she didn't have to do anything the solicitor suggested, if she didn't want to. Jane prayed to the same person she'd called upon before. This time she asked for the strength to not only listen but act on the advice she was sure they would give her.

Jane gripped Toby's hand tighter "Can my friend come in with me? I think I need the moral support." She was sure she'd heard him wince slightly at the force she'd used to hold his hand, but he'd never complain, it wasn't in his nature. He merely squeezed her hand back in unity.

The woman smiled. "Of course he can. If that's what you want. Please, this way." She motioned for them to follow her down the corridor. Twenty-three footsteps later—yes Jane counted every single one of them—the receptionist knocked once on a solid brown wooden door and pushed it open, stepping aside for Jane and Toby to enter.

Toby smiled down at her. "I can wait here if you prefer, right outside the door, Janey." It was clear he didn't want to, but regardless, he gave her the option to face her demons alone.

She clung tighter to his hand. "You promised. Toby, you promised you'd come in." Fear was thick in Jane voice now, causing her voice to wobble with the threat of tears. Her whole body shaking as she begged him to stay with her. Jane was certain he could feel her trembling as the vibrations shook through her arm.

He nodded, smiling reassuringly at Jane. "Alright, darling. Come on then." He placed his hand in the small of Jane's back, guiding her into the large room. If he hadn't, Jane didn't think her legs would have made it across the threshold. As it was she felt like she'd left her stomach back in the car. This whole situation felt alien to her.

Sitting behind the large wooden desk was a large lady with soft features and greying hair cut into a very neat, shoulder-length bob. "Mrs Ryan. I'm Helen. Please take a seat, can I get you a coffee?" Her glasses sat high up on the bridge of her nose and she had a notebook open in front of her with Jane's name written clearly in capital letters across the top of the page along with the date and time.

Ten-seventeen am.

Jane heard Toby say from beside her "I think just some water, please, if that's okay?"

Jane nodded in confirmation. "Oh sorry, yes just water.....please." The enormity of the situation was overwhelming her.

Helen addressed the young woman who had shown them in. "Kate, two glasses of water please." She then smiled warmly at Jane. "Mrs Ryan, take a seat, please." The solicitor gestured to the second seat, indicating for Toby to sit too.

Jane looked across at him as she reached across to take his hand again. It was then that Jane noticed the lady sitting across the room in the corner. She stood to introduce herself as the support worker, from the Domestic Violence Support Unit that Jane had called the day before. She informed both Toby and Jane that she would just listen in for now and if needed, they could talk afterwards. Jane's voice wouldn't work; she could only manage to nod vaguely at the very smiley woman who was there to help her through her tangled mess.

Evidently sensing her discomfort the solicitor

asked softly, "Mrs Ryan, are you okay, do you need anything?"

Jane spoke in a quiet voice. "Jane, it's Jane, Please don't call me Mrs Ryan. I don't like it anymore." "I...I...How does this work, exactly?" She asked, looking up at the matronly figure sitting behind the desk.

Helen McCarthy sat back in her chair, her hands gently cupped in her lap. "Well, Jane. I have some basic details from Ms Clay, from the phone call you made to them yesterday." Helen smiled at the lady from the refuge. "I just need you to verify firstly that they are correct." She looked down at her notepad and read aloud a transcript from the phone call Jane had made to the advice line. "The final point on the list is the rape that took place eight days ago. Is that correct?" Toby's gasp was audible to all in the room, Jane felt his body tense beside her. The solicitor continued. "Is there anything else you need to add?"

Toby gripped her hand tighter and she realised she hadn't told him that Dave had raped her, after locking Freya in her room. Ashamed that the truth had been exposed, Jane now wished she had let Toby wait outside.

With her cheeks glowing and bile rising in her throat Jane turned to face Toby. "Y-you can leave if you like." She released his hand giving him the get out clause she thought he might need. She'd come this far, she could go on.

Toby shook his head. "Not going anywhere, Janey." Toby reached across, taking her hand in his again. Only this time he held it tighter than before. He lowered his head slightly and took a large breath before relaxing his shoulders and clearly preparing himself for whatever else his friend hadn't divulged.

From the tightness of his grip on her hand she guessed Dave had better make sure his path never crossed with Toby's again because it appeared Toby may not be able to keep his hands to himself any longer. Jane knew he'd only managed to so far out of respect for her and Freya, but she knew hearing Dave had raped her would tip him over the edge.

Jane returned her gaze to fix on Ms McCarthy, sitting opposite her. "It is rape, isn't it?" Her voice wavered as she spoke. "He can't do that, can he, if I say no? I mean, I *did* say no over and over again. I asked him to stop, to leave me alone. It is rape, isn't it?" She desperately needed clarity from this woman. She needed to hear someone who knew what they were talking about, tell her that she still had the right to say no to sex with her husband. Say no to someone that she had willing had sex with many times.

Ms McCarthy fixed her attention firmly on Jane. "Yes it is. You *always* have the right to say no. No-one can make you do that if you don't want to. It is recognised as marital rape in a court of law now. Was it just the once, Jane, or did it happen often?" she enquired gently, pen poised ready to capture any small detail Jane gave.

"Once," was the only reply Jane could manage.

The solicitor nodded, going over the notes she had made on the page with Jane's name across it. Seeing the pad made it all seem real; having everything written down on paper gave it some kind of weight. It wasn't just the little bubble Jane had created anymore.

Ms McCarthy placed her pen down and linked her fingers before resting her hands on the desk. "Okay, Jane, here is what we need to do next."

For the next ten minutes the solicitor went over all the options available to Jane, starting with a safe house that she and Freya could go to that afternoon. Jane sat quietly, praying that Toby was taking all this in, because she wasn't sure she would remember everything later. She was pretty sure she'd missed a lot of it anyway.

Jane realised the room was now silent. They were obviously waiting for her to make a decision and when one didn't come Toby prompted her. "Janey, do you want them to arrange a safe house for you today?" He was looking at her with a hope-filled gaze now.

Jane lifted her chin. "No, I don't want to leave."

Toby looked downcast, complete confusion crossed his face as Jane realised she hadn't made herself clear. "No, Toby, I mean, why should *I* leave *my* home? I want *him* to leave. You said that was an option, didn't you?" Jane questioned not only the two women directly but herself also, needing clarity.

"Yes, but I can't push for that today, Jane. That option will take me a few days to put in front of a judge. You could go with Ms Clay today, to a place of safety." Helen the solicitor smiled, hopeful that Jane would agree.

Summoning strength from somewhere deep within Jane replied defiantly, "I don't want to. I'm not running anymore. No, I want *him* to get out of my home. I want a divorce." Toby stared at Jane as a huge grin slowly spread across his face almost splitting it in two in the process. Jane folded her arms across her chest. "What? I'm not going, Toby." Where the new found confidence had come from, she didn't know but she *did* know it felt pretty good to be finally taking charge; to be taking back some responsibility.

Toby chuckled. "Who are you and what have you done with Janey?" Shaking his head in what looked like disbelief. Or was it relief? Jane wasn't sure. Jane had uttered the words she knew he'd only hoped to ever hear. It was the beginning of what she was certain would be a difficult path for her but she knew he'd be there all the way for her.

Ms Clay coughed lightly bringing the pair back to the meeting. "I could make a phone call, get a locksmith out. The police can arrange for a panic alarm to be in place in the next day or two. Could Toby stay with you until then?" She raised an eyebrow quizzically at Toby, phone in hand, ready to make the promised call.

Toby didn't give Jane chance to open her mouth. He shrugged his shoulder indicating it was a stupid question that didn't need to be asked, let alone answered. "Of course. She's my friend. I'll stay as long as she needs me. That's a given."

Jane didn't know what she'd done to deserve such an amazing friend in her life but she was glad she'd found him. Because it had been difficult to talk to Lindsey about it all, they were too close somehow, Jane still hadn't filled her in about all the gory details of her marriage. Although Lindsey would be a little upset that Jane hadn't gone to her first, she knew she'd be glad she was getting help now.

Ms Clay asked, "Is that okay, Jane? Shall I make the phone calls on your behalf?" Jane nodded allowing the woman to step out of the room, her phone already pressed to her ear.

Helen closed the notepad on her desk, signalling

the meeting was nearing an end. "All that's left now is for me to collate all the information. I'll get the papers drawn up and you should receive your copy in the next few days. We'll petition Mr Ryan at his work address this afternoon, instructing him not to return to the marital home. It'll get lodged with the court, and we'll have to wait for Mr Ryan to get a solicitor. But it should be pretty straightforward. Jane." Smiling, Ms McCarthy stood and escorted Jane and Toby to the door. Toby took her extended hand, thanking her for her time as he led Jane from the room still holding her hand. "If you have any questions about anything we've gone over today, Jane, just give me a call and we can arrange a further appointment."

Jane nodded, there was probably a lot of questions that would arise over the next day or two, things she'd need clarifying. But for now, Jane took solace in the relief she felt. Knowing she'd made a positive step in the right direction felt astonishing.

As they entered the waiting room, the support worker was finishing up the calls she had promised to make. "That's all sorted, Jane. The police will come here this afternoon to collect the petition. They'll deliver it to Mr Ryan at work, before end of play today. There'll be an officer outside your address for a while this evening too but that's nothing to worry about. The locksmith is on his way now so we need to meet him there, okay?" Ms Clay asked Jane.

It was in that moment that the fear decided to rear its ugly head again. Gripping tightly around Jane's chest. Dave would know today. He'd find out that she had filed for divorce. He'd be angry and wouldn't take this lying down. Jane knew all too well what happened when he didn't get his own way. She'd be on the receiving end of his swift right hook again. She had no doubt about that.

Toby waited for Jane to answer; when she didn't he simply took over and gave driving directions for Jane's address to Ms Clay or Judy, as they now knew her to be called. He informed her they would need to collect Jane's car and Freya on the way, but that they'd meet her back there as soon as they could.

Placing his hand in the small of her back once more, Toby gently pushed Jane forwards, making her legs work. Jane knew she wouldn't have moved if he hadn't taken control of the situation as he did.

He asked, "Janey, can we pick Freya up now? Will that be okay?" His questioning was gentle but persistent as he guided her back to the car that waited across the street. "Janey, I need you to snap out of it. Come on, you've come this far, don't bolt on me now, darling!" Toby held tightly onto Jane's shoulder, compelling her to focus on him. Forcing her out of the bubble she'd locked herself away in again.

Jane lifted her chin to look at him, bewildered. "Oh my God, what have I done? This is going to be so bad, Tobes." Tears ran freely down Jane's cheeks again. "He's going to know what I've done, they're going to tell him I want a divorce because he hit me." Jane's stomach rolled, if she'd eaten at all today the contents would have been forced from within.

Toby fixed her with a stern gaze. "It's going to be bad, yes, but I'll stay with you and no-one is going to touch a hair on your head, I promise you. He won't get within six feet of you. Judy said there'll be police there too. You've nothing to be scared of, I'll look after you." He smiled sweetly at her, as he helped her into the car and leant across to fasten her seatbelt again. Once he too was seated in the car he reached over and patted her knee. "Do you want me to ring LJ and get her to pick Freya up for you, might be easier than explaining to the old folk just now?" Jane nodded her response as Toby started the engine and headed off towards Jane's home. "We'll leave your car at the café for now. I'll pop back later and get it, okay?"

Panic erupted violently spilling from Jane. "NO! You can't leave me alone, Toby. He'll wait until you leave and then...I don't know what he is going do." She could see it playing out in her mind; Toby would leave to collect her car, Dave would be lurking somewhere and then *wham*, she'd be doubled up in pain again at best. She couldn't risk that.

Toby nodded and smiled reassuringly. "Okay, it's okay, don't panic, I'll stay, LJ can go get the car. You trust her to drive it, don't you?" He giggled; Lindsey's driving skills left a lot to be desired. They had joked on more than one occasion, that even the army wouldn't let her drive a tank because she'd manage to smash it up.

Realisation once again hit and Jane's insides knotted. "We have to tell her, don't we? I didn't think about telling everyone. They're all going to think I'm so stupid. Either that or they won't believe me." Sobs wracked through her body, the inevitability of it all hitting home hard. "Nobody will believe me, will they, Toby?" Horror bubbled through her voice; she had no idea what to expect once Dave knew what she'd done. Jane just knew it wasn't going to be alright. He wouldn't simply walk away from this and if he had anything to do with it, neither would she.

Once again Toby's voice calmed her inner turmoil. "Listen, we can just tell LJ for now, we don't need to tell anyone else anything at all, darling. You don't have to explain to anyone, if you don't want to. It's *your* business, nobody else needs to know a thing." He was right.

They drove the rest of the journey in silence with

Toby making covert glances at her the whole time. Jane sat and stared out of the window, contemplating how the next few hours would play out. Judy was going to stay with them to talk to the police when they arrived; assuring Jane she wouldn't even have to answer the phone if she didn't want to. Judy and Toby could take care of everything, leaving Jane to look after herself and Freya.

She was vaguely aware of Toby talking over the hands free to Lindsey, giving her specific instructions to tell Jane's parents that she had gone home from work ill. He would explain everything when he saw her, he told her. There he was, Jane's knight in shining armour, taking care of business for her again.

Chapter twelve

Jane didn't know what she expected to see as they rounded the corner onto the street where she lived, but seeing the police car parked outside her front gate made the reality of what she'd done hit home even harder. There was no choice now but to see it through. The officer was standing outside the house talking to a man who Jane presumed was the locksmith, and as promised Judy from the Domestic Abuse Unit was there too, conferring with both men.

Jane hadn't noticed Toby's car come to a stop, or the fact that he was now standing beside her, holding the car door open, waiting for her to get out and unlock the house for everyone. She inhaled deeply and moved her legs around to the side. She clambered out of the car in a daze but Toby's arm wrapped around her shoulders tightly, providing the support she evidently needed.

She could see the neighbours' curtains twitching;

they must have been desperate to know what was going on in their quiet, sleepy little street. Realising that she was under scrutiny made her want to turn and run, run and not stop, but she couldn't. Instead, she moved slowly up towards the house, past the locksmith who tried to make some kind of conversation with her but Jane just needed to get inside, get away from the prying eyes. She couldn't even look at the poor man, never mind make small talk with him. Once inside she placed her keys on the side table, the small hallway felt cavernous somehow, Jane wrapped her arms around herself protectively. Jane glanced around her surroundings as though taking it in for the first time again. She was vaguely aware of Toby talking to someone on the phone, was it *her* phone? Did he just answer *her* house phone? She couldn't unravel the thoughts in her head, they swam around in chaos like litter on a breeze as Jane tried to work through her emotions.

When Jane realised it might be Dave on the other end of that call terror rose again in her throat. She couldn't let Toby deal with Dave's abuse. Jane reached out to take the phone from Toby, only to be guided down the hallway by Judy. "Just let him deal with it, love. Let's get you sorted with a drink first, eh?" Judy pulled out the chair and motioned for Jane to sit at the table. She put the kettle on and searched through the kitchen cupboards for cups, talking as she did so, as if to fill the silence and distract her ward. "Now, there's nothing for you to worry about, Jane. Ms McCarthy, Helen, has just called me; the papers have been collected from her office, so Mr Ryan will be notified very soon that he isn't to come home today. All we need to do is sit tight here; make sure that you and Freya are fine. The police officer will be here for a short time too. Just in case. Now just try to drink this for me." She placed a steaming cup in front of a shaking Jane.

Jane wrapped both hands around the cup to steady it; she was suddenly so cold—probably the shock of it all, she surmised—her hands wouldn't stay still long enough to allow her to lift the cup to her mouth. Judy found a blanket in the clean washing pile and wrapped it loosely around Jane's shoulders, before disappearing off to talk to the officer again. Leaving Jane alone with her thoughts.

Toby came into the kitchen carrying a very giggly Freya in his arms, with Lindsey hot on his heels; the tears streaming down her cheeks were a dead giveaway that she knew *everything*. Jane held out her arms for her daughter to be handed over. She just needed to hold her, smell her, feeling her warmth as she cuddled into Jane's side brought her back to the here and now.

"Mummy, Unca Tubs funny! He blow berries on

me!" She squirmed and giggled on her mother's knee, trying to hide from Toby as he tried to tickle her again.

"Freya, why don't you show Uncle Toby that new Froggy game you have? I bet you could beat him at it." Jane lifted the little girl from her knee and passed her to Toby, who without question headed off in the direction of the playroom. Jane knew she owed Lindsey an explanation and the last thing she wanted was Freya overhearing any of that conversation.

Jane watched as Freya wriggled out of Toby's arms, down to the floor. "Unca Tubs, I can walk, I a big girl! Come on." She gripped his hand and walked down the hallway beside him, babbling away. Seeing Toby's huge hand wrapped around the little girl's tiny fragile one almost broke Jane. It took all her strength to push down the fear she held inside for Freya's future with a single mother.

Lindsey sank to the floor, kneeling beside her friend, pulling her in and holding her tightly. Tears fell freely from both women. "I can't believe he's been hurting you." Lindsey spoke through her own tears as she clung on to Jane. "Why didn't you tell me? You could have told me, I would've understood, I could've helped. I *want* to help." She mumbled into Jane's shoulder. "Toby told me everything, please don't be mad at him. I *made* him tell me what he knew because I could tell things weren't right, I knew you weren't ill or just having a day off work today. I had no idea things were so bad, honey." She pulled away and tucked a stray hair from Jane's face behind her ear and wiped the tears that were now flowing like a river down Jane's cheeks. "I'm so sorry, Jane, I should've realised that something was wrong earlier. I'm such a shit friend. I just thought that you had a bit of an odd relationship, not that he was knocking you around. Why would he *do* that to you? You wouldn't hurt a damn fly, for fuck's sake!" Jane took it as a rhetorical question and let Lindsey continue. "Well, I've called Sam and he's going to drop me some things off later. I'll stay with you for a few days. I know Toby will be here, but I want to help take care of you and Freya, if you'll let me." She was searching Jane's face for some reaction while trying to get a grip on her own emotion. Unsure of what Lindsey needed from her, Jane simply smiled, nodding her agreement. She didn't have the energy to argue anymore. She only wanted today to be over and to be able to breathe a little more freely again.

Judy paid the locksmith, despite Toby trying to beat her to it. Apparently Jane's safety was covered by some emergency funding that was available and needed using before the end of the month. It was also cheaper to pay the locksmith than it was to put a mother and child up in a safe house for a few nights, she informed him, so the money they'd saved could go to help another woman in danger. Jane could hear Judy and the locksmith talking in hushed tones at the end of the hallway for a few minutes before she walked back through to the kitchen to tell Jane she had to leave. She said she'd return the following day but in the meantime that she was only a phone call away, should she need to talk. Jane thanked her but made noises that indicated she'd be fine with Toby and now Lindsey staying with her.

Twenty minutes later the phone calls started.

Dave began pleading with Jane at first, begging with her to let him come home so they could talk it over. Asking for her to *at least* let him talk to Freya. He cried when Jane refused point blank, finding the strength from somewhere deep inside. The phone calls that followed became progressively angrier, varying from questioning what it was that he had done wrong, to telling Jane it was entirely her fault he had to hit her, pointing out that if she'd have just done as she was told, none of this would have happened. When he accused Jane of ruining Freya's life by filing for divorce from her father, she lost it completely. She screamed down the phone that she had left him to make sure Freya was safe from *him*, to make sure *she* didn't have to be afraid in her own home. Dave had merely mocked her.

After witnessing the awful scene, Toby took the telephone from Jane and firmly placed it back in its cradle. As he comforted Jane in his arms on the floor where she'd slumped to sit with her head in her hands, the phone rang again, and refusing to let her suffer any further, Toby answered it instead. Jane could hear the shouting coming from her now estranged husband on the other end of the line.

Toby listened calmly until the noise stopped and then simply stated, "Bring it on, big man." Before replacing the phone and unplugging it from the socket.

It was going to be a long night.

With her little girl safely tucked up in her bed, blissfully unaware of the chaos surrounding her, thanks to Lindsey and Toby, the trio sat down with a takeaway as Jane's friends tried to make sure she ate something, if only just a few mouthfuls, of the mountain of food that was laid out on the dining table. The conversation was less than easy, both Toby and Lindsey tried to keep things light and skirted around the real talking point. They both took turns in reiterating that Jane had done the right thing, praising her for finding the courage to finally make the break and seek help. Jane could tell that Lindsey was still a little upset she hadn't figured it out sooner.

"I really wish you had talked to me, you know. I feel like I've been a really crappy friend to you knowing that you felt you couldn't tell me. I'm so upset that you've suffered in silence until Toby figured it out, it should have been me that noticed the bruises. I'm so sorry, honey. I know I can be a bit full on at times with my opinions but I would have listened and I would have believed you. I would have understood. Why didn't you tell me?" Lindsey asked as Toby stood to clear away the leftovers.

"LJ, it doesn't matter now, does it? She's been through enough today. She doesn't need to justify herself again today." Toby raised an eyebrow in Lindsey's direction.

"Talk to you? Tell you that my life was a mess. Tell you that for most of the time I have known you, I have been covered in bruises that I had to hide from not only you, but my parents? Is that what you want to hear? Or did you want me to tell you that he beat me up once, because you came to visit and I forgot to ask permission beforehand? When I married Dave, it was for life, not for a few years, not to put me on until something better came along. I'm sorry, really sorry I didn't tell you but I had enough going on just surviving each day." Jane stood and walked out of the kitchen away from the situation, as she always did. The way she had been conditioned to behave, not to confront or make things worse. That was how she dealt with everything these days. Back down, walk away, and keep the peace. Jane could hear the pair of them arguing in the kitchen, Lindsey's voice getting higher and higher, Toby trying to talk over the top of her, "Happy now, LJ?" Jane heard him say as he came out of the kitchen, heading in Jane's direction.

They both heard the back door open and click shut again quietly.

Toby huffed the air from his lungs. "Think she's gone for some fresh air, I think I said a bit too much to her, Janey. Sorry, babe. You okay?" He sat beside Jane, pulling her into his side as he planted a soft kiss on the top of her head as Jane let out a sigh. He rubbed Jane's arm reassuringly. "I know why you stayed with him for so long; I understand it was hard for you. It doesn't start out bad, does it, darlin'?" The tension began to ease out of her shoulders finally.

"Look what happened when I tried to leave him last time, he reacted by taking an overdose, what was I supposed to do? I couldn't leave him then, could I? You're right, it wasn't *all* bad, we had some really great times. I have some good memories. When we first met in high school he was lovely, he looked after me, made me feel so special. He made me feel like I was the centre of his universe. I never had to open a door myself, never paid for a meal. He took care of everything. Everyone loved him; he is just one of those guys that people liked. He made the proposal so special, you know. He took me to this beautiful, secluded beach one night, when we got there he had laid a blanket out with loads of candles, I mean loads. He got his sister to set it all up while he drove me there. We had a picnic and then he produced this big box for me to open. Inside it was a balloon, one of those helium ones, with a weight attached at the bottom. It had 'Marry me?' written across it and my engagement ring was threaded onto the ribbon on the balloon. I was so happy that night." Jane smiled at the memories.

Toby listened intently. "It sounds really nice, Janey." Jane knew he was allowing her to talk through her memories, she knew he didn't want to hear how perfect her life used to be. She knew Toby's ultimate fear was that she'd take Dave back, that her resolve would wain and she'd give in to his pleading.

"It was. For such a long time too. When Freya was born, God, if you could have seen him. The tears running down his face, the pure joy of seeing his daughter born. He spent hours thanking me for such a perfect gift, said he could never repay me for producing such a beautiful little girl. His universe, he called us his two angels. He promised to move heaven and earth for both of us. I don't know when it changed really. Things just shifted a bit, you know? Like, he would tell me he didn't like the top I was wearing and ask me to change into one *he* had bought, because I looked more beautiful in the one he suggested. Then he started answering for me, not letting me speak out for myself, in case I got embarrassed or flustered, he said he didn't want me to feel awkward if I didn't understand the question." Shaking her head in disbelief as it all unravelled before her. "Soon, I didn't dare open my mouth, unless he gave me a nod to say it was alright to speak. But he made it look like he was just looking out for me. He became very controlling. Manipulative. I realise that now; about what I wore, whom I spoke to and who I was friends with. He used to take my phone from me and read my text messages and call logs. I used to delete most messages I sent and received, just in case it made him angry. I memorised your number off by heart, so I didn't need to program it in, Lindsey's as well, there's actually very few numbers in my phone if you check it." She fumbled in her pocket and produced her mobile phone, holding it aloft for Toby. "You can check it. I don't mind if you want to. Did I tell you that I had to give him the bus tickets, as proof, if I said I went on the bus somewhere too? On one occasion, he slapped me in front of his work friends on a night out because I answered him back. That's when I should have left, isn't it?" Toby stayed silent, not adding anything to the one way conversation. Instead he let her clear her mind.

A loud clapping made her jump. "Oh, bravo! An Oscar-winning performance I'd say, Jane." Toby and Jane both spun around to find Dave standing in the doorway. He sneered. "Now, I'd like you to take your arm from around my wife and get the hell out of my house. I won't cause a scene." He was glaring at Toby with his fists now clenched at his side.

Toby stood and pushed Jane behind him. His attempt at keeping her safe. "Looks like you're going to have to cause a scene, because I'm not leaving her here with you. Janey, go call the police. Tell them the psycho's here and he's refusing to leave."

With a pounding heart and shaking limbs, Jane moved out slowly from behind Toby and began to make her way to where the phone sat a few feet away.

Dave moved towards her. "I wouldn't do that, Jane. I just need to talk to you, sort all this mess out that you caused, baby." Toby got to her first, standing once more between her and danger. Fear gripped her with an iron fist. Her first thoughts were of Freya sleeping upstairs, could she get to their daughter before him? She wasn't entirely sure she could co-ordinate her limbs into some semblance of movement if her life depended on it.

"Ring them, Janey." Toby insisted. "Look, Dave, you need to leave now, mate. Or I might have to make you leave."

As Jane picked up the phone Dave lunged forward, straight into Toby, who in return knocked Jane off balance. Struggling to stop herself from falling over, she grabbed at Toby's shirt to steady them both but to no avail. Jane crashed to the floor, hitting her head on the television stand on the way down. *Shit that hurt*, her hand instinctively reached up to check for the blood as her surroundings began to spin. She could feel the sticky liquid on her fingertips as she pressed onto the area where her head had connected with the piece of furniture. Vaguely aware of Toby and Dave scuffling on the floor beside her, Jane listened as the sirens in the distance grew louder and louder until they suddenly stopped and chaos ensued inside her house.

Two officers dragged the men apart, forcing their hands behind their backs while they put handcuffs on them both. Lindsey was by Jane's side, appearing from nowhere, helping Jane to sit up now as everything came to focus in front of her.

The enormity of the situation hit Jane as she took in the sight of Toby in handcuffs before her. She frantically explained to the officer that Toby was innocent, begging him to remove the cuffs that restrained her saviour.

Toby was panting, out of breath as he told her, "Janey, it's fine, honey, calm down, you're safe now." He tried to soothe her as they removed his restraints and he rubbed his wrists.

Dave, on the other hand, was fighting and kicking out at the officers, as they tried to lift him out of the house and into the back of the van that awaited him. "Get the fuck off me, you bastards! She's my wife, for fuck's sake." He screamed over his shoulder, "Jane, tell them it's a mistake, tell them we're okay, Jane!"

She didn't speak. She sat there on the floor huddled into the corner, holding her head in her hands as her friends tried to calm her once more. "How did they know, I didn't ring them?" she asked.

Lindsey stroked her arm. "I did, Jane, I walked out after Toby told me a few home truths. I went for a smoke to get my head around everything. When I came back I saw Dave's car parked outside and it was all kicking off in here. I rang them and told them about the idiot. I'm so sorry, Jane. If I hadn't walked out, this wouldn't have happened and the big hero here wouldn't be nursing a fat lip." She nodded across at Toby, who was trying to smile without moving his lips too much. The giggles that erupted soon turned into howling laughter. None of them were sure the officer who had returned to check on Jane and get their statements quite understood what was so funny.

Lindsey eventually stood once the hysteria had calmed. "Drink, anyone? I could sure use something *very* alcoholic right now." She stood and headed off to the kitchen leaving Jane with Toby and the officer.

Chapter thirteen

Ironically, the finalisation of Jane's divorce occurred on her fourth wedding anniversary. The date seemed fitting for the marriage to be finally ended somehow.

Maybe now, all the fighting would stop. Maybe Dave would cease turning up at all hours to cause problems for Jane or her parents. As far as she was concerned the day marked the start of the rest of her life. The bad stuff was over and done with and never again would she be known as Mrs Ryan. There'd been no doubt about returning to her maiden name as soon as the divorce was finalised. Her only regret was that Freya would no longer share the same surname as her, but it was a small price to pay for her freedom. The freedom to breathe and live a normal life.

Her closest friends had organised a bit of a get together with work colleagues and family. A *divorce celebration*, they had called it, and Jane couldn't wait, it would be a fantastic night to mark the beginning of the rest of her life. Her parents were looking after Freya for the weekend; something both Freya *and* her grandparents were excited about, so much so that Freya had packed her overnight bag a week ago to make sure she had everything she could possibly need. It had been a really distressing time for Jane's parents too; they of course, blamed themselves for the situation their daughter had found herself in. They had thought that their now ex-son-in-law, had been the perfect partner and father. They had, of course, gone through the emotional rollercoaster with Jane, suffered the highs and the lows, but they had stood by her side supporting her through each hurdle, until Jane was once again strong enough to ride it alone. Her dad had said once that they felt he had not only hurt Jane with his violence, but them also; they too felt as though they had been punched and kicked in the gut. That he had let *them* down. Jane understood that to some extent. They'd spent their whole lives making sure she wanted for nothing; that she grew up in a safe loving environment where she'd been free to explore and become the confident young woman they'd handed over on her wedding day. They'd spent years making Dave feel like a part of their family with birthday tea's and carefully selected gifts. There'd been lunchtimes in the pub with Jane's dad while Jane and her mum had a catch up; he was very much a member of their family in their eyes, getting to know him and accepting him as a son they'd never had. It all seemed like such a waste to them now.

Elaine had been distraught at the thought of her daughter being hurt by the man they had so lovingly accepted all those years ago. Jane had to somehow make them understand that she didn't tell them in order to protect them from the hurt she knew would follow once they knew the truth. It had been a fraught conversation, to say the least, but they hadn't once questioned her actions or her decision to divorce him, as she first worried they might. Instead they vowed to give her the love and support she needed to get through it. And she had indeed survived her first weeks alone.

Jane was back at work, Freya was settled and happy, more carefree than Jane had even seen her. She hadn't noticed at the time, or maybe she had and had tried to ignore the signs, but the last year had affected her badly but the little girl was now well on the way to being her funny little self again. She was, however, still afraid of the dark and completely refused to have her bedroom door closed, preferring to hear her mum pottering around at night, Jane understood that. It somehow made the nights easier for her, knowing Freya was there listening out for her. By rights it should have been the other way around but kids have a way of taking control of a situation and making it right. Even when the bleakest days hit, Jane knew Freya could pull her from the dark depths once more. The little girl was like a little ray of sunshine on even the drabbest of days. That bright little smile and those chubby little arms locked around Jane's neck in the tightest of cuddles went a long way towards erasing a lot of pain.

Toby had become a constant part of their lives. He regularly spent the night on Jane's couch after they'd eaten too much Chinese food, or drank too much wine; Freya adored her Uncle Tubs, as she called him, just as much as Jane did. They wouldn't have got through the last few months if it hadn't have been for Toby seeing straight through the web of lies Jane had weaved so intricately. Recently though, Jane had become aware of how dependent she'd become on him. The last thing she needed was to step out of a controlling relationship and then rely on Toby to make everything alright again, she knew that was down to her. So with that in mind, she began to push him into resuming his own social life. She knew he couldn't look after her forever, however much she wanted him to, it just wasn't fair that he had put his life on hold for her this last few months. They'd only ever be friends, Jane was more than aware of that. Anything romantic between them would just be weird, he was like a brother to her.

After much persuading, Toby announced that he would be bringing a couple of his friends from back home with him to Jane's celebratory divorce party and they were going to be heading off to a club afterwards. Jane had her invitation to go along with them, of course, but she'd declined, reassuring him that Lindsey would be staying with her, making sure she got home safe and sound. He had taken some convincing but Jane managed eventually, promising him he could come visit her the next day. Jane was well aware he needed to start living his life again, just as much as she did, even though the thought of him not being with her the whole time, was causing one huge big knot of anxiety to form in the pit of her stomach. He had been her rock for such a long time, but she looked forward to the day when he found his own partner in life, someone he could live out his life with. Jane just hoped whoever he ended up with was worthy of him.

It was a little after seven when Jane and Lindsey reached the bar they had picked for the night. It was one of the quieter ones in Leeds City Centre but that didn't mean it would stay that way all night. Especially not once they'd taken up residence in the place. As Jane pushed open the door to the bar, she recognised the tune playing. Pink's So What washed over the room, filling it with its upbeat vibe. Jane couldn't stop her head bobbing along in time with the music. *Yep. It was going to be a good night.*

Lindsey steered her across to where they'd

managed to reserve a corner with a few tables so they could really relax and let their hair down without fear of disturbing the other patrons. Toby had already arrived with his friends in tow.

After his usual kiss to her cheek Toby introduced the men with him. "Jane, this is Ollie," he indicated to the tall, sandy-haired man with the most amazing crystal blue eyes Jane had ever seen. She was sure they actually sparkled in the pub lighting.

Ollie raised his beer bottle slightly in greeting. "Nice to meet you, Jane." Small wrinkles appeared around his eyes as he smiled broadly. If Lindsey hadn't have nudged her discreetly, Jane's jaw may have actually hit the floor as she gazed in appreciation at the fine specimen.

Those pesky butterflies began to float around Jane's stomach again, only this time they were soaring in a beautiful formation. "You too." The coy smile giving away the fact the she found him a little attractive. Oblivious to her reaction, Toby continued around the small group, introducing Jamie, the shorter more athletic looking one and finally Dan who looked a little lost amongst his peers.

Jane placed her sparkly black clutch bag on one of the tables where a silver bucket sat holding a bottle of champagne. "Oh, it feels like a proper VIP party now!"

She giggled as Toby uncorked the bottle and poured her and Lindsey a glass.

The smile appeared to be almost splitting Toby's face in two as he raised his own glass. "Cheers," he clinked his glass against Jane's. "You did it. You really did it. I'm so proud of you."

A warm fuzzy feeling welled in her, the realisation that she'd come through what she was certain was the worst year of her life, caused a giddiness to bubble in her chest. "You bet I did!" She giggled, her shoulder bumped Toby's before lifting her glass to her lips, draining the contents.

Lindsey gasped. "Woah! Easy there, Tiger. We have all night!"

"Oh I know, but I, for one, intend to enjoy myself." Jane reached for the champagne bottle again, topping up hers and Lindsey's glass.

Destiny's Child and Survivor began to play, the beat vibrating through the floor. "Jane! They're playing your song!" Lindsey grabbed the glass in Jane's hand, placing in back on the table alongside hers. "C'mon, we have to dance to this." Jane followed her friend out onto the dance floor and with carefree abandon, they both leapt around singing along way too loudly to the lyrics. As the song came to an end and Kelly Clarkson's Since You Been Gone began to play, Toby, Jamie and Ollie joined the girls on the dance floor. They were intent on making sure Jane had the best night and as she bounced up and down, Lindsey and Toby held each of her hands aloft in a triumphant gesture, encouraging every single second of the merriment she intended to partake in.

The night of celebration had been amazing. The chance to let her hair down and dance the night away enabled Jane to brush away the months of stress and anxiety. Hopefully all that was behind her now and she could move on with her life. She'd already started to make plans for a little holiday, just her and Freya, maybe just a few days for their first trip away alone but she was excited about what the future held for her now. Toby had made sure Jane wanted for nothing throughout the evening; he'd barely left her side the whole night. When he needed to go to the bathroom he left Jane with one of their many friends, not that she needed babysitting. It was just his protective side, a side that he never seemed to bat down where Jane was concerned. Her safety was always paramount. Toby's friends, Dan, Jamie and Ollie had turned out to be the life and soul of the party, Jane could see exactly why Toby was friends with them. Jamie and Lindsey had spent the night laughing together, whilst trying to drink each other under the table. Dan and Ollie seemed the more reserved of the four firm friends but, nonetheless, they knew how to party, and party hard they had.

Lindsey sat opposite Jane at the kitchen table. "Oh my God! What a night, did you enjoy it, honey? I think Sam is a little mad with me though, did you see him kick off when I was dancing with you, Jamie? God, he needs to get a grip sometimes!" Lindsey was giggling into her morning coffee, while Jane made bacon sandwiches; Sam was still asleep on the ready-bed in Freya's room. Toby and his friends had ended up almost knocking Jane's door down at two in the morning, apparently they didn't have enough cash for a taxi home, so decided to walk to Jane's instead as it was nearer. Somehow, Jane didn't believe him and she would tell him so, when everyone had gone.

Jamie glanced across at Lindsey. "Is he always that much of a killjoy, babe?" He asked as he tucked into his breakfast.

Toby laughed loudly as he pulled Jane over to sit on his knee, nobody batted an eyelid at the gesture, it was just Toby's way. "Not so much a killjoy, more like plain old boring!" Toby couldn't help himself when it came to winding Lindsey up about her ever-exasperating husband; Sam was not what you'd call a cool dude, more of your uptight kind of boy next door. But he had a heart of gold and Jane liked him.

Lindsey slapped Toby's arm hard. "Did I tell you

he's started taking his laptop to bed now, so he can update the spreadsheets he's set up for the monthly bills and groceries? Exactly, who else has a spreadsheet for grocery shopping? I can see you're all jealous." Lindsey waved a pointy finger around the gathered group as she gave into the giggle fit "I mean, really!" That was enough to produce a round of whooping and laughter, not to mention choking noises from everyone around the table. Even Jane struggled to keep a straight face amongst the merriment.

Sam's voice stopped the jollity when he interrupted. "What's so funny?" He stood in the doorway looking like he was about to throw up. Green around the gills from all the alcohol he'd consumed the night before. He wasn't a big drinker normally but he'd insisted he wasn't about to miss out on Jane's *big night* as he'd put it.

Taken by surprise a little, Jane smiled broadly. "Nothing, it's just this rowdy lot. Come on, sit down I'll make you some breakfast." Jane jumped up from Toby's knee, gathering the ingredients she needed.

Sam waved one hand and covered his mouth with the other. "No honestly, just coffee for me. I don't feel fantastic. You nearly ready to go, Lins?" He walked over and stood behind his wife, rubbing her shoulders "I just phoned for a taxi, should be here in five."

He bent to kiss Lindsey's head but she moved away

not allowing him to connect the kiss. "Actually, I was going to spend the day with Jane…" She looked to her friend with a pleading expression waiting for her to speak.

Flustered and with an expression that slightly resembled a deer caught in headlights, Jane quickly answered. "Erm, yes we were going to erm…clear out all that rubbish in my room, and I was going to take you to lunch remember." Jane couldn't look at her, why did she put her on the spot like that when she knew she couldn't handle lying?

Sam looked a little upset but he obviously didn't want to cause a scene in front of Toby and his friends. "Okay, well if you must, do you want me to pick you up here later then?"

With a brisk shake of her head, Lindsey assured him she didn't need collecting. "No it's fine, Tubs will give me lift, won't you?" Jane saw her kick Toby under the table prompting him to mutter in agreement that he would, indeed, take her home.

When she had waved Sam off at the door, Lindsey breathed a huge sigh of relief and headed off to find Jamie in the kitchen whilst Toby and Jane cleared away the sleeping bags in the lounge, opening windows as they went. The stale alcohol fumes hung heavy in the air, that and the scent of four grown men.

The giggling alerted Jane to Lindsey's presence in

the doorway. "Right, Jane, we're heading out. Thought I might show Jamie around town. I'll ring you later!" Jamie winked at Toby, whose jaw had just hit the floor; it was Jane's turn to kick him now. The door shut firmly behind them, leaving Toby, Jane and Ollie staring after them.

"Awkward, much?" Ollie stated calmly shortly before they all collapsed again in giggles.

Jane managed to speak through her laughing fit. "I am so going to kill her when she rings!"

Toby stated plainly "She won't ring. Jamie won't give her a minute to open her mouth, well no, that's not strictly true, he'll want her to open her mouth, but not to talk to you!" They were both hysterical now, rolling around on the floor holding their sides.

Jane slapped Toby's arm hard, to which he promptly stopped laughing and looked sullenly at her. "Okay, okay that's my friend you're talking about and she IS MARRIED or had you forgotten?"

Toby fake pouted. "Sorry, Janey. Come on, lunch is on me seeing as *your* BFF stood you up for *my* BFF. Are you coming, Ollie? And where's Dan?"

With a quick shake of his head, Ollie declined the offer. "Nah, mate, my train leaves in just over an hour, I'll have to get a move on." Ollie pulled Jane out of Toby's arms and into his. "Jane, it's been a pleasure, thanks for putting us up. If you ever get fed up of this big thug, then give me a ring. I programmed my number in your mobile last night. Hope you don't mind, but I got yours from Lindsey too," he confidently told Jane with a wink. "I think Dan's still snoring," Ollie muttered as an afterthought before planting a huge wet kiss on Jane's forehead.

Toby put his best hurt face on. "Are you hitting on my woman, mate? You know she'll never call you, 'cos she'll never get pissed off with me. So jog on, matey!" He playfully punched Ollie on the arm, before pulling him in for a man hug. "Take care, I'll let you know when I'm heading home next, okay?"

"Sure, just make sure you bring Jane with you next time." Ollie smiled widely.

With her hands held up questioningly, Jane addressed the pair. "Er, I am still here, you know! Ollie, it's been great, any time you're around I expect a call, okay?" Jane hugged Ollie one last time as he headed towards the door.

"You can bet your life on that one," Ollie winked cheekily at Jane before turning his attention back to Toby. "See you soon, mate." With a nod of his head, Ollie headed out of the door to catch his train home.

Chapter fourteen

Lindsey sat across from Jane in the canteen, shovelling down chocolate like it was going out of fashion. "I left Sam. Last night. I can't stand the suffocation anymore. Do you know, he followed me to my friend's house last week? Like, properly followed me, all covert like. Said he didn't trust me anymore. Can you believe that? The idiot." Lindsey shook her head in disbelief. "Well, I don't care anymore. It's over as far as I'm concerned. He can go home to mummy now. Do you know, she puts lavender on his pillow every night to help him sleep! Why did I marry him? He is so not my type." The words spilled from Lindsey in one long rant. It was blatantly clear she didn't really want any answers to her questions, nor did she want her decision validating.

Jane just sat listening to her, of course Sam didn't trust her anymore, she went off with one of Toby's best mates whom she'd only just met and did God knows what for six hours. Although both of them denied any wrong doing.

Jane wasn't sure her friend had thought her decision through. "Lindsey, are you sure you're doing the right thing? I mean, you don't know Jamie that well, it's just, I see the way Sam looks at you, like you're his world, you know? Are you sure you can't fix this?" Jane felt her friend needed a reality check. "It's not easy being on your own, you know. If you try to work things out I'm sure he'll see things differently. Don't you want to make a go of your marriage?" After everything she'd been through, Jane knew getting a divorce wasn't a walk in the park. She didn't want her friend to go through what she'd experienced if she didn't have to.

Shocked that Jane had questioned her, Lindsey retorted. "Are you kidding me? I'm not leaving him for Jamie, jeez, that was dead in the water before it even started. We had lunch, talked and yeah fooled around a bit but that's all. We're friends. Jamie's not someone you leave your husband for, and yes, I've talked to him a lot this last few days because he listens without making judgement." Lindsey raised her eyebrows, knowing that was maybe a dig too far. "I've left Sam because I don't love him anymore. You know my philosophy on life, if it ain't working, then walk away. I can't stay with him just because we got married; it's not a life sentence anymore. I want to be on my own for a while, I want to live a little, have a bit of fun before I sign up to the whole settling down for life, I'm really not ready for the two point four and a dog thing yet. Sam's old before his time, he thinks we should be in bed by midnight every night and out visiting his family at the weekends. Yes, he may be a lovely guy, but maybe he's too *nice* for me. There's just too much I want to experience before I die, Jane. I thought you of all people would understand," Lindsey stated glumly.

Jane reached out to pat Lindsey's hand. "I do understand. Sorry, I just don't want you to make a mistake, that's all; I just wanted you to be sure. Where are you going to live now?" It suddenly hit Jane that if her friend had walked out on her marriage last night, where the hell had she slept. "Do you want to stay with me for a while?"

Lindsey shook her head. "Don't worry, it's all sorted. I move into my new flat today, after work. I'm so excited, you want to come see it later? It's perfect, just what I need right now, somewhere small and all mine." Her eyes were gleaming now with the sudden change of subject.

Jane realised her friend really had thought this through after all, maybe she'd underestimated her. "Of course I do! But when did all this happen? When did you rent a flat?" Lindsey proceeded to tell how that she had rented the flat from one of the guys in accounts; it had apparently been on the noticeboard for weeks. She had, of course, managed to barter him down on the rent, making it more than affordable for her on her own. He just needed to get it rented out so he could move in with his soon-to-be wife. If there was a deal to be made, you could bet Lindsey would make it. She was the sort of person who'd argue about the sticker price on a chocolate bar if she could.

"Hello, hello, what's going on here then?" Toby pushed his way through the busy canteen to sit beside Jane, as usual planting a kiss on her forehead as he did. His arm, which now lay across Jane's shoulders, was heavy and warm.

Everyone was used to the way he treated Jane, nobody gave them a second glance anymore. Jane didn't think anyone quite believed the whole *just friends* scenario, but if the last few months had taught Jane anything it was to stop caring what other people thought. She loved Toby like a brother; there was nothing she liked more, than to be tucked up under his arm. He made her feel safe and cared for. Something she hadn't had for a very long time.

Jane squeezed Toby's bicep, giving him a wink. "I'm helping Lindsey move into her new flat tonight, you busy or are you gonna lend some muscle?"

"I'd love to help, but I'm babysitting Freya tonight, you donut!" Toby watched with a smug expression on his face as realisation slowly dawned on Jane. She'd totally forgotten about her plans for the evening. One of the guys from the team opposite to hers had offered to take her to see a movie; Toby had been more excited than Jane about the whole thing when she'd talked it over with him. It had been a long time since anyone had asked her out on a date, the etiquette of the game was not her strong point. Toby had been the first person she'd spoken to when Ryan had asked her out and she'd practically run from the office in a blithering mess. The poor guy must have thought she had a screw loose.

Taken aback by Toby's revelation, Lindsey quizzed her friend. "Where you off to Jane? You didn't tell me you were going out, you only ever go out with me or Toby. I'm moving flat and he's babysitting, so spill, lady!" She had that look in her eye that meant Jane couldn't squirm out of telling her. Lindsey wouldn't let this drop until she had the gory details and lots of them. The fact that she was rubbing her hands together in glee like some maniacal cartoon villain didn't help either.

"Janey has a date!" Toby chanted as he sat there grinning like a Cheshire cat.

Fixing him with her 'mum stare' Jane fought to defend her decision to accept Ryan's invitation. "What are we, a bunch of two year olds now?" She turned her attention towards Lindsey. "It's not a date, just a....movie, with a *friend*, that's all. I can cancel, Lindsey, it's not a problem." Jane slapped at Toby's arm as she tried to remove it from around her shoulder, edging over to the other side of her chair. She glared at him, disappointed that he felt it was okay to make fun of her. He, of all people should've known how much courage it had taken her to agree to go out with Ryan in the first place. Her churning stomach had kept her awake for a whole night after she'd agreed.

Toby looked at her, with his mouth twisted up slightly at the corner in contemplation. "Movie, dinner and drinks equals a date in my book and I'm pretty sure Ryan sees it like that too. I spoke to him earlier by the way; he's very excited about your *date*. He asked what kind of movies you liked, so I told him you absolutely love those scary, slasher ones!" He guffawed at his own joke, and Jane wasn't even sure she knew who was sitting beside her anymore.

She was livid now, as Toby's loud laughter attracted more attention than she felt comfortable with.

She hissed at him, "You'd better be kidding me! That's it, I'm going to go cancel right now, and you know I didn't want to go, *you* said I should. You convinced me it'd be okay and now look at you. I'm not going now." Jane crossed her arms in front of her chest in defiance, pouting like a petulant child. If she could've stamped her foot, she would have.

A look of anguish spread across Toby's face as he realised he'd actually upset his Janey. "I'm joking, just winding you up, don't cancel. He's a really nice guy, you'll have fun. Please, I'm sorry. Take no notice of me." He really did look as though he meant it.

Lindsey waved her hand in front of Jane. "Don't you dare cancel to help me move. Jamie's coming to help anyway. You need a night out without us, you never know, you might even enjoy yourself. Ignore the big idiot. I'm just pissed you didn't tell me. Come on, spill the beans, Missy." Lindsey was practically jumping up and down in her seat, barely able to contain the excitement in her voice.

Jane took in the sight of the pair of them and thought the whole world must have gone mad. She was going to see a movie with a guy she worked with, nothing more. She certainly didn't think it was a date.

"Okay, but there's really nothing to tell."

Toby shook his head; as he stood to leave he leant over to kiss Jane again. "We okay? I'm really sorry, it *was* just a joke. I thought you'd have told LJ already." A pain filled expression crossed his face. He was hopeful, she could see it in his eyes. Although the thought of making him pay for hurting her feelings did cross her mind.

With a chuckle, Jane dismissed his worry. "See you at six, Tubs, and don't be late. It appears I have a date."

He turned, winked at Jane and left the canteen, leaving her to fill in all the details for her very giddy best friend.

The 'date' was not the best Jane had ever had. Ryan had been lovely, a perfect gentleman, opening doors first to let Jane walk through, paying for everything despite her constant protestations. But it had felt weird and uncomfortable. The conversation had flowed without any awkward silences but Ryan had been more interested in the relationship she had with Toby than he appeared to be in Jane. Apparently nobody understood them, everyone was convinced that they had been dating, that Toby was the reason Jane's marriage had ended. She hadn't wanted to divulge the whole reason behind the breakdown of her marriage to some bloke she barely knew but he left her no choice. She wasn't about to let Toby take the blame for that one.

Once Jane had explained to Ryan that her ex was a violent, nasty man that now only had supervised access to their daughter and a restraining order to stay away from her, the night ended pretty quickly. She didn't blame him—who would want to start a relationship with someone with that much baggage? After pulling his car up outside her house, Ryan had kissed her politely on the cheek. His eyes flitted backwards and forwards nervously between Jane and the road ahead. His fingertips tugged at the collar of his shirt as he waited for Jane to exit the car. She couldn't understand where his obvious and sudden onset of nerves had come from, until she turned to walk up the drive and saw Toby peeking through the lounge curtains, spying on her.

Jane thought that perhaps she was destined to a life of platonic relationships and Toby, her ever present rock. It didn't matter, she knew life would be good and she could survive quite happily as long as Toby was in her life, take-out nights with her buddy were the best and that was all she needed, right?

Toby glanced across the room at Jane. "You need to get back on the horse, my lovely lady. It's been months since Ryan-gate. I know you've had other offers, people talk at work, you know."

It was movie night. The takeaway had been eaten and the film had finished ages ago. Jane and Toby were on their second bottle of wine with both of them admitting to feeling a little squiffy to say the least.

Jane groaned. "Oh no, don't start that again. I'm happy just the way things are right now. Dave seems to be towing the line lately. He hasn't said or done anything stupid for weeks now. I haven't had a smashed window, funny phone call or a new dent on my car for ages. I don't want to rock the boat. Anyway, I thought you liked having me all to yourself, not having to scare away potential suitors." She teased him, in her semi-drunken state.

Jane leant forward to top up the glasses again, as Toby sat staring at her. "I love having you all to myself, but it isn't healthy for you to just have *me* in your life. LJ is too busy with 'JimJam' these days. You two haven't had a girly day for God knows how long. You need to spread your wings, learn to fly again, angel." Jane wondered how much he'd had to drink exactly if he was spouting rubbish like that. But his words were gentle and meant as encouragement. "Or just go out and have fantastic, mind-numbing sex with someone!" He roared with laughter at his own comedy. Okay, so he was definitely the more drunk of the two of them.

Shocked at his words, Jane gasped. "I don't want mind-numbing sex with *just anyone* okay? And I can't believe you're telling me to sleep around!"

Toby stopped laughing as Jane's face became serious. She suddenly felt very sober. Having him in such close proximity and the alcohol running through her veins gave her some kind of confidence boost. If she just leaned in a little she'd be able to kiss him, to feel his warm lips on hers. He would wrap his arms around her and hold her tight. How had she not seen the man he was before now? In her now alcohol fuelled, confused state, he was just what she needed; kind, caring and very protective. She could see how easy her life would be with Toby there to take care of everything; to take care of her and Freya. He adored Freya, after all. The little girl doted on her Uncle Tubs as she called him, he was the father figure she'd lacked.

Toby sighed and closed his eyes briefly before fixing his gaze on her. "Janey...please don't look at me like that. I can't be that man for you. I love you too much to mess this up." He wagged his finger back and forth motioning between the two of them. "You know since Abbie died, I can't do this stuff. She'll only ever be the one for me. But I do adore you, if I had met you before, then maybe, but I just can't, babe." He looked dejected as his shoulders slumped, his whole body seeming to fold in on itself. "I didn't mean to make you believe otherwise. That was the last thing I wanted to do. I think since Abbie died, I've kind of declared myself off the market. For good." Toby shrugged his shoulders, smiling reticently. "You'll meet someone who will treat you so good, take care of Freya like she's his own. I'll always be in your life making sure he takes care of my two favourite ladies. But you need to move on." Toby held Jane's face in his hands, refusing to let her turn away from him; embarrassment and shame heated the skin of her cheeks. She knew he was right, the two of them together would be so wrong. He was like a brother to her, she'd allowed the line to become blurred for a moment.

Toby was her best friend and she didn't want to ruin that for anything in the world. "Toby, I'm so sorry, I think I drank a little too much wine." She averted her eyes, too humiliated to look at him now. "God, how bad does this look? See, I'm still a total disaster area. You're right, I know you're right, it's just…" The words fell short, leaving her unable to finish her sentence. It was probably for the best.

Toby lifted Jane's face up and planted a soft kiss on her lips. "Don't apologise, I'm truly flattered. I love you so much, but I'm just not *in love* with you, I'm still in love with my dead wife." His eyes were glassy and red rimmed as he fought to hold it together. "And you're not in love with me, not really.. I'll tell you what we're going to do, we're going to forget the whole thing ever happened, we go back to being Tubs and Janey, and get smashed, while we fill in that online dating thingy I caught you looking at the other day. I'll find your Mr Perfect if it kills me."

Toby stood to fetch the laptop, pausing in the doorway. "You know how much resolve it took me not to kiss you back, don't you? I'd only hurt you though, Janey. You deserve so much more than a guy like me."

As he disappeared into the hallway Jane wanted to slap her own face. She wasn't in love with Toby, just the idea of *being* with someone she could entrust her life to. She knew that, she really did but it didn't make the embarrassment of the whole stupid trying to kiss him thing any easier either. She vowed right then to never drink alcohol again. Her stupid broken, battered little self obviously couldn't handle the whirlwind of emotions the wine had brought to the forefront.

Chapter fifteen

It was Friday night. Having finally managed to convince Lindsey that she and Jamie could actually leave the house/bedroom for a few hours and spend a night with the rest of them; the gang of friends were heading out for the night. Jamie had jumped at the chance to move up to Leeds when his company expanded. In fact he'd volunteered, leaving Lindsey to conveniently let him crash at her new flat; it became evident quite quickly that it had been planned for a long time. Lindsey and JimJam, as she insisted on calling him now, were a firm couple.

Jane was happy for them seeing as Lindsey appeared to be head over heels in love with Jamie. It was almost nauseating to watch them together. They had to be in constant contact with each other; if she sat down it was on his knee. If he stood, she stood ensconced in his arms. It wasn't all one sided though, you could see that Jamie worshipped Lindsey. He followed her around like a puppy dog most of the time. Her wish was his command.

Toby had invited Ollie over for a long weekend too; conveniently they were both staying at Jane's for the duration, no doubt everyone would end up spending the majority of their time there. Toby had actually moved in a few weeks ago, just after the embarrassing kiss thing. His lease had run out on the house he'd been renting and he'd been unable to renew it because the landlord wanted to sell up and make a bit of cash instead. It had seemed to Jane like the logical thing to do; he needed somewhere to stay and she needed the rent her spare room could generate; besides, who better to house-share with than her lovely man, and best friend? Freya thought it was great to have someone different to wake up at some ungodly hour on a weekend. Although Jane wasn't sure how long he would last living with them if she carried on. Toby insisted he loved her and it was all good, and Jane had found them eating cereal out of the box together on the sofa on more than one occasion. She'd have to have a word about house rules at some point, but seeing him with her daughter melted her heart.

"You ready, beautiful? Taxi's here," Ollie shouted up the stairs at the same time as Jane emerged from her bedroom. She hadn't been prepared for the wolf whistle Ollie gave her.

Ever so slightly flustered by the attention, Jane changed the subject swiftly. "Yes I'm ready, urgh, do you think you two could maybe clean up that mess you left in my spare room tomorrow, it stinks in there!" She chuckled as she pushed gently past Ollie. He winked and playfully nudged her shoulder with his as she squeezed through the gap between him and the doorframe.

"Sure thing, boss. Come on, or those two will be at it on the restaurant table if we don't get there soon."

Jane groaned in agreement. Ollie was right, Lindsey was in full on relationship mode. Jamie hadn't really had a say in the matter. Then again, Jane didn't think either of them had come up for air since Jamie had moved up to Leeds. Lindsey spent all her work breaks either texting or on the phone to Jamie, although texting was the wrong word. Jane was sure it was more like sexting that was going on, but fair play to them, they were having fun and if it all ended tomorrow, Jane was ready with a shoulder to cry on if that's what Lindsey needed.

Toby was already in the car as Jane locked the door and he scooted over to let her in, forcing Ollie to sit up front.

"Well, we're only twenty minutes late if he puts his

foot down," Toby indicated to the taxi driver hopeful of making up a few of the lost minutes. "You look fab by the way, darling." He threw his arm across Jane's shoulders, pulling her into his side. It was a place she was most comfortable.

Ollie shuddered as he crossed his arms over his chest. "Oh, that's it, if you two start I'm getting out and going home on the next train, give it up already," he grumbled turning slightly in his seat to stare out of the window focussing on the scenery as it whizzed past the window in a blur. "I can just about cope with the other two lovebirds but you two…"

Jane wriggled with embarrassment, trying to free herself from Toby's firm grasp but to no avail. Toby just clung on tighter, laughing at Ollie. "Best friends, buddy, that's all, no snogging or sexy time going on over here."

Jane had never felt more uncomfortable. Perhaps Toby was a little overbearing with his affection sometimes, she certainly didn't want Ollie to think there was anything more than a strong friendship between them. She nudged Toby in the ribs gently, "Stop it. Do you *have* to say things like that? You can be so embarrassing sometimes." She turned her attention to Ollie now. "Sorry Ollie, ignore him." The need for the journey to be over already was strong. In fact she even considered asking the driver to turn around and take her home. If that didn't mean staying home alone all evening, it might have been the better option. They rode the rest of the way in an uncomfortable silence, reaching the restaurant just as Jamie was ordering drinks at the bar.

Lindsey waved wildly at the small group of friends from a table in the middle of the restaurant. It was clear she and Jamie had been there a while. The amount of empty glasses that sat on the table were a clear indication of the night that stretched before them.

Lindsey moved her coat, freeing the seat up for Jane to sit beside her. "Hey, what took you so long? We thought you'd all changed your mind and ditched us!"

A brief chortle escaped Jane's mouth. "Nah, I just took longer than planned choosing the dress, sorry." Jane waved her hand up and down her own body, brushing away at non-existent fluff along the way. The low cut grey dress had been a quick panic buy during her lunch break two days before. It was a colour she wouldn't normally go for and it was a tad on the short side too. Short enough that Jane felt the need to keep pulling on the hem, hoping it would somehow miraculously grow a few inches longer and cover the essentials a little more adequately.

Lindsey squeezed her friend's hand. "That dress is amazing, you look fabulous. I couldn't carry that colour off but on you it's stunning. Just do me a favour and stop pulling at it. If you're going to wear a dress like that, wear it with confidence." Lindsey hoped to ease her friend's anxiety a little.

Jane pulled at the hem of her slate grey dress once more. "That's easy for you to say. This is me we're talking about. I wish I'd worn trousers now."

Ollie leaned across right on cue. "Well, I for one, am pleased the dress won the outfit war." He placed down a glass of red wine in front of Jane and told her, "You look lovely."

Jane's cheeks flushed crimson again. She wasn't used to receiving compliments, they made her feel slightly uneasy. "Thank you." She smiled shyly before lifting her glass to her lips and taking a sip. The wine would surely help to settle some of the butterflies that seemed to insist on showing up every time Ollie was near.

The group moved into the bar once they'd finished eating and had split and paid the bill. Toby was flirting with one of the waitresses, as he had been for most of the night and Lindsey was all over Jamie like a rash, leaving Jane to chat to Ollie.

Exasperated by his friend's actions, Ollie tipped his head in Toby's direction. "Doesn't it bother you that he's been trying to get into her pants for most of the night?" he asked as he glared at Toby over his bottle of beer.

Jane scrunched her brow. "No, why would it?

Ollie, we're just friends, close friends, yeah, but that's all we'll ever be. Let him have some fun, he deserves it. He's spent the best part of the year looking after me, picking up the pieces and helping me to put my life back together. He needs some down time." After a quick glance over her shoulder, Jane turned her back on Toby, giving him a little space to use his best chat up lines on the starry-eyed girl that was lapping up the attention he was lavishing on her. And who could blame her? He was a good catch in anyone's eyes.

"Well, if you get lucky too, I guess I'll be riding home alone tonight." Jane teased Ollie before she lifted her glass to the barman, signalling they'd like another round.

Ollie waved a twenty at the bar tender. "My round, Jane, here." He handed over the cash to pay for the drinks.

Lindsey came up for air. "Aww, look! The Tubster might get some action finally!"

Jamie snorted with laughter, before pulling his girlfriend back down onto his knee; they signalled to Ollie and Jane, drawing attention to a free table for the four of them which was far away enough to give Toby a little privacy to get his groove on. Jane knew he wouldn't have left her with Ollie if he didn't think she'd be safe and Jane trusted him. She wanted with all her heart for Toby to have some fun.

Toby came to check on Jane twice on his visits to the toilet, forever putting her first. She honestly couldn't fathom a time when that wouldn't be the case, he was part of her family now. And family was important to both of them. As Toby headed back from his second visit to the toilet, Ollie told him to go enjoy himself, assuring Toby he would see Jane had a good night and got home safe, if he chose to take the waitress up on her less than subtle offers of a nightcap after hours. Toby looked a little torn, until Jane stood to hug him, telling him she was fine, she wanted him to have his own life.

"Go spread your wings, learn to fly again," Jane whispered his own words back to him, smiling.

Toby questioned Ollie with a somewhat narrowed eyes. "You promise me you'll make sure she gets home? She's important to me. If anything happens to her, I swear..."

"Nothing's going to happen to me, I'll be fine. Ollie's staying at ours anyway. Go, go have fun and enjoy yourself." Jane spoke with more confidence than she felt. On any night out she always went home with Toby or Lindsey, this would be the first time she'd go home alone. It was a huge step.

Ollie placed a protective arm around her back, indicating he took his responsibility seriously. "You have my word, she's safe with me. You know that. In fact, I think we're going to head home after this drink, if that's anything to go by." He nodded his head in the direction of Jamie and Lindsey; the pair really *did* need to get a room.

"Well, if you're sure." Toby was apparently reluctant to leave but Jane was happy enough, tucked into Ollie's side. Toby and Ollie had been friends for a long time so there was no doubt about the trust they had built. Standing in line for the taxi at two-thirty in the morning, Jane thanked God it was a mild night or they might all just freeze to death, looking at the length of the queue ahead of them.

A very giggly Lindsey wandered out of the queue. "Me and Jimjam are going to walk, it's only ten minutes from here for us. Will you be alright with Ollie?" Lindsey hugged Jane to her, rubbing her hands up and down Jane's back.

Jane nodded emphatically. "Yeah, of course. Go, have mind-blowing sex. You two have hardly been the best company anyway and as for Toby, well I don't know why any of you bothered leaving home tonight." she joked with her small group of friends.

Jamie laughed at her comment. "What can I say? Do you want me to kill Toby for dumping you? Crazy man." Toby had left over an hour ago with the little dark-haired waitress, who looked like she had won the lottery when he walked out the door behind her. But not before he had threatened Ollie with his life if anything were to happen to Jane.

"Jamie! *Friends*, we're just friends and not the type with any added benefits either, to answer the question you're *not* asking. We're not joined at the hip, unlike you two. He isn't my significant other," Jane stated crossly. Defending her relationship with Toby was becoming tiresome, people believed what they wanted to believe, despite the protestations.

Lindsey shook her head at Jane. "I don't understand you two." She didn't need to, nobody did. Toby and Jane knew the score.

Jane waved her hand in dismissal as she spoke. "I don't understand you either sometimes, but that doesn't matter, does it? Go; take the man to bed before he explodes!" She didn't want to continue with the twenty questions anymore.

It took another thirty minutes before it was Jane and Ollie's turn to climb in the taxi that pulled up at the front of the queue.

As they rode back in the cab, Ollie turned to Jane and stated "You really are just friends, aren't you? I didn't quite get it before, but I think I do now. Toby's talked to me a lot recently, said you're like his sister or something." Ollie was gazing at Jane, waiting for her to verify his thoughts.

Jane shook her head as she laughed lightly. "You

know if I had a pound for every time someone asked me that, I'd be a billionaire!" Jane smiled, "I don't know how much he's already told you, but yeah, friends is all we'll ever be. He means too much to me to risk ruining it by trying to have a different type of relationship with him. I don't think of him romantically at all and I know you all find that difficult to process. It's just how it is, I love him but I'm not *in love* with him, there's a difference."

"He told me about your ex-husband. I hope that's okay?" Ollie seemed a little uncomfortable admitting that Toby may have somehow betrayed her confidence. "He told me you had it rough for a while, you're divorced though now, aren't you?" Jane nodded, gazing out the window. She still couldn't talk about things with just anyone, Ollie seemed to pick up on her unease immediately. "Sorry. It's none of my business. Did you have a good night? I did. I like being here with you two. I miss Toby and Jamie sometimes, or should I call him Jimjam now." Jane turned to face Ollie again, allowing him to flash a bright smile in Jane's direction. He pleaded "Please don't think up a nickname for me, will you, I don't think I could carry on being your friend if you did." He laughed. He was right though, it was a ridiculous nickname. Nobody was even sure Jamie liked it either, he seemed uneasy every time Lindsey said it but she refused to call him by anything else these days. He was her JimJam.

"Coffee or bed?" Jane asked Ollie as she opened the front door.

"Now there's an offer I can't refuse!" he waggled his eyebrows suggestively before sitting down to remove his shoes. "Kidding, just kidding, Jane. Coffee would be great. You sit down though, I'll make it for you."

Jane followed him down the hallway into the kitchen.

"I'm glad you and Toby are just friends, I'm sorry if I upset you earlier in the cab, it's just...you know, it's just you're both a little full on with each other and well..." Ollie looked embarrassed, awkward even.

"Well, what, Ollie?" Jane retorted in response, standing in front of him now with her arms crossed in her signature stance, as Toby called it.

"Well, if you were more than friends, I might be in a bit of trouble for having some of the thoughts I have running around in my head about you. I'd definitely be in trouble if I did this, too." Ollie leant in towards her, cupping her face. He hovered, his lips mere inches away from hers. He paused, giving her every chance to move away, and when she didn't he gently placed his lips over hers, kissing her softly. Jane placed her hands on his chest, holding tightly onto his shirt. He moved away fractionally, only for Jane to grip his shirt tighter and pull him back towards her.

Jane smiled up at him. "Do it again, please?" Ollie let out a sexy little moan, sliding his tongue along her bottom lip this time. She opened her mouth slightly, giving him just enough room to slip his tongue onto hers. Her arms wrapped around his neck involuntarily, holding him in place this time, as he deepened the kiss. When the kiss ended, Ollie was grinning broadly.

He shook his head and kept the handsome smile firmly in place. "I've wanted to do that for so long. Now, about that coffee." He pushed Jane away gently. "Go sit down, I'll bring it in." Allowing her to take a minute to process what they'd done.

Jane's heart skipped excitedly as her head swam with memories of the kiss, she tucked her feet underneath her legs on the well-worn sofa. Not only had she just kissed Ollie, but more importantly it had felt so right. Not like the times she had been kissed on the few dates that had happened since her divorce. Kissing Ollie felt natural, not forced at all. She wanted more of them.

As they sat cuddled up on the sofa, Ollie wanted to make sure he hadn't overstepped the mark. "Was it too much, too soon? I'm sorry, shall I just head off up to bed, leave you alone?" He looked a little sheepish to say the least.

"No! Don't do that, I didn't exactly stop you, did I? Come and drink your coffee, at least." Jane patted the sofa next to her. When he had drained his cup he motioned for Jane to snuggle up to him. She obliged willingly, she felt just like she did with Toby. Safe.

More relaxed now, Ollie pulled Jane in closer still so he could rest his cheek on her head. "So, can I take you on a date tomorrow? Would that be okay? I have to go back home in a couple of days, so I don't have much time." He asked. "Is Freya staying at your mum's all weekend? The three of us could go out for the day tomorrow if she's coming home." He stroked little circles on Jane's arm as he spoke.

Jane loved the fact that he wanted to include her daughter, it made her heart swell with hope. "No, she won't be back till Monday. It's her weekend to see her dad. He visits her at her grandparents; they kind of chaperone him. Tomorrow night would be nice, if you still want to..." She couldn't look at him, fearing that the reminder of her past would bring him smack bang back to reality and he'd retract his offer of taking her on an actual date.

Ollie nudged her shoulder playfully. "I only just asked you; Of course I still want to." He laughed at Jane's insecurities as she covered her face with her hands.

Jane squirmed behind her hands. "Sorry, it's ...well, I don't think I'm very good at this sort of thing."

Ollie gently pulled at her wrists, uncovering her now bright red face. He smiled as he lifted her chin with his finger. "You're just a little out of practice. Perhaps I could help with that." He bent down, planting another soft kiss on her lips.

A loud cough came from the doorway, startling them both, Ollie almost jumped six feet and landed on the floor in front of the sofa.

They turned to find Toby laughing hysterically. "Ahem! What's going on?" Ollie bent double taking in deep breaths. "What the actual fuck? Shit. You scared the life out of me, creeping around. What the hell are you doing here anyway?"

Jane reached for his hand pulling him back to the sofa, next to her. "Just friends, remember, Ollie." She grinned at his overreaction to the arrival of their friend.

Toby held his arms out to his sides as if the answer were obvious. "Erm, I live here, last time I checked; you on the other hand appear to be hitting on my girl, buddy!" He leant over the sofa to give Jane her usual kiss. "You want me to throw the kid out, babe?" he whispered using his best old movie gangster accent, just a little too loudly in Jane's ear, making sure Ollie had heard him.

Jane kissed him back, throwing her arms around his

neck, almost pulling him over the back of the sofa. "Luck run out then, Tubs?" Jane laughed as he pouted, pretending to be sad.

Toby shrugged in response. "Nah, just missed you. I'm off to bed and I do *not* want to hear any sex noises, from either one of you or I may just have to drown the pair of you."

Oh, he didn't just say that, did he? Jane threw a cushion at Toby's receding back as he shouted goodnight over his shoulder, shutting the door loudly behind him. Jane and Ollie sat in silence for a few minutes, listening to Toby perform his nightly ritual of teeth brushing, toilet flushing followed by his door banging shut and him shuffling around his room before he finally fell silent.

Jane glanced up at Ollie, whose gaze was fixed on her; that lovely slanted grin on his face. "Jane, you're blushing. Don't worry; I'm heading off to bed in a minute. Alone. I just wanted another kiss first if that's okay?" He didn't wait for permission, not this time. Not asking for entry now, he planted beautiful gentle kisses on her now dry mouth. "Tomorrow it is, then." He winked at her as he ran his fingertips over her cheek, before he stood and headed off to bed.

Jane was awoken just before lunch the following day by the most glorious sight a woman could ever wish to see: her best friend standing beside her bed with two large cups of tea, bacon sandwiches and the papers.

"Shift over, fatty!" Toby grunted as he climbed onto bed with her. Offering her his cheek, he begged for a kiss before he would hand over her much longed for breakfast. Jane, of course, obliged lovingly and took her sandwich from the tray.

"Your mum called. Freaky features has been and gone already. Freya's fine, and she said would you bring that book back you borrowed, when you pick the munchkin up on Monday after work." Toby relayed the information freely as he munched on his breakfast and flipped through the pages of the morning paper.

There was a time when Jane would've chastised him for calling her ex 'Freaky' but she didn't even flinch these days. He wasn't freaky; more like unhinged.

With a wicked grin, Toby wagged a finger in Jane's direction. "And, madam, do we need to have the safe sex talk this morning? I hear you have a date tonight, with my mate." The tea Jane had swallowed moments before now ran down her nose. Toby guffawed loudly. "Attractive, Janey, real attractive. Shame Ollie missed that one, might put him off and I wouldn't need to give him 'The Talk' later. Speaking of the love god, he said to tell you he headed out for a while. Something he had to do, but he'll be back to pick you up later. Think he was worried you might freak out on him, have second thoughts, or whatever."

Her heart fluttered madly with the mere mention of Ollie's name, making Jane feel like a crazy teenager in the first flush of love. Acknowledging she had heard what Toby said, Jane busied herself munching on her breakfast and snuggling in for a cuddle under Toby's arm. How time's changed.

Chapter sixteen

The date had gone really well, too well in fact. Jane couldn't stop thinking about Ollie, he occupied her thoughts day and night, even more so with every day that past. They'd gone out for a curry and then on to the local pub where there was a quiz night on. Staying local meant they could both drink and not worry about driving home, or calling taxis.

The conversation had flowed easily the whole time with Ollie regaling her with stories of his Uni days with Toby, causing her to laugh loudly for most of the night. Ollie listened as Jane talked happily about Freya and all the things she wanted for her now, but he never once questioned her about her marriage failure. Jane was sure Toby had given him the 'big brother' talk earlier whilst she was getting ready. She had overheard the heated voices from the kitchen below her room. When she had appeared at the door a few minutes later, however, all she witnessed was the two men enjoying a beer each with no hint of animosity at all.

Sunday had rushed by way too fast, with the group of friends all heading to the pub again for lunch before walking back to Jane's the long way round, chatting loudly about their plans for the rest of the day ahead. Ollie had held Jane's hand, squeezing it every now and again, the whole time they were out, despite Lindsey's ribbing and the fake puking noises she insisted on making. Jane didn't care, she felt happy and content. Maybe it was a little odd that she felt this way so soon but, why not just go with it? As Lindsey said, life's too short.

Monday arrived and Jane was back at work. She was doing her best to try and distract herself from the fact that Ollie was leaving today to head back home. He'd be gone before she got home from work, and she already missed him.

Right on cue, Toby walked in to the canteen just as she was pouring the hot water into his cup, making his morning cup of tea. Jane was sure he could smell the kettle being switched on.

"Why is Ollie here? You must have really left your mark on him." Toby questioned, his eyebrows drawn inwards.

Jane's eyes narrowed in confusion. "What? He isn't here, idiot. You just can't help yourself can you?

The constant ribbing gets boring, you know." The phone in the staff room rang, making Jane jump. She reached for the receiver. "Hello...yeah, okay, I'll be right down." A grin spread across her face and her heart rate picked up as excitement flooded her body. "He *is* here, Toby!"

Toby was jumping on the spot, mirroring her actions and clapping his hands like a teenage girl. "I know, I know! *I* told *you* that already!" he said, putting on a stupid, girly voice before stopping abruptly and rolling his eyes. "Grow up, woman, and go see your man, will you? I can spy on you from here, you can see the car park from this window." He pushed Jane out of the door.

As she opened the door to reception, Jane could hardly breathe. She mentally chastised herself, pulling herself up on the nerves that were more than evident in her shaking hands and hot cheeks. Jane had only spent a handful of days with this man, and yet he had her heart racing every time she thought about him.

Ollie's cheeks coloured to match the heat rising in Jane's. "Hey, is this okay, me popping in like this? I just didn't want to leave without saying goodbye properly." He grabbed her hand and she guided him out the front door, picking a quiet, discreet spot under the canopy, mindful of prying eyes from the floor above.

Jane smiled up into the cerulean eyes that gazed

down at her. "It's fine. You won't miss your train though, will you?"

He shook his head as he moved in closer to kiss her, waiting as usual for Jane to give him permission, before finally closing the distance between them. "So, can I call you tonight? I know that we only went on the one date but…I kind of hoped that this might go somewhere. I'm only an hour away on the train. You could drive it in less than that. If you wanted to, that is." Ollie searched Jane's face as if looking for some kind of sign. Something that told him he hadn't misread the signals. It was clear he didn't want to push her into anything she was uncertain of. She was so grateful that he was mindful of her likely fear of history repeating itself but he seemed to be doing his best to prove to her that not all men were bastards.

Jane worried away with her teeth at an imaginary hangnail, trying to figure out how to say what she needed to say. "Ollie, I come as a package deal. You don't just get me, you get Freya too." She held her breath for what seemed like an eternity, she waited for him to digest what that actually meant.

Evidently he didn't need think about it. "I can handle that, if you give me a chance to. She's a cute little thing, just like her mum." He smiled warmly. "I talked to Toby last night. I know a lot of what went on in your past. How much you got hurt, physically and emotionally. I want you to know that we can take things slow, see what happens, if you want to, that is."

Jane could just imagine how that talk went. She was glad he'd had a sounding board in Toby; if he was serious, he needed to fully understand the extent of what being with her entailed. The emotional baggage she carried around was huge.

Ollies smile remained warm, "I really like you, all I ask is that we try it out, Jane, I have the weekend after next off, and I thought that maybe you could come over, bring Freya with you, we could go show her the castle, have a picnic..." He looked adorable with his shy smile and that hopeful glint in his eye as he struggled to find the right words to make her agree.

Jane didn't need to think too hard about his suggestion. "Look, I tell you what, you ring me tonight and we can take it from there. If you still think it's a good idea in a few days, then I'll come for the weekend. But, I think I should leave Freya at home this time. You can show *me* the castle, instead."

Ollie blew out a large sigh, as the smile spread wider across his face. "Okay, but can I get another kiss? Before I have to run." Jane reached up on her tiptoes to meet his large frame, her arms wrapped around his neck as his snaked around her waist. She covered his lips with hers, tasting him as she did. She could feel him smile against her mouth.

Jane skipped all the way back to her desk, wishing that Lindsey wasn't away on holiday, she would be livid at missing out on the gossip. The butterflies she'd had fluttering in her stomach for the past few days had now settled and where happily flying in a beautiful formation instead, leaving Jane lightheaded and happy.

The day dragged on as Jane tried to keep her mind on the monotonous job before her. Customer service jobs really did suck, perhaps a change of job in the New Year was something to think about. She didn't know who she was trying kid, while ever Toby worked there she'd stay. The thought of not spending her days with him still alarmed her somewhat.

Later that night Jane sat tucked up on the couch with a large glass of red wine, her new favourite tipple, trying to concentrate on the programme that blurred away in front of her. She could feel Toby, peering over his book at her every now and again from where he resided on his end of the couch. Jane had already mentally judged the distance between both them and the phone just in case Ollie rang. The last thing she needed was the wind-up merchant to beat her to it, although she knew she was being a bit optimistic. What man in his right mind would take on a twenty-eight-year-old divorcee, with a preschool child and a nutcase for an ex-husband, who didn't think twice about threatening her or her friends even now? No,

Ollie wouldn't ring, he'd no doubt had enough time on the train ride home to sort his head out and see sense, and Jane didn't blame him.

Toby topped up her drink. "If he messes you around, he has me to answer too."

Jane feigned confusion. "Eh? What you going on about?" Her cheeks heated; she couldn't lie to him for toffee.

Toby rolled his eyes but grinned. "Yeah, okay, Janey. Your eyes haven't left that bloody phone for the last hour. Here's a novel idea, why don't you ring him? It's allowed in this century you know."

Jane almost covered Toby in the red wine he had just poured her. "Leave it. He didn't say he'd definitely ring today. Anyway, I'm heading off to bed." She tried to play down the frustration she felt. She'd attempted all day not to get her hopes up but inevitably she had. She made her way across the room and kissed Toby goodnight as she passed by, picking up the empty wine bottle as she went. No point in dragging out the disappointment anymore; sitting by the phone waiting was doing her no good.

After brushing her teeth and removing the day's make-up, Jane snuggled up in bed with her book. What more did a girl need? As she reached over to switch off the light, her mobile phone buzzed on the nightstand. Three missed calls and three texts, all from Ollie:

'Hey, called a couple of times, you avoiding me? Lol',

'Ok, so either your phone's off, u left the country or you changed your mind. Hope it's not the last one. Ring me.'

God, she felt like such an idiot. Of course he would ring her mobile and not the house phone, he wouldn't want Toby to answer it instead of her. Why had she not thought about that?

'Just txt T so I know you're there, I get it don't worry about it'

Great, now Ollie thought she didn't want to talk to him. As Jane started to text Ollie back her phone buzzed with a message from Toby.

'Do it Janey, it's all good xx'

Jane quickly sent a reply to Toby, and then started on her message to Ollie. *Should I just call him? No...no a text is better*, she decided. *I suppose that way I don't have to listen to him make excuses about how he's changed his mind.* Jane: *'hey you, sorry phone been on charge! Thought you would ring landline, how was the trip home?'*

Ollie: *'long & boring. Worried T might answer landline, wanted it to be just me & you, how did work go'*

Jane: *'long & boring. Aww you old romantic.'*

Ollie: *'that's me! so about next weekend???'*

Jane: 'what about it? you only just left!'

Ollie: 'k but not letting it drop yet. Wish I was still there'

Jane: 'me too. T been a pain now you're gone'

Ollie: 'T always a pain, it's his job. Gotta go J early start can I ring you tomorrow?'

Jane: 'k, speak soon x'

Ollie: ' keep your phone with you then'

Jane: 'lol yes sir! Night'

Ollie: 'nite J'

Jane put her phone back on to charge and switched off the light. She had a feeling it was going to be a long night. As she closed her eyes thoughts of Ollie flooded her mind, some of the thoughts weren't PG rated either. Jane drifted off to sleep with images of a semi-naked Ollie filling her dreams.

It turned out to be a long week of Toby and Lindsey tormenting her about the late night texts and calls to Ollie. The fledgling couple talked every night for at least an hour, followed by around twenty texts every day where he asked her to visit him in every single text. Jane finally agreed to get the train over the following Friday, much to her two BFFs' joy. Jane, on the other hand, was not so sure it was a good idea; she still had reservations about where this was going. She wasn't sure she was ready for the whole thing. She made the mistake of voicing her concerns to Lindsey,

"What if it doesn't work out?" Jane had asked Lindsey. "What happens then?"

Lindsey's brow furrowed a little before she answered. "Are you being serious? Are we talking about the same guy here? If it doesn't work, then you go back to being friends, but that's never going to happen. Have you seen the way he looks at you? I mean, those eyes though." Her own eyes had taken on a dreamy state now.

Jane nudged her friend playfully. "Hey, you have Jamie. Seriously though, what if it all goes disastrously wrong and he hates me? There'll be all those awkward silences when he realises we have nothing in common, and then there's Freya to think about too..." she fiddled with a small piece of skin by her nail.

With a chuckle Lindsey dismissed her doubts. "Why is it going to go wrong? He invited you to stay because he likes you, he wants to spend time with you away from me, Toby and everything else. Just the two of you. And you'll have loads in common, you don't seem to struggle for conversation when he's here so why would it be any different because you're at his place? As for Freya, well, she already seems to like him. You're not silly, and neither is Ollie, Freya will adapt if you give her time. You're overthinking it." Lindsey gave Jane a reassuring nudge. "What was it you said to me? Oh yes, go have mind blowing sex before he explodes. I think those were your exact words. Well, right back atchya, Jane. Go have a little fun."

Jane threw her head back and laughed freely. "I am not going to jump into bed with him! He won't want to sleep with me." Worry etched Jane's brow now as that thought swam around her head. "Will he?" Jane had very limited experience with men, and it had been a long time she'd taken part in the dating game, so to speak. The thought of getting naked with someone new was a little scary.

"Oh, Jane." Lindsey chuckled as she shook her head. "It might be someone different but the bits are all the same! At least I'd hope they were."

Friday arrived and as she packed her weekend bag, Toby returned from dropping Freya at her parents' house. He'd offered to do the drop off so Jane could have some space to pack without tiny little hands helping.

Toby gawped at the large bag sitting on the bed. "So, what time am I dropping you at the station?" He gestured at the bag and laughed. "Jesus, woman, are you going for the fortnight? How much crap have you got in there?" He struggled to lift it from the bed and let it thud onto the floor, heavily.

Apprehension ran through Jane now that she had time to think. Her brow crumpled in confusion as she chewed at the inside of her cheek. "Too much? I don't know if I should go, Tobes. I mean, he'll probably be bored of me in a week or two…In fact, he'll probably stick me on the first train home in the morning." She made a move to grab her bag back from where it sat on the floor. "That's it, I'm not going. This is such a bad idea, and you should've talked me out of this days ago." Grabbing at the zip, she fumbled, trying to undo it.

Toby tried unsuccessfully to remove the bag from Jane's reach. "Don't you dare start with all that nonsense now. For God's sake, it's a weekend away, you're not eloping…are you?" He looked serious for a minute, while he scrutinised Jane emptying the bag completely. As he watched her unpacking he pulled his phone from his pocket and appeared to be making a call. "Yeah, mate, you need to ring Janey, she's currently unpacking her bag and ranting that it's a bad idea. 'K, talk to you later." He ended the call and just stared across the room at Jane.

She stood in open-mouthed disbelief at his audacity. The urge to throw something at him was just about to take her over when her phone began to play the now familiar ringtone.

Toby picked the phone up from the night stand and held it towards her, waggling it in the air. When she didn't take it, he clicked the answer button and stuck it on speaker.

Ollie's voice rang around the room. "Jane ... take me off speakerphone, please,"

Jane took the phone, cancelling the speaker as she did. "Hi."

Jane listened to Ollie, soothing her nerves once again. "Hi, babe. What's wrong, why are you unpacking? It's okay to feel bit nervous or uncertain, but I've been looking forward to seeing your beautiful face all week. Your train leaves in little while. Did I do or say something to put you off coming to visit for the weekend?"

She hated the uncertainty she'd caused him, hated the anxious tone she could hear running through his voice. He was disappointed and she'd been the cause.

Jane sighed deeply. "You didn't do anything wrong; it's just, I don't know, I just feel a bit strange, that's all." Jane couldn't explain how she felt to Ollie, he would never understand. She just knew there would be repercussions from Dave if he found out that she was seeing someone. Then there was Freya to think about. Jane would always have to put her first, in any decisions she made. She wasn't sure that Ollie was quite ready for that. In fact, Jane wasn't sure that she was ready for Ollie, come to think of it.

"Of course it feels strange, this is new to both of us. I feel a little nervous too, you know. But I can't wait to see you. I want to show you where I live, take you out and spoil you a little, if you'll let me. If I promise not to bite, will you get on the train?" She laughed at the little sad voice he was putting on; she could just imagine the puppy dog eyes too. He sighed. "That's better, now go pack some of that crap you have lying all over the bed, back in your bag and get T to drop you at the station. I promise I'll be there when your train gets in, okay? Put him back on for a sec." Jane handed the phone back to Toby, as she started to hastily repack, but only looking for essentials now. She honestly didn't need four pairs of shoes for a weekend away. *Did she?*

As Jane pondered the pile of clothes before her, Toby spoke to Ollie. "Yeah, don't worry, she's packing. Yeah, yeah, I hear you. Okay, mate.... talk soon, buddy." Once the call had ended Toby popped her phone in the top of the handbag that sat next him on the bed. Then without speaking further he collected her overnight bag and headed down the stairs, not giving Jane a chance to pack anything else or change her mind yet again. Jane prayed he wouldn't ask her if she was okay because she knew she'd say no and go into immediate melt down mode again. There wasn't any time for that, not now she had decided she was definitely going. Right now, she needed to finish packing, get into the car and to the station. *One step at a time, Jane, one step at a time.*

Jane called after her Toby as he made his way

downstairs. "I need to pack a few more bits, Toby!" It was no use; he was already by the front door, holding it open, with Jane's coat, keys and bags in his hand. He motioned silently for her to move her butt out through door so she reluctantly did, huffing like a surly teenager. Toby locked the door and they both climbed into the car.

It wasn't until they'd been driving for a few minutes, that Toby finally spoke. With a quick glance in Jane's direction, he asked, "Calm now, are we? You know, I wouldn't be encouraging you go if I thought you had anything to worry about. He's one of the good guys, you'll be fine." He reached over to give Jane's hand a small squeeze while she gazed out the window, refusing to turn around. The nerves were getting the better of her again. She was looking forward to spending the weekend with Ollie but the enormity of what it stood for weighed heavy on her mind. That didn't mean she was going to let it stop her though. From here on in, her life was for living and that's exactly what she intended to do. She was going to live it to the full. She didn't know why she was crying, they weren't tears of sadness; that she knew. Maybe she simply felt the need to release all the pent up emotion she felt. Yes that's what it was.

The nerves mixed with the excitement Jane had begun to feel in the car reached fever pitch as she glanced around the huge, freezing cold train station. There were loads of people milling around, all of which seemed to know exactly where to go, which train they needed to board. Jane had no idea, she quickly glanced at the announcement board, looming large above her. Just how anybody understood any of that garbled crap was way beyond her. She knew which station she needed to get off at, but they only listed the end destination. Jane didn't know what the end destination of her train was. How was she supposed to figure it out? There was a reason Dave never let her go anywhere on her own, he knew she was useless at it. Jane could feel one massive panic attack coming on now. She felt sure her vision would go blurred any minute and then she'd likely pass out. She could just feel it coming. Jane looked around her taking in the unfamiliar, daunting surroundings, she just wanted to turn around and go home. *There's no way I'm giving in now*, Jane thought, giving herself a shake as she turned to look back up at the board more determined than ever.

Toby appeared behind her. "How you doing, you okay?" Jane nodded her head slowly.

She glanced down at the ticket in her hand and back up at the board. "I think I need platform two, right?" Jane watched as the listed destinations flashed up in order on the display.

Toby checked the board with her. "Yup, that looks right to me, come on, let's get you on that train." He lifted her overnight bag on to his shoulder and followed Jane through the station in search of platform two. "Ollie said to tell you he'll be at the station waiting for you, when you get in. You don't have to change trains or anything so once you're on the train, you can just sit back and relax for an hour. Read your book, or listen to music, or whatever will help you pass the time." He was being so nonchalant about the whole journey, his calmness was beginning to rub off a little on Jane. She still felt the knot in her stomach and the sweat beading at the base of her neck but with each step nearer the train she took her confidence grew. She was doing this.

Toby tightened the grip around her shoulders and kissed the side of her head. Jane knew it seemed silly to be scared at her age, she could freely admit that. But, she hadn't been allowed to do anything on her own for years. The furthest she had been allowed to go by herself had been to work, which took roughly ten minutes. If you didn't count dropping off Freya at her parents' house. Her self-confidence was almost non-existent and spending an hour on a train was a whole new ball game for her. Jane could feel the anxiety still gripping her throat with the amount of people milling around the station. Her palms were beginning to sweat and the dizziness had begun now too.

After guiding her down the platform, to the right train, Toby handed her the overnight bag and the hot chocolate he'd bought for her. He bent to look Jane in the eyes as he quietly said "You'll be fine. Breathe, Janey. Give me fifteen minutes to get home, then ring me if you want to okay? I'll help the time pass a bit, if you want."

Jane really did love him with everything fibre of her being. "Okay, but you're right, it'll be fine." Jane gave him a quick hug before boarding the train and finding a seat by the window. Toby remained rooted to the spot until the train moved slowly backwards, away from the station. True to his word, Jane's phone rang in her bag, a little over fifteen minutes later. Toby stayed on the line talking about nothing at all for almost forty minutes. Jane knew he was just trying to keep her mind from worrying about being alone and away from all that was familiar.

"Right, sweetie-pie, I gotta go. I got stuff to do. Listen, I want you to have fun for a change, live a little, you deserve it. Just be you, okay? Text me when you get there. Love you." Excitement overtook the nerves she'd felt earlier. In thirty minutes time she'd be with Ollie; that thought made her heart race a little quicker. The memories of the last time they'd been together swam around her mind. The gentle kisses and hand holding made her pulse race.

Jane's text alert went off five minutes later, fishing out her phone, Jane smiled inwardly knowing it would be Toby checking up on her again.

'I'm here J, didn't want you to worry so got here early, the board says you'll be here in 20 mins. See you soon, Ol x'

Jane couldn't help but smile, like she'd escaped the asylum, at the unexpected but welcome message.

Chapter seventeen

As the train pulled into the station the anxiety within Jane rose sharply. Her hands felt clammy and her stomach appeared to be gearing up to perform a little dance to its own tune. Jane couldn't decide if it was excitement at seeing her new man or the small amount of fear she still felt about negotiating her way through the station. She could see there were a lot of people suddenly swarming on the platform. How the hell would she find her way out of the station? Did Ollie say where he was parked? *God, I think I am going to throw up any minute now. If I just stay sat on the train, will it just take me back to Leeds, or do I need to change trains? This is awful.* The thoughts ran quickly through Jane's head. Dragging her overnight case down from the storage rail, she took a deep breath while mentally scolding herself for being such an idiot. She was an adult, she could manage to negotiate a train station, surely? As she stepped onto the platform, concentrating solely on making sure she put one foot in front of the other, her text alert went off again. After rummaging in her bag, she clicked the message icon.

'Hey, beautiful x'

Jane looked up to find the gorgeous, sandy-haired man, beaming at her from behind the ticket barrier, the golden flecks in his hair shone like treasure as the sun illuminated his features, he was less than fifteen feet away. All the nerves she'd felt about the journey, travelling alone and having to negotiate the station where suddenly swept aside by that bright, warm smile and those striking eyes. She couldn't keep the grin from her face. Pulling up the handle on her luggage and wheeling it behind her, she hurried towards him. When she reached him, Ollie snaked his arm around her waist, pulling her in tight to his chest. Jane tilted her head upwards, she needed to look into those mesmerizing blue eyes of his. Without hesitation, Ollie lowered his head, his lips met Jane's in a heated embrace. No thought given to the crowds of people that milled around them in the crowded station. For once, Jane didn't care who was watching, as she allowed herself to get lost in the moment.

Ollie drew his head back a fraction before tenderly kissing the tip of her nose. "I missed you."

The words wouldn't form in Jane's throat, it might have had something to do with that huge ball of emotion that seemed to be lodged there. *He'd missed her*. Hearing him say those words made her heart skip a beat, and her skin tingle in all the right places.

As they drove back to Ollie's flat, it was as though they'd never been apart, there were none of the awkward silences that she'd worried herself sick about for the last week. It was as though they'd known each other for years, instead of a few weeks.

Jane's phone rang, just as Ollie parked the car. Taking her phone from her bag, Jane answered Toby's call. "Are you okay? Did Ollie pick you up yet?" Toby was trying to keep his voice light, but Jane could sense the worry in him.

"Yeah, Tobes, we just got to Ollie's flat."

Toby let out an audible sigh. "Ah, great. Well go have fun, lovely."

Jane glanced over at the handsome man sitting beside her, staring at her with a hint of a smirk on his face. "Sorry, he's such a worrier." She shook her head and rolled her eyes. "Anyone would think I wasn't capable of traveling alone."

Ollie leaned across the centre console of the car, his hand slid around Jane's neck. With a gentle pull he brought her face closer to his before tenderly kissing her again. "Yup, but I like that he cares. I know no one will even try to hurt you with him around." The wink he gave her caused every inch of her body to heat instantly. "Come on, you want a cuppa before we head out for the afternoon?" Ollie exited the car, heading around to the passenger side in order to open Jane's door for her. Taking her hand in his, he led her along the side of the old converted church which housed his flat.

Once inside he gave her a quick guided tour, as he pointed out all the essentials. "Bathrooms through my bedroom, its en-suite," Ollie waved his arm in the direction of the oak door to his right. "But there is a cloakroom in the hallway." He dropped Jane's overnight bag by the bedroom door before moving towards the kitchen area of the large living space, and switching the kettle on. While he waited for it to boil, he pulled Jane in tight, allowing his arms to wrap around her protectively. "I was scared you wouldn't get on the train."

Jane lifted her head from his chest where it rested. "That was never an option," rising up on her tiptoes, Jane's lips found his again. The boldness of taking what she wanted in the moment filled her with joy. "I just got a little spooked."

He had the whole weekend planned out perfectly, including a picnic by the castle the following day. First, they were heading out for lunch, followed by a walk around the old style market square. The cobbled streets wound like a maze around the historic buildings that surrounded the market on all sides. This smell of potatoes baking on the stalls filled the air, mingling with the sweet aroma of the freshly baked goods that were also on offer. There were row upon row of market traders selling their wares, with anything from hand knitted items to fresh produce available to purchase. Jane bought a little ragdoll for Freya from one of the vendors, knowing that she would love it. Ollie guided her to a lovely little café just off the main square, the bistro tables allowed them to sit outside and enjoy the street entertainers. Jane appeared mesmerized by the eclectic looking man blowing giant soap bubbles for the children to chase after. She could picture Freya running around trying to catch one while squealing with glee. They seemed to sit there for ages talking and drinking lattes and sharing a huge piece of chocolate cake.

As the daylight dimmed, they made a move to walk back to the flat. "So, what are we doing tonight then?" Jane asked as they walked arm in arm back through the narrow streets.

Ollie glanced down at her. "I've booked a table at that Italian restaurant I told you about. Is that okay, or do you fancy curry or something else? Just name it, this weekend is about you, having fun and relaxing." His eyebrows lifted questioningly.

"Italian would be great." Jane reassured him.

They arrived back at the flat with a couple of hours to fill until their dinner reservations, Ollie poured Jane a glass of wine before selecting a relaxing playlist on his iPod. As Sam Smith drifted from the speakers, they sat cuddled on the couch together. Small lamps dotted around the room offered ambient lighting, providing a warm comforting backdrop to the generous sized lounge-come-kitchen diner. Jane loved the open plan layout of the flat, which was surprisingly modern considering it was part of an old church conversion. The mixture of old and new fitted together seamlessly.

One solid arm tightened around her shoulders, enclosing her a little more. His nearness flustered her, his body heat caused her pulse to race. So far out of her comfort zone but yet Jane yearned for him to kiss her again. She chanced a coy glance up at his rugged features.

Ollie cupped her cheek in his hand, "What's wrong?"

Jane swallowed hard, trying to keep her voice steady and even. "Nothing, why?"

He ran his thumb gently across Jane's cheek, "You look like a rabbit caught in headlights, your cheeks are flushed and I'm pretty sure I can hear your heart racing." Ollie's fingers glided from her cheek to the back of her neck, he held her tenderly as he leaned in closer still. When he finally kissed her Jane felt her whole body relax into him.

Tentatively Jane allowed her hand to roam over Ollie's toned stomach, her fingertips taking in solid muscle she could feel hiding beneath his shirt. As she tightened her grip on his shirt, Ollie deepened the kiss. His tongue begging for entry, sweeping softly across the seam of her lips. Lost in the moment, Jane reached up, running her fingers through his hair, revelling in the way he made her feel beautiful and desirable once more.

Ollie grinned against her lips. "I think we need to slow this down a bit," he suggested. His smile was breath-taking. She could have kissed him all night *but* he had made dinner reservations, and she was sure she'd heard his stomach rumble.

With a coy smile Jane leaned back. "Well, if you insist. I suppose we ought to be getting ready to go out."

She hadn't missed the admiring glance he'd given her when she'd appeared in his lounge, complete in an off-the-shoulder blue dress and silver strappy heels. "Woah, you look stunning," Ollie smiled warmly at her.

A coy smile appeared on Jane's face, "You don't look so bad yourself." If truth be told she thought he looked gorgeous. He wore a light blue shirt which he'd left open at the collar, paired with a pair dark trousers. His sandy hair had been swept back, showcasing the golden tone as it shimmered under the light.

The restaurant was lovely. There were a few tables in the main seating area downstairs, but they were seated in the balcony area, overlooking the main room. It was quiet and intimate, perfect. The food was out of this world. The company, as ever, was charming. Ollie was very attentive as he held her hand across the table, he didn't seem to care that they were in a public place and not tucked away back in his flat, and he was more than happy to let everyone know she was with him. He made sure Jane's wine glass was always topped up, checking her food was to her liking. The weekend was turning out to be a huge success.

With his napkin on the table beside him, Ollie signalled the waiter. "Right, are you ready if I pay the bill? Thought you might like to go for a walk before we head back to mine, is that okay? Will you be alright in those shoes?" He peered under the table to check out Jane's footwear again.

Jane lifted her hand vaguely in dismissal of his questioning. "I can walk, don't stress. Where are we walking *to*? And here, I want to pay for dinner." She felt just a little tipsy from the constantly filled-up glass he'd provided. Perhaps that would hinder her walking ability and not the footwear.

Ollie baulked at the thought of Jane picking up the bill. "Not a chance. This is my treat, you deserve spoiling a little." When Jane tried to protest, he offered a compromise. "Tell you what, we can walk home past the late night shop. You can buy another bottle of wine for us to drink back at mine, if you want. Come on." He held out his hand to Jane as she put her coat on, before guiding her out into the now cool night air. The streetlights were lit, shedding a warm light along the cobblestoned streets. Gone were the daytime entertainers, they'd been replaced by couples and small groups of friends who's chatter filled the evening air as they spilled from the local bistro's and small bars.

Jane leaned over and planted a kiss on Ollie's cheek. "If I forget to tell you later, I had a lovely night, thank you."

He let go of Jane's hand, placing his arm around her shoulders instead, pulling her in to the safety and warmth of his side. "You're more than welcome. Glad you had fun. Are you warm enough?"

Jane knew the chattering of her teeth had given her away. "A little cold but much better now you have your arm around me." She smiled shyly at her own words and how brazen she seemed to be becoming these days. Ollie responded by hugging her tighter before he rubbed his hand up and down Jane's arm, warming her.

As she stood in Ollie's bedroom, Jane searched

her overnight bag for something to change into. She just wanted to get out of her dress and feel comfy. If only Toby had let her finish packing, instead of just shoving random things back in her bag, she might be able to find something of use. She abandoned her attempts, instead pulling on her favourite pyjamas and then heading into the bathroom to brush her teeth. She could hear cupboards and drawers opening and shutting in the bedroom next door as she removed her make-up. *What was he doing?* She stuck her head out of the en-suite door in time to see him heading back into the lounge, with a blanket under his arm.

"What are you doing?" Jane called after him. She found him a few seconds later, making up a bed on the couch.

Ollie let his gaze roam over Jane appreciatively as she stood barely inside the doorway in her silky pyjamas. As he turned to grab the pillow from the floor Jane saw him adjusting himself inside the tracksuit pants he'd changed into. "Just making up a bed." The tone of his voice seemed a little huskier now than before. She felt a little warm and fuzzy knowing that *she,* of all people, had flustered him.

Jane had assumed she would be sleeping in his bed, with him but this was probably a better idea after all. She couldn't help but feel slightly relieved actually.

Not sure that she was ready to take things that bit further yet.

Jane moved to take the duvet from him. "Thanks, but I could have done that myself, you know."

Ollie looked at her blankly. Then realisation appeared on his face that she was talking about the makeshift bed. "No, this is for me. You're in my room," He grinned as he headed over to the kitchen to put the kettle on. "Fancy a decaf, before you go to bed?"

Jane sauntered over to join him at the breakfast bar.

"Ollie, you're not sleeping on the couch, it's *your* home. I'll be fine out here honestly. But a cup of tea would be nice, thanks." Jane rested her arms on the countertop, watching him move around his kitchen, her gaze lowered to take in his very pert, well rounded bottom. She did appreciate a nice bottom.

He made her a drink. "I don't want you to sleep on the couch. I want you to sleep in my room. I won't take no for an answer." He smirked as he placed the cup next to Jane. "Why don't we stick the telly on, see what trash we can find to watch. I'll let you snuggle under the duvet with me." Ollie winked, grinning goofily at Jane as he placed his cup on the coffee table and sat on the sofa. He climbed under the covers and lifted it up Jane to get in next to him. She obliged and snuggled under his arm, feeling safe and more than a little comfortable. Her mind began to drift along with her eyes as she struggled to keep them open after the busy day they'd had.

Jane woke with a start when she felt Ollie lift her from the sofa. "Come on, sleepyhead, bed for you. I have loads planned for us tomorrow."

Jane rested her head against his chest, not wrestling with him to put her down. "I can walk, you know." She muttered sleepily. "But I must admit, you gotta love a man who can carry you." Ollie threw his head back, laughing loudly as Jane continued. "I feel like that woman in that cheesy chick flick, the one where he carries her out of the factory and everyone applauds them." She giggled uncontrollably now as Ollie kicked open the bedroom door, walked in and placed her on the bed.

Ollie beat at his chest. "Me man, you woman." His best cavemen impression had Jane in hysterics. He bent to kiss her, "Sorry, but no navy uniform for you tonight. Sleep well and I'll see you in the morning." He turned to leave the room.

Jane could hear her heart beating loudly in her ears, it was now or never. She needed to seize the moment and tell him she didn't want him to go. "Ollie, you don't have to sleep out there, you know. I don't mind if you want to sleep in here."

He shook his head, defiantly. He wasn't giving in. "You are *not* sleeping on my sofa."

Jane lowered her head, avoiding any eye contact for the minute. The nerves forced her fingers to worry at the duvet, as she plucked up the courage to continue. "I didn't mean that…I meant you could sleep in here, with me…well if you want to that is. I don't mind. But… I think I'd like you to." There you go, it was out there. Jane had asked him to share the bed with her. She really didn't know where to look now, so instead of looking at Ollie she busied herself picking at yet more imaginary fluff.

Heat rose in Ollie's chest. He ran his hand through his hair in frustration at the words he was about to say. "You know what? I'd really like that too, but I'm going to sleep on the sofa tonight. I don't want you to think you don't have an option. That isn't why you're here. Of course I want to take the next step with you, but there's no rush, is there? I'm just glad you came to stay, that you're here. Why don't we take things slowly for now?" Humiliation took hold of Jane, forcing her cheeks to heat. Maybe making the first move was a mistake, perhaps she should have waited for Ollie to decide when the time was right instead? "Hey, don't look like that. I don't want to ruin this but jumping into bed too soon, that's all."

Jane fake pouted at him and his gentlemanly ways. "A kiss then, instead?"

Ollie made his way back to the bed, he climbed on top of the duvet and lay down beside her. "Anytime." He ran his hand up her arm before letting his hand settle on her cheek. Jane gazed into the bluest eyes she'd ever seen. Sliding her arm around his neck, she let her fingers nestle in his hair, pulling him in slightly, she was eager to feel his lips on hers again.

Ollie gently sucked her lip into his mouth, nibbling slightly as he did. Jane responded instantly, running her tongue along his top lip begging for entry into his delicious mouth. He didn't disappoint, sliding his tongue onto Jane's, caressing it gently, and deepening the kiss.

Ollie pulled back to plant a kiss on the tip of Jane's nose. "Night, beautiful," he whispered. The effect she had on him was audible in his throaty voice and it pleased her.

"Night." She sighed dreamily as she watched him leave, before wriggling down under the covers. After replaying their passionate exchange a few more times in her head she closed her eyes and let the warmth surround her as it lulled her off to sleep.

Chapter eighteen

"NOOOOO! Get off me!" Jane screamed loudly, sitting bolt upright in the unfamiliar bed, her eyes searching for something recognisable in the darkness. Her body was drenched in sweat and her pulse raced. Fear gripped her heart tightly causing it thud at her ribs.

The door flew open and Ollie ran in. "Jane? What's wrong, babe?" He slammed the overhead light on with his fist, instantly flooding the room with light. In seconds he was by Jane's side, pushing the sweat-soaked hair back from her face as Jane struggled to bring her breathing back under control.

Jane reached up to take Ollie's hand, squeezing it lightly. "Sorry, nightmare, that's all. Sorry." Mortification swamped her small frame, great, just what she needed, Ollie to hear her crying out for help in the middle of night with no real explanation why. Yet more messed up madness she carried around daily.

"Hey, don't apologise, it's absolutely fine." He reassured her. "God, you're shaking, come here." Ollie slid under the covers, pulled Jane into his chest and held her tightly. He made soft shushing noises as he gently rocked from side to side. "It's okay. I've got you, babe. There's no-one here, just me and you. It's just me and you. Can I do anything to make it better?" He asked between the soft, tender kisses he was placing on Jane's forehead.

She shook her head and forced a smile. "No, no, I just..." She inhaled a deep, calming breath. "Sorry, it's just sometimes I... I don't know why they happen, they just do. I'm so sorry I woke you." She turned her face into Ollie's chest and tentatively slid her hand underneath the T-shirt he was wearing. She wanted to feel closer to him. "Would you turn the light off please, Ollie?" She didn't want him to see the tears that had spilled over her eyelashes and trailed down her cheeks.

He reached over and flicked a switch next to the bed, leaving them in total darkness. "You want the bedside lamp on?" he asked gently. Jane didn't speak but shook her head, squeezing him even tighter as she did.

They laid together for ages until her heart rate returned to normal. Only then did Ollie move, and it was merely to adjust the pillow beneath him. Then he pulled Jane back into his arms. "Try to sleep, babe, it's almost four in the morning."

Jane closed her eyes and deeply inhaled the newly familiar scent of the man holding onto her for dear life. He adjusted her leg so it draped across his and sighed softly. It wasn't long before they were both drifting off to sleep again.

Breakfast was spent trying to avoid the subject of Jane's nightmare. It wasn't until they'd both showered and dressed that Ollie dared to bring it up again, asking quietly if *he* had done anything wrong, triggered something off, or upset her in any way.

Over breakfast the next morning, Jane tried to explain that it was nothing to do with him or his actions, they just happen sometimes. "Flashbacks, that's all. I don't know why they happen anymore, it's not like I dwell on the past. I don't really know how much you know. I mean, I know Tobes told you a fair bit, but we haven't really had that conversation, have we? If you want to know anything, I'd prefer it if you talked to me, not Toby though. Does that make sense?" He nodded and she continued. "You can't stop the nightmares, Ollie, nobody can. The doctor said they should just stop in time. I'm sorry if I scared you." The cup she gripped tightly held her gaze. "Do you want me to get an earlier train home? I can go this afternoon instead of tomorrow morning if you want. If you're having second thoughts, I understand, I know that I have a lot of emotional baggage to deal with. It's not easy for me, so I know how hard it must be for you to wrap your head around. You didn't sign up for any of this." She continued to stare down at the cup of coffee, stirring it continually.

Ollie smiled as he reached over, placing his hand over Jane's "No, I don't want you to go home. You just scared the living shit out of me last night. But hey, at least you got me to share the bed with you." Jane knew his attempt at humour was aimed at dismissing her uncertainty. With a gentle squeeze of her hand, Ollie continued. "Jane, can I do anything? I won't ask you about your ex or what happened, but I'd love it if you trusted me enough to tell me, when you're ready, that is. I want to protect you, keep you safe but I don't know what to do or say now. Please, don't go home today. I've booked tomorrow off work too; let me drive you home then, instead of you getting the train back?" He lifted Jane's chin with his finger so he could look her in the eyes. "Will you please stop stirring that bloody coffee, you're going to wear a hole in my cup."

Jane smiled back at the handsome man opposite her. "Okay. If you insist. Jeez, have you seen the time? How long have you let me ramble on for? It's lunchtime already. Now, about that picnic. In case you hadn't noticed, it's pouring down."

Ollie glanced out of the window. "Lounge picnic it is then. If you're game?" He leapt out of his seat and headed out the front door, returning moments later with a picnic blanket tucked under his arm. He pushed the sofa back towards the wall, moved the coffee table to the side and proceeded to lay out the blanket in the lounge area. Jane watched in amusement as he started to mess with the controls for his iPod. A moment later music began streaming from speakers that weren't visible in the room. He threw cushions from the sofa onto the blanket and motioned for Jane to move to the lounge.

The picnic he'd prepared while Jane showered sat in a basket on the kitchen counter. Ollie grabbed the basket, joining her on the tartan rug. "Can I interest you in some wine, madam?" He handed her a glass as he opened a bottle of white, before pouring it into their glasses. Ollie emptied the contents of the basket onto the rug between them. "Dig in." Jane's gaze roamed over the goodies, unsure what to choose first. The delicious looking crusty rolls or the little salad pots and dips with strips of pitta bread he'd selected. He'd obviously gone to a lot of trouble and Jane felt spoilt for choice.

As the hours passed, Ollie kept feeding Jane little samples of food as they chatted. She wanted to know everything about him. He'd been only too happy to oblige with tales of his childhood, from growing up in the same small village he still lived in to how he'd come to set up his own IT business with his brother, Jason or Jay, as Ollie lovingly referred to him. He was passionate when he spoke about work, his eyes lit up with excitement when Jane appeared to take an interest. As he turned to top up Jane's wine glass she laughed loudly as The Wanted began singing about Lightening. "I did not expect that on your iPod! The rocky kind of stuff, yeah, but this?" The giggles wouldn't stop. "Who are you and what have you done with Ollie?"

He snorted with laughter as he leaned over to tickle Jane. "Do not diss my music, missy!" Jane squealed loudly as she tried to roll away from his grasp but he was too quick for her, grabbing her arms, pinning her to the spot as he leant in to kiss her. "It reminds me of us. I think I may set it as your ringtone now too." Laughing, Ollie released her arms, allowing Jane to wrap them around him.

She raised her eyebrows and smiled widely at him. "I think you should, then I can ring you when your mates are around and embarrass you!"

There was no answer; he just gazed into her eyes as he lowered his face, kissing her on the lips once more. Jane tangled her fingers through his hair, pulling him closer. She needed him, he enabled her to breathe right now. Jane closed her eyes as Ollie's hand slid up under the hem of her shirt.

He began drawing small circles with his fingertips along her stomach, eliciting gentle moans as she shivered at his touch. He gradually kissed across her jaw and down the side of her neck. She permitted her hands to roam down his back, feeling the muscles ripple as he moved. As he gently sucked, then nibbled his way around Jane's shoulder and collar bone, she grasped his t shirt and pulled it up over his head. Allowing her to take the lead, Ollie helped to remove the offending item. His hands drifted to the buttons on Jane's shirt, but before going further he stopped to look at her, giving her a chance to stop him if she wanted to. Giving him the permission he sought, Jane fumbled with the button on his jeans.

Ollie placed his hand over Jane's, introducing a temporary stop to her actions. "Jane, are you sure, there's no rush, babe. We don't have to do this; I can wait until you're ready. It doesn't have to be right now."

Jane silenced him with a kiss, and he moved to position himself above her. A not–so-soft groan escaped his lips as Jane slid her hands down below the fabric of his underwear, feeling warm skin under her touch. Pulling him nearer to her, she tried to close the remaining distance between them. Returning his gently probing kisses, pushing him onto his back softly,

Jane began trailing soft kisses all down his chest and across his firm abdomen as she worked his jeans free of his legs, along with his underwear. As she sat astride him, she removed her now unbuttoned shirt, discarding it on the sofa behind.

Ollie ran his hands up her sides, causing goose bumps to swell across her body. He sat up and wrapped his arms around her waist pulling her in closer still, Jane relished the skin to skin contact as he gazed adoringly into her eyes. She had no idea where all this new found confidence had come from but she chose to embrace it.

Ollie kissed her again, his teeth gently pulling at her bottom lip before he smiled and spoke. "I think I'm at a disadvantage here, you're wearing far too many clothes for my liking." He reached behind her back to unclasp her bra, pulling the straps down and off her arms. He trailed soft bites down her chest and across her breast before capturing a nipple with his mouth. He gently swirled his tongue around the hardened bud he'd created.

Jane could feel her heart pounding against her ribcage; almost sure Ollie could hear it too. It felt as though it might crash through her ribs at any minute. He gently lowered her back down onto the rug, sliding her underneath him. Her mind raced; she'd never felt like this before about anyone. He licked, sucked and nibbled his way down, across her abdomen, as he nipped at her hip bones Jane lifted her bottom slightly allowing him to remove the remainder of her clothing.

As he gently positioned himself between Jane's thighs, careful to hold his own weight on his arm, he reached down to pull her leg around his waist and whispered against her lips, "You can still say no, Jane. We can stop at any time…"

It was then she knew for sure she didn't want him to stop touching her, not now, not ever. He was giving Jane something she'd never had or experienced throughout her adult life. Control. Jane was the one calling the shots, it was her decision to carry on or stop. She pulled him in tighter. The kisses grew more urgent as she tried to convey her message. Their breathing became more rapid as Ollie slowly pushed inside her, letting out a guttural moan as Jane lifted her hips to meet his, taking him deeper inside. Ollie gazed deep into her eyes, his expression one of adoration, trust and longing. He stilled his movements, pausing to kiss Jane's eyelids. His hand slid beneath her and he pulled her closer to him, trying to push even deeper as she wrapped her legs tightly around his waist. Ollie pulled back, almost leaving her completely then rocked his hips back slowly. Burying himself deeper inside her, the moan that escaped Jane's mouth was almost unrecognisable. Her eyes fluttered open, taking in the sight of Ollie above her. Crystal blue eyes gazed back at her longingly as he rocked in and out of her slowly. Her whole body felt alive for the first time, the tingling sensation spread from her fingertips to her toes building from a tiny spark to a long slow burn that would sending her flying over edge before long. With slow rhythmic thrusts Jane matched his movements, hips grinding together as she pushed to find the release she desperately needed. Ollie sat back on his heels, taking Jane with him. His hands gripped her hips now, helping her to find her rhythm as she rocked in his lap. The change in position was all she needed. Ollie thrust upwards twice more before the waves crashed, taking them on an earth-shattering journey that would leave Jane's body feeling boneless.

When they had floated back to earth, their breathing returning to normal, Ollie gazed lovingly down at her. "Wow! That was...God, I mean are you okay?" Ollie searched Jane's face for some kind of sign, kissing the tip of her nose, and eyelids as he waited for her to speak.

"I think my legs may never work again." Jane giggled as Ollie grinned a very self-satisfied smile. Pulling her into his embrace, he held her as he stroked soft circles down her bare back and she snuggled into his chest, breathing in his scent. She ran a lazy hand over his well-toned chest, enjoying the feeling of the toned muscles beneath her touch.

They laid in contented silence for what seemed like ages before Ollie spoke again. "You want to put some clothes on and go out for a drive with me?" *Did* she want to move? No, she wanted to stay there wrapped up in this man's arms for eternity. *Should* they go out for a while? Probably.

They didn't rush to shower or dress. Both instead, taking their time, playfully grinning at each other like teenagers. Jane watched in awe as Ollie stood and walked across the room to get a drink. His pert buttocks wiggling with every step. He really did have a stellar backside.

The rain had slowed when they eventually headed off in the car in the direction of the castle, where Ollie had wanted to have the picnic if it hadn't been for the weather. Ollie messed with dials and controls galore in his car as they waited for the traffic lights to change to green.

"Put a CD on if you want, or if you scroll through the screen, you can access my iPod playlists, if there's something on there you fancy? Here, have a play." After a few simple instructions Jane happily scrolled through playlist after playlist of songs she had never heard of until she came to The Wanted song again, chuckling away to herself, she pressed play on the little interactive screen and turned to watch Ollie's expression change to one of amusement as the song began to play. "I'm never going to hear the end of this, am I? If you tell Toby I'll have to inflict great pain on you." He laughed as Jane threw her head back hooting with laughter. The imminent ribbing was inevitable.

Jane glanced around her sleek surroundings. "This is such a cool car. If you drive this why do you come to visit Toby on the train? Are you mad? There's no way I'd spend an hour on a stinking train when I could drive this." She didn't know too much about cars; she just knew this was cool and looked expensive, with loads of added extra bits, like the iPod thingy which changed into GPS, radio, and apparently a DVD player at the flick of a switch. She could almost guarantee the tyres on this mean machine cost more than her car. She gasped suddenly. "Oh my God! Are these seats heated? My backside is getting awfully warm right now."

Ollie grinned. "I would let you have a drive but I've seen you drive yours, so I think you'll have to forgive me for wanting to keep this in one piece." Feigning annoyance, Jane reached across to swat his arm at the insults and letting out a really unattractive snort as she giggled loudly. He laughed and tried to dodge her hands. "Come on, the rain's almost stopped.

Fancy a walk through the grounds? I'll buy you an ice cream if you're good."

The castle grounds were beautiful. There was lots going on that Freya would love, lots of woodland walks and a petting zoo she would adore. Jane was already mentally picturing bringing her here, if she got another invitation. If she didn't, she was sure she could easily hope on a train and bring Freya herself. It would be great to see her little face light up as she ran freely around the place. There were so many things she wanted to do now she had the freedom to get out and do them without the guilt and explanations that had always gone before. She sighed in contentment as she revelled in the fact that she could now be herself and live a life she'd never even anticipated

"So, do you think you might like to come to stay with me again sometime soon?" Ollie asked interrupting her thoughts; almost as though he was able to read her mind. "I get most weekends off, just sometimes I have to go away for a week or two at a time. But if you wanted to, we could work something out."

Jane knew his job took him away and that the last time he had to go anywhere it was France where he spent almost three weeks sorting some IT problem out for his main clients. Toby had told Jane how jealous he was, that his friend got to travel the world with the IT consultancy company he had set up with his brother.

Ollie had been all over the world, setting up new systems or troubleshooting old systems for clients. He was more than a little excited about his upcoming trip to Dubai, to discuss the needs of a brand new contract that his brother was hopeful they could secure. That was as long as Ollie didn't do or say anything stupid once he got there. He was due to leave at the end of the month and would be away for just over a week.

Jane's eyebrows knitted together in contemplation. "Aren't you going away at the end of the month though? It'll be a good few weeks before we can arrange some time together, won't it?" She felt a little sad as the words came out of her mouth. This was all very new. She didn't want to rush things but could feel herself falling for this man, and she was falling fast.

"How about next weekend? Bring Freya next time. We could have a drive to the coast with her, or bring her here to the zoo thing. She likes animals, she must do, she loves Toby." Ollie sounded hopeful.

Her wide eyes along with the quick intake of breath gave away the surprise she felt at his suggestion to include Freya. It wasn't that she didn't want him to more that she worried about the affect it would have on her young daughter. "Is it not a little too soon for you? I mean, bringing my daughter into this." Jane waggled her finger between the two of them. "I know it's a lot to take on, someone like me, with a child. It's probably not your parents' idea of the perfect relationship for you." Jane watched as he ran his hands through his hair, blowing out a large breath.

Ollie guided her to a bench a few steps away, pulling her down beside him. "Jane, we're the same age. Yes, this isn't exactly what I envisaged, when I thought about falling in love with someone. I didn't think about a child being involved at the start but that's not to say that I don't like it. I just never thought about it until now. I want to see where this goes; I want to spend time getting to know you and Freya. What did you tell me before? Oh yes, the package deal thing. Well, I think I might like this package deal, and it's my decision to make. It's up to me to decide who I fall in love with, not my parents. So, are you up for seeing how it goes? And for letting me get to know Freya a little better?" Ollie held her hand tightly as he waited for her to reply.

Did he just say falling in love with someone? Focus, Jane. Almost gulping down air and trying to compose herself she answered, "I er... I don't see why not. I mean she has to always come first, you know? I'll always have to put her needs before my own, but I know she likes you, so that's a good start. She doesn't like everyone despite what you see between her and Toby. That took a lot of work on his behalf. Maybe next weekend is a little too soon though?"

Ollie's shoulders slumped as his brow crumpled. Jane could see he was disappointed. She bent her head down to capture his gaze. "I didn't say no. Why don't you come visit us? Toby's away with his mum next weekend, some birthday thing, I think. We would have the house to ourselves; Freya will be at my parents' Friday night until Saturday afternoon. So it could be just the two of us that night. We could still drive to the beach, it's not too far from my house." Jane paused, giving him a chance to reply.

Without hesitation, Ollie replied. "Sounds good to me. I've a meeting on Friday morning, but how about I come over after that? I could be at yours by the time you finish work." And just like that the glum expression was gone and that handsome smile she loved was back once more.

So, it was agreed. No more dilly dallying around. Jane intended to take life by the horns from now on.

The afternoon sun began to dip, casting a soft glow across the castle grounds. The gentle hues danced over the small lake. Ollie stood, holding out his hand for Jane to take. "C'mon, let's head back."

The drive back to Ollie's flat was fused with fleeting glances and loving touches. They hardly made it through the door before Jane leapt into his arms, kissing him thoroughly. Ollie responded willingly, his hands gripping her bottom, he pulled her in tight against him. He carried Jane through to the main living space, making a beeline for the kitchen counter, where he placed Jane gently down.

Jane faltered. "Don't you want to take this to the bedroom?" she asked.

Ollie shook his head, the fire in his eyes burned brightly. His fingertips roamed up Jane's thighs, before they found the waistband of her jeans. As he pulled down the zip, Jane lifted her hips allowing him to remove her jeans completely. "I like it here,"

Jane watched as he moved into the space between her legs, with his hands firmly planted on her bottom again, he edged her forwards. Her hands found his zipper, freeing him from the confines of his trousers. Jane gazed at him through her eyelashes as she heard the breath leave his body. With her hands gripping his shoulders, she allowed him to slide inside her in one long slow movement. "Ollie," Jane gasped as he began to slide in and out of her. It was fast and frantic but amazing. Jane had never experienced anything like it, her whole body shook with pleasure.

As their breathing slowly returned to normal, Ollie lifted her from the countertop. He carried her across the lounge, kicking the bedroom door open as he went. "I'm not finished with you yet."

The rest of the weekend went by so quickly. Jane hardly had time to blink before Ollie was loading her bag into his car. "I would have been happy on the train, you know." Jane told him.

"No, you wouldn't. You hated it; I saw your face when you got off the train on Saturday. Anyway, I want to drive you home; I know a nice pub we can stop at for lunch on the way. That way I get to extend our weekend by a few hours too." The smile on his face was beautiful and breath-taking as he started the engine and headed for the motorway.

Jane had to admit that she did indeed, much prefer this mode of transport to the smelly old train but she was still determined to stand on her own two feet more. "Okay, you can drive me home on this occasion, seeing as you can't bear to be apart from me." She giggled.

Ollie winked at her. "Hey, you know the feeling's mutual." She couldn't deny it.

Instead of hitting the motorway after lunch, Ollie opted for the back roads instead.

"You know it will take you much longer, going this way," Jane mumbled as she scrolled through her texts. Toby had messaged to let her know he'd picked Freya up already and that she could go straight home. *One less job to do*, she thought.

Ollie coughed. "Ahem, am I talking to myself now?"

She cringed and stuck the phone back in her bag.

"Sorry, sorry! I'll put it away. It was just Toby letting me know he's collected Freya."

"Aw, that's good of him. That means you can go straight home." He paused and Jane could sense he had more to say. She watched him expectantly and he sighed. "Have you and he never...you know...had anything more than friendship? I know it's none of my business but I see the way you two are and I just can't help but wonder why you're not together."

Jane laughed at the thought "We're just not attracted to each other. He's like the brother I never had...and sometimes don't want." She laughed. "He's been my friend for so long that I just don't even think about it anymore. Don't get me wrong he drives me crazy sometimes but I know he's always got my back. He was the driving force behind me standing up to Dave and I'll be forever grateful for that. But you have absolutely nothing to worry about. We have a strong friendship that feels more like family but neither of us would ever want to cross that line. It just wouldn't work. And besides, I'm rather fond of this other guy I've been seeing recently."

Ollie reached over and squeezed her hand tightly. "Well I can tell you for certain that the guy you're rather fond of is rather besotted with you too."

Jane rested her head back and smiled as desire rose

within her and heated her blood. "So you're not jealous?"

He shook his head and shrugged. "I don't have anything to be jealous of. Not anymore." And that was the end of that. Jane was relieved that for once someone had accepted the truth about her relationship with Toby without feeling the need to dissect it further and play the Freudian. Their relationship was exactly what she had described. Toby was family. But Ollie, she hoped, was her future.

"Come outside with me? I have to get going in a minute." Ollie held out his hand for Jane to join him. Toby stood, sharing one of those manly pats on the back/hug kind of goodbyes that men did with their friends. "Drive safe, mate." Jane closed the door quietly behind them, walking Ollie down the garden towards the mean machine that was his car, all sleek, black and shiny looking.

He leant against the car door pulling her into his chest. "I feel like a teenager with his first crush." he breathed into her ear and kissed her cheek softly, as she snaked her arms around his neck and returned his kiss. He sighed. "I'm not ready to let go yet, Jane. I really wish I didn't have work tomorrow. I want to stay.

Holding you, keeping you safe. I can't wait for the weekend now."

If he pulled her in any tighter she wouldn't be able to breathe. "I don't need you to keep me safe, silly. I need someone to have fun with, someone to share my life." Jane said although she wasn't ready to say goodbye either. "Come on, its four days. We can make four days." She was trying to convince herself as much as him. She pushed herself gently away from him, giving them a little distance to breathe freely again.

Ollie blew out a breath, grabbed her hands in his and squeezed lightly. "It's going to be the longest four days of my life. I'll ring you when I get home. Go on, get inside it's starting to rain again." He climbed into the driver's seat and Jane pushed the car door closed behind him. She leaned down to kiss him through the window, before stepping back and watching him drive away.

Once his car was out of sight she turned, wrapping her arms around her body and dashed inside her warm dry home. She locked the front door behind her as she shuddered from the cold wet night.

She hated the rain.

Chapter nineteen

It'd been three hours since Jane had kissed Ollie goodbye and watched his car disappear down the street and out of view completely. She'd spent that time with Freya, playing with the ragdoll Jane had bought her as a gift when she was at Ollie's. Happy that Freya was content with her new doll, Jane headed into the kitchen to open a bottle of wine to share with Toby, it was time for a catch up with her friend.

Toby sat at the kitchen table. "LJ just texted to see if you were back. Told her to drag her and Jamie's sorry asses over here for a few drinks. That okay with you?"

Jane nodded as she reached up to pull out the extra wine glasses they'd need, when an almighty crash came from the lounge. Freya's screaming followed quickly. Dropping the glasses to the counter instantly, Jane set off running in the direction of her daughter closely followed by Toby.

Freya sat on the lounge carpet surrounded by

broken glass. A large rock sat no further than a foot away from her. Toby ran out the front door as Jane picked her way across the glass to lift her daughter from danger. Jane shook with anger as she whipped Freya from the carnage and into her embrace. "It's okay, baby girl. Mummy's here. I've got you." She soothed the toddler.

Hugging Freya tightly, she followed Toby outside. "Did you see anyone?" She frantically ran her hands over Freya, checking for any blood or injury she may have.

Toby turned to his friend with a sorrowful look in his eyes. "Yeah, I did. Sorry Janey, it was Dave. I saw the car. It was definitely him."

Jane watched open-mouthed as Toby dialled the emergency services and asked for the police. She couldn't quite believe that her ex-husband was insane enough to pull such a stunt. Jane's priority was her daughter's safety. They needed to report the damage quickly, that way there'd be more chance of catching the scumbag responsible.

Toby spoke to the call handler. "Yeah, I saw who it was, well I saw the car anyway. Yeah, I got the reg number too. It was Dave Ryan, the ex-husband of my housemate. There's a restraining order on him. Okay, thanks." Toby pushed his phone back in his front pocket, turning to check if Jane and Freya were both okay.

"Dave? Really?" Jane was astounded that he would do something so stupid, when he knew his daughter would be in the house.

Nodding, Toby guided her back inside with Freya. "The police will be here in a few minutes, they said. Come inside, is Freya okay, is she hurt? She's shivering." His eyebrows knitted together in concern.

Jane reassured him. "Yeah, she's okay. Well, she isn't hurt but I think she's a little shocked."

Once he was satisfied there was no physical damage to Freya, Toby busied himself cleaning up the glass, while Jane stood clinging onto Freya again with all her might. Fifteen minutes later the police arrived along with Lindsey and Jamie. Toby made tea for them all while Jane spoke to the officers first and then he gave his statement. Jane listened as Toby informed the police that her ex-husband had been sitting outside in the car when he'd run out the front door. Dave had even shouted out to Toby, asking him to tell Jane, 'This is just the beginning, no-one is going to play at being Freya's dad!' Then he had driven off at normal speed down the street, like he hadn't just committed a criminal offence.

Jane fought to take it all in; the sheer stupidity of it

was overwhelming. Her whole body shook violently as she played out, in her mind, what might have happened if the rock had landed a foot to the left. Surely Dave had known Freya would not only be at home but still playing when he decided to put the front window through with half a damn brick? Jane struggled to take in anything the police advised her as her head swam with what ifs. The relief she felt was immense when she heard them say they had picked Dave up a few streets away, thanks to Toby giving them the licence number of his car. Surely now they would have to detain him? Jane was hopeful the police could keep her and her daughter safe now he had violated his restraining order.

The sudden urge to vomit overtook her, thrusting Freya into Toby's arms, Jane covered her mouth with her hand and ran at breakneck speed to the kitchen, just making it in time to the sink before emptying the contents of her stomach.

Lindsey followed Jane in to the kitchen, reaching over to rub her back, whilst holding her hair out of the line of fire. "Tobes rang Ollie. He's on his way over. We told him not to but he insisted. God, Jane, I could hear Ollie shouting down the phone from the other side of the room." Dipping her head, Jane rested it on her arms across the sink, her tears joined the water that Lindsey was now running to clear the vomit away. "Better?" Lindsey handed Jane some kitchen towel to clean herself up then gathered her friend into a huge embrace.

Lindsey smiled sympathetically. "He can't hurt you now. The officer said he would probably get a custodial sentence. What with the court order thing and everything. He'll probably go straight to court tomorrow from the station." Jane knew her friend was trying to reassure her, but all that ran through her mind was the feeling that she was right back in the violent throes of her marriage again. The uncertainty of when it would end swamped her, Jane's whole body slumped as she folded her arms around herself protectively. Lindsey brushed Jane's hair back from her face. "I'll put Freya to bed; she must be shattered with all the carry on. Come and sit down, sit with Toby. Let him take care of you for a minute." Lindsey guided Jane back along the corridor, aiming her at the sofa next to Toby.

Jane was numb. She felt like she was watching some harrowing movie, not sitting in her own house, where she was supposed to be safe, surrounded by chaos and police officers who kept talking into earpieces and writing down notes. How had this become her life again? Why could her ex-husband not walk away or just behave like any normal human being?

By the time Ollie arrived, Jane's feelings had gone

through fear to anger and back again. He'd no sooner walked through the door or closed it behind him before Jane launched herself into his arms, not even giving him time to drop his bag on the floor.

Ollie held her tightly in his embrace. "Shh, babe, it's okay. Shush now, come on, I'm here now." Ollie held on tightly, trying to soothe her with his words as she sobbed, unable to form any sort of coherent sentence. As he held her, Jane released the last of her angst. Her breathing became shallow and she gasped for breath as stars began to appear in front of her. Ollie held her at arms-length, his brow crumpled in worry. "Jane, look at me, take a big breath, honey, I can't understand you. I need you to calm down for me. Can you breathe with me, slowly in, now out, that's it. Slowly, slowly." He was regulating his own breathing making Jane copy him, making her hold eye contact with him as they breathed together deeply. "That's it. Is Freya okay? Was she hurt, are you hurt?" He ran his hands over Jane's arms, checking her over visually as she assured him they were both fine.

"I want to kill that bastard!" he growled at Toby over Jane's head as he held her close again. "Did they arrest him? They fucking better have had, I want to rip his fucking head off right now." Toby tried to calm Ollie down, telling him that wasn't the answer; Jane didn't need to hear that sort of thing right now. Jane stiffened in Ollie's arms, the tension in the air acting as a trigger to her insecurities.

Ollie picked up on the change in his girlfriend instantly. "Sorry Jane. I'm just mad at the idiot."

Lindsey walked over to where Ollie stood cradling Jane. "We all are, Ollie, but she's terrified, look at her. She needs you to stay calm and just be here with her. Okay?" Lindsey ran a hand up his arm, soothing him as she spoke. "We all need to calm down, keep things normal for Freya, if she hears raised voices it might upset her again. That little one's been through enough today." Jane felt Ollie relax a little around her. She knew he wanted to protect her but right now she only needed him to be there for her.

Jamie was busy opening and shutting cupboard doors searching for alcohol. Toby pointed him in the direction of the cupboard that held a stock of the good stuff. "Vodka, mate, she likes vodka, or that foul American bourbon crap if you pour it neat."

Lindsey cleared a space on the coffee table, allowing Jamie to put down the glasses while he poured long shots of whisky for each of them.

Ollie sat down on the nearest chair, with a quick pat to his leg, he gestured for Jane to sit on his lap so he could hold her tightly still. "Here, drink this straight down. Then you need another one, okay?" Jane took the glass from him, almost throwing the amber liquid down her throat. She winced from the after burn it left behind. Jamie topped up her glass, pushing it back towards her.

Ollie watched as she drank from the glass. "Better?" He asked as she snuggled into his chest.

Jane buried her head into his neck allowing herself to inhale his scent. "Hungry, actually, we didn't eat yet, did we, Tobes?" It was as much a question as a statement. In all the chaos Jane couldn't quite remember if they'd got round to eating or not.

Toby grinned in response. "I'm on it, darlin', just ordered pizzas for everyone."

The guy arrived to board the front window up at the same time as the delivery guy. The group of friends sat huddled around the kitchen table eating pizza, listening to the banging of the board going up. Jane sat on Ollie's knee as he refused to let her go. She was glad he held on to her, given half a chance, Jane might take off running and not be able to stop.

Ollie slipped the window man a hefty tip for coming out late on a Sunday night. As Lindsey and Jamie said their goodbyes, Toby made his excuses heading off to bed, not long after. He kissed Jane as he passed her. "Love you, night, darlin'. You going to be okay?"

Jane nodded, smiling at him, trying to appear braver than she felt. "Yeah, of course. Love you too,

Tobes, night." She didn't relish the thought of being downstairs by herself, but when Ollie left she'd head up to bed, at least to try and get some rest.

As the door to the lounge closed behind Toby, Ollie breathed out deeply. All the tension from the night had built up inside him.

"You need to get going soon, you have work tomorrow." Jane kissed him lightly, trying desperately to not to let fall the tears that threatened. She really didn't want him to leave. Everything seemed better when he was near.

Ollie recoiled at the idea. "What? You think I'm leaving you alone now? I'm not leaving you tonight. I brought everything I need with me; I can go to my meeting from here, just need to head off thirty minutes earlier. No big deal." He shrugged his shoulders.

As Jane was about to protest she realised it was futile, she didn't want him to leave either. "Okay, if you're sure, but can we go to bed, I'm shattered and I'm not sure how long Freya will sleep for, she was still upset when Lindsey put her to bed I think." Jane stood and held out her hand for him to follow. Once in bed, Ollie held her close. Jane rested her head against his chest listening to the slow rhythmic beat of his heart, she allowed the gentle thrum to calm her as she drifted off to sleep.

As he'd said, Ollie left early the next morning,

leaving Jane in bed with the cup of tea he'd brought up for her before kissing her goodbye. The promise he made to call later eased her battered emotions. Freya had slept all night and was still dozing as Jane sat sipping her morning cuppa in bed, reflecting on the night before. The glazing company were booked to replace the front window later that afternoon and Jane knew already she wouldn't be able to look in lounge until the window was restored. The sight of the boarded up frame would be too much for her to bear. A tap on the bedroom door snapped her from her reverie.

Toby's head appeared. "How you doing this morning? Or is that a stupid question?" His body followed and he climbed onto the bed beside Jane.

"I'm okay. Surprised Freya's still asleep and gutted that Ollie's left for work but apart from that, I think I'll live." The small smile she offered her friend betrayed the attempts to down play her anxiety.

Toby tried to play down her obvious angst. "Hey, you've been through worse. At least now he's in custody. Look at it that way." Toby sipped at his own drink. "He can't hurt either of you while the police have him locked up."

Jane focused on the negatives as she'd been conditioned to do for so long. But he was right, while ever the police had Dave, she was safe and that brought her a great deal of relief.

The next few weeks passed in a daze. Dave had been formally charged with criminal damage and breaking the conditions of his restraining order, the day after he broke Jane's window. He'd appeared in court and was now being held at Her Majesty's pleasure for the foreseeable future, leaving Jane space to feel safe again. Ollie had only been home twice since the window incident. He clearly didn't want to leave his girlfriend alone. He'd apparently decided it was his job to protect her now, not Toby's. She was secretly delighted to have her boyfriend around so much. If nothing else, it was giving Freya time to get to know Ollie better and it seemed to be going really well. The little Princess already had him wrapped around her finger, making him read her bedtime story, but only every other night because she wasn't quite ready to trade Toby in full time yet. Ollie put in loads of effort, making up funny voices for the characters to make her giggle, as he read.

"I'm not going to Dubai next week. Jay's going instead," Ollie stated nonchalantly as they ate the curry he'd made from scratch; the boy was good, Jane made a mental note to remember to thank his mother for teaching him to not only cook but do his own washing and ironing. It was a revelation.

"Why is he going and not you? Please tell me you

didn't turn down the job for me. Ollie, you were looking forward to going. You should go." Jane pushed her plate away, unable to eat anymore. She didn't want Ollie to make such big changes to his life on her account. It was important to her that he kept doing everything he'd normally do. She didn't want him to resent her, weeks or months down the line.

He shook his head vaguely, dismissing her concern. "It's no big deal. Jay was getting a little jealous of me doing all the overseas contracts anyway, and I don't want to be that far away from you or Freya just now. I can do the next trip, if it needs one." He didn't look up from his meal, he simply carried on as though he hadn't just dropped a bombshell.

Jane stared open-mouthed at him, stunned by his statement. "I can't let you do that. This is your job, your company. You worked hard to build it up and I will not let you wreck that." Jane had his attention now, forcing him to look up, annoyance hit when she saw him smiling at her gentle outburst. She was a little offended he found her so amusing.

Ollie raised his eyebrows quizzically. Making her feel like a toddler throwing a tantrum. "Honestly. It's really not a big deal. I've had a few years of travelling with the job, I want to stay at home more now we're together and there's Freya to consider, that's all. Jay's single and very happy to go instead, it makes sense right now." He paused to let that sink in, Jane studied him intently. He had something else on his mind, she could tell. He was so easy to read, the little twitch that appeared under his eye when he was about to say something she might not like was doing a merry dance. "While we're 'discussing' things, I'd really love it if you would give some thought to moving in with me properly. Instead of me staying over when I can. I can move up here if you want, I don't mind, or if you need a fresh start, which Toby and I think you do, we could look for a house somewhere else." Ollie placed his clasped hands on the table before him. There, it was. The thing she could tell he'd been worrying about.

Jane opened her mouth to tell him he needed to slow down but she couldn't seem to form the right words let alone get them out. Of course she saw living with Ollie as her future but was now was the right time? She wasn't sure. When Jane didn't respond, Ollie continuing his prepared speech. "We've talked about it, this isn't something I've plucked from nowhere. Toby said he can find somewhere else to live. He can even come live with us, if you *really* want him to." Ollie shrugged his shoulders. "I honestly don't care about the details, I just want us under the same roof, as a family. But I don't want to live here, in his house, Jane. I can't, and I think this place holds too many memories for you and Freya. I want to be able to give you everything you've ever wanted; I want to look after both of you, for the rest of my life. I earn enough to look after the three of us, without you having to worry anymore. You can stay home, look after Freya full time, or carry on working. Whatever makes you happy? It's your decision." Jane could tell he'd thought long and hard about the finer details

Jane let out a sigh as she stood up from the dining table clearing away their plates. "Ollie, it's too soon. Don't you think it's too soon? I need to learn how to be on my own again. Can you see that?" Jane had her back to him now, running water in the sink, keeping herself busy as she heard Ollie's chair scrape across the floor before making his way across the room. They may have talked about their future together on numerous occasions but to have it laid out on the table for her to take was a scary prospect, even if it was exactly what she wanted.

He placed his hands on the work surface on either side of Jane, encompassing her in his arms. He bent down to place a kiss on the side of her neck. "You already are a strong, independent woman, you deserve the best in life, that's what I want for you. I love you, I tried not to let myself fall so quickly but I have and I do love you and that adorable little girl. I just want you and Freya, all your flaws, mistakes, smiles, giggles, sarcasm. Everything. I love you and I don't see why we shouldn't be together. I'm not going away, so you're stuck with me forever, if you'll have me. But I don't do things by half; you should know that by now. I actually don't care if we do this now or in a few years if that's what you want to do, but why wait? Why put it off any longer?" Ollie let her take in what he'd said, as he rested his chin on her shoulder, he waited for her to answer him. "So, what do you think?"

Jane turned in his arms to look up into those mesmerizing ice blue eyes, searching for some kind of sign, something that would tell her what to do. Jane knew he was right, she needed to find the courage to grab life with both hands and run with it. Feeling out of her comfort zone with the declarations of love, her poor battered heart was confused but not enough to stop her knowing that she loved Ollie.

What was the point in denying it? "I love you too." As the words left her lips Ollie breathed a sigh of relief, taking her face in his hands and cradling it gently as he kissed her. When the kiss ended she gazed up at him. "Ollie, can we just take this a little slower though? I mean, moving in together is a big deal. What about Freya?" If it didn't work out, the effect on Freya could be huge. Jane didn't want to confuse her.

Ollie rested his forehead on Jane's as he spoke quietly. "I love her too. Jane, she's so young, she'll adapt really easily. Better than we will. She'll be my priority just as much as you are; but we can give her everything she needs, together. We can make a whole better life for her, if you just give us a chance."

Jane slid her arms around his waist, nestling her head against his chest. Ollie undoubtedly knew how to say the right thing. Freya was her weak spot and Jane would do anything to give her the life she deserved. She had been through so much in her short life and Jane felt she had a lot to make up to her. She took a deep breath, steadying her nerves before she spoke, not daring to look up at Ollie's face.

Oh what the hell, she had nothing to lose by chasing her dreams. Toby had assured her Ollie was one of the good guys and he'd done nothing to prove otherwise. "Okay, we can look for somewhere to rent together. But I don't want to be too far from my parents or my friends. Forty minutes away, no further, okay? As for Toby, he doesn't need to live with us; I don't need him to live with us, alright?" Jane faked a shudder at that thought.

Ollie grabbed her and swung her around in the air as she laughed freely, feeling like a schoolgirl again. "You mean it? Really? We can look for our own place? You should ring Toby and tell him, ring him now, here!" Ollie thrust his phone into Jane's hand, urging her to make the call.

She wanted to share the news with anyone that'd

listen. She'd just agreed to live with Ollie, she'd agreed to let him build a new family with her, to make a new start. Right this minute though, she wanted to enjoy the moment with her boyfriend. "Oliver! Calm down, I just agreed to move in with you. I don't want to ring Toby now. I can tell him later, when he gets home. I want to celebrate with you, just you."

Epilogue

Two Years Later

Jane stood out on the deck of what was to be her home for the next few days. Champagne glass in hand, she looked out over the ocean. It was the most beautiful day; she was in the most magnificent place, Negril, Jamaica, of all places. The long white sandy beach stretched for miles as the water lapped at its shoreline. It was idyllic. The villas along the coast were all private, separated by lots of green leafy trees and plants. Each little home feeling like it stood all alone on the island, instead of being a short walk to its neighbour. The peace and tranquillity they gave was way more than the brochure had promised they would offer.

Jane's family and friends were all gathered in neighbouring apartments, getting ready for the big day; at least they would be later. It was still early. Freya had woken at some ungodly hour, wanting to build sandcastles on the beach. It was her first time holidaying outside of the UK, and not in that damn caravan of her grandfather's. The pair had spent the best part of two hours playing together in the shaded area, in front of the villa, before Toby had joined them from next door. Bringing with him a bottle of what tasted like very expensive champagne to celebrate and some juice for Freya. The friends had chatted, laughed and cried together until Jane could take no more.

"Am I really doing this again? Do you think I'm crazy?" Jane had positioned herself on the sand next to Toby, head rested on his shoulder, beginning to doubt the whole thing for the millionth time that week.

Toby shook his head. "You're not crazy. Ollie is the best thing that could have happened to you, apart from meeting me, that is. He's a good guy; he adores you and that little girl. What more do you need, eh?" He nudged her with his shoulder, making her spill her drink. "Oops. Sorry. Good thing you're not dressed yet. Or were you planning on wearing those shorts later?" Toby joked trying to ease the pressure his friend evidently felt.

Jane laughed. "No! Of course not. Did you not see that white thing hanging in my bathroom? It's called a dress. I'm not sure you're familiar with that term but yeah, I have a dress. Lindsey's coming over soon for breakfast, and then the ritual begins. Apparently I have a make-up woman, a hair woman and some other woman coming over in about an hour. It takes that many people to make me look anywhere near respectable these days." It was Jane's turn to shoulder-bump him now, as he fell back laughing on the sand. "Stay with us for breakfast, Toby? I'd really like you to be here this morning, if Jenna doesn't mind that is, bring her over too." Jane couldn't imagine spending her wedding morning with anyone other than her best friend, it was ridiculous that they'd tried to plan it any other way. He was her family in all but name. His rightful place was by her side, and that's exactly where she wanted him during the pre-ceremony celebrations.

Jenna had been with Toby for a while now; they met on some team building course for work, something Toby had attended under duress and extreme pressure from his boss. Jenna was gorgeous and the complete opposite of what Jane or anyone had expected Toby to fall for. Small, petite features with waist-length, chocolate brown hair. She brought out a side in him that everyone thought was gone forever. He adored her; it had been obvious from the start that she was a keeper in his eyes. Jenna, like everyone else, had struggled with Jane and Toby's relationship just as most other people did in the beginning, but it hadn't taken many weekends of everyone being together until she relaxed, accepting them for what they had together.

Toby smiled broadly, the love he felt evident in his eyes. "I left her asleep. There's a note telling her to head over here when she wakes. But I'll go get her in a minute, just wanted some alone time with my best friend before she becomes Mrs Miller."

Jane gasped. "Oh. My. God! That sounds so weird. Mrs Jane Miller!" That was going to take a little getting used to. She'd not envisaged being Mrs Jane Anybody ever again, not after her first disastrous experience.

Jane and Toby sat watching the ocean together in silence a little longer before he stood, pulling Jane up with him. "I'll go grab Jenna, if that's okay then. You okay? Nerves holding up, are they?"

Jane and Ollie hadn't rushed into the marriage; the proposal had been a long time coming but once Ollie had proposed it had been all systems go. They'd only been engaged for a few months but he'd said he didn't see the point in waiting or dragging out the inevitable. There was also one very excited little girl desperate to be a bridesmaid to contend with. Making Freya wait any longer had been out of the question for Ollie. Whatever Freya wanted, Freya got. He'd proved his worth when he not only proposed to Jane but took the time to ask Freya's permission to marry her mum. The child had been overjoyed, wanting to scream it from the rooftops. Persuading her it was best to keep it a secret until he actually asked Jane to marry him had been a little hard.

Jane shoved Toby gently, smiling contentedly as she spoke. "I never felt better actually. You know what? You're right; meeting you was the best thing that could ever have happened to me. Ollie is just the icing on the cake." Jane hugged her best friend tightly before kissing him firmly on the cheek. Was that a tear she saw in his eye? "Now go, before Jenna thinks you've deserted her."

The next few hours were a little chaotic, having her hair and make-up done professionally seemed a little extravagant but Jane had been convinced fairly easily when Ollie pointed out she was only doing this once. It was the last time down any aisle for her, so she might as well enjoy every second of the pampering he intended to lavish on her for the day.

Lindsey held the top of Jane's wedding dress steady, allowing her to step into the lavish white satin gown. She smoothed out the fabric as she slowly pulled the zip up at the side. It was a simple design, strapless and fitted with a little glitzy embellishment across the bodice. The fabric skimmed over the curve of her hips, before gently filling out around her lower body. Simple and understated elegance. As Jane looked in the mirror she revelled in the fact the dress made her look at least a dress size smaller, and a hell of a lot taller once she slipped on the heeled sandals her and Lindsey had picked out only a week ago.

Lindsey shook her head and sighed. "Jane, you look amazing. So beautiful." She wiped tears away from her eyes before pulling Jane into an embrace.

Jane held Lindsey at arm's length. "So do you. That dress is perfect." Lindsey wore an olive green, silk, knee-length dress with a dark green sash that sat just under her breasts. Freya wore the same colour calf length sundress that made her look like a princess. They both had a single white Calla lily to carry too. No big fancy bouquets to contend with. Jane would have been happy with a quick trip down to the local registry office with their friends in tow, but everyone else had been horrified at the mere thought of that.

"Are you kidding me? If I turn to the side I look like an unripe tomato! Sorry, sorry. I love the dress, it's just... who knew this baby bump would be so bloody huge, and I'm only half way through this pregnancy thing I seem to be tied up with right now!" She pouted as she stared at her reflection in the mirror. She didn't look at all like an unripe tomato. She looked stunning, and pregnancy suited her.

Jane winked at her friend. "Well, just stay front end on for the photos then, eh?" She teased Lindsey trying to make her laugh. The pregnancy had been a surprise to everyone but especially Lindsey and Jamie. They'd only been married for five months. They went off to Vegas for a long weekend, astounding both family and friends when they called from their hotel to break the news that they had paid for a drive thru wedding on the second day there. The baby had been conceived the same weekend; Jamie put it down to too much alcohol and sun, but a lack of common sense and condoms had paid a huge part in it. But they were both blissfully happy, now they had got used to the whole idea of introducing a small person into the mix.

Lindsey scrambled around in her small clutch purse. "Here, I almost forgot! I'm supposed to give you this, from Ollie. He said you could only have it once you had your dress on." She held out a small box tied with a silver ribbon and a card addressed to, 'The Soon To Be Mrs Miller'.

Jane put the box on the dresser, ripping open the card first. Inside it read;

You're the most beautiful person I have ever met, you make me whole, I could search my whole life over and I would never find anyone as special as you. I love my life because it gave me you; I love you because you are my life. All my love Ollie x

Jane had to read it twice through the tears that had formed in her eyes, before she handed it to Lindsey to read whilst she giddily opened the gift. Inside the box was a white gold bracelet, with three small heart-shaped pendants next to the clasp, each one was engraved with an initial; J, F and O on one side and 'forever' on the reverse. Jane held it out for Lindsey to fasten around her wrist, the tears flowing freely now.

"Flashy bastard!" Lindsey muttered through her own tears. "Come on, let's do this." Lindsey led the way out of the bathroom, into the bedroom that now housed Jane's parents, Jamie, Toby and Jenna.

Freya was happily bouncing on the bed, way beyond excited. "Look, Mummy! Uncle Tubs gave me a flower to put in my hair. Does it look pretty?" She stopped bouncing briefly to allow Jane to see the white flower that adorned her daughter's curls.

Jane leaned to kiss her daughter. "It's beautiful, just like you, baby." She kissed her cheek as she lifted the bundle of happiness off the bed, handing her over to Toby to calm her down. He was the only one she was listening to today, she'd made that very clear.

A few moments later they walked the short distance to the beach together; Jamie, Jenna and Elaine, Jane's mum, took their seats under the newly erected canopy.

Her dad took a step back as Toby leaned in to kiss Jane on the forehead, his signature move. "You look beautiful, Janey. He is one lucky man. I love you, now go make me proud." Short and to the point, because that was Toby. Jane knew he was struggling to hold back tears of joy. They were there in his eyes for all to see.

Toby hugged her tightly then bent down to whisper in Freya's ear, making her chuckle softly. "Uncle Tubs! You are silly. Of course I'm going to marry you when I'm all bigger but you'd better tell Jenna that too. Oh and I didn't tell mummy the secret thing. Did you put the picture I made in the letter?" She kissed him full on the lips in earnest. The little girl waited for Toby to confirm everything was as it should before she continued, "Now go sit down, I gotta get Mummy and Ollie married." Toby grinned, winking at her as he walked over to sit with Jenna and Jane watched as he took Jenna's hand in his and, bringing it to his lips, kissed the back of her hand as he sat.

Jane and Ollie stood before their gathered family and friends surrounded with love and happiness. The officiant addressed the small assembly. "Today there will be no dearly beloved, no betrothed and no other ancient rhyme of the married. Today, promises become permanent and friends will become family," The officiant placed a steady hand on Jane and Ollie's shaky joined hands. "Today is about love. Love isn't just a word; it's an action. It's something you do, if you cherish it, it will never die."

Ollie turned to face Jane before he spoke. "I

believe in you, the person you will grow to be and the couple we will be together. With my whole heart, I take you as my wife, acknowledging and accepting your faults and strengths, as you do mine." He paused for a moment to gather his thoughts and to get a check on his emotions. "I promise to be faithful and supportive and to always make our family's love and happiness my priority. I will be yours forever, in sickness and in health, in failure and in triumph. I will dream with you, celebrate with you and walk beside you through whatever our lives may bring. You are my person—my love and my life, today and always."

Jane wiped an errant tear from her cheek before she recited the words she'd written for Ollie. "It is clear to me now that everything in my life has led me to you - I think back on all my choices and consider even the bad ones blessed, because if I had done even one thing differently, I might never have met you and become your wife." The tears flowed a little more freely now as Jane carried on her heartfelt vows. "I have to catch my breath to believe this is real, that I'm marrying my true love. I love that we will live out our lives together. Somehow my life has come to this amazing moment and I will always share it with you. You are my guide, my every wish come true and the person I want to grow old with."

As the small congregation cheered, Ollie leaned in

to kiss his new bride. The ceremony was short but perfect. The officiant brought Freya up to join the young couple. Ollie lifted her into his arms, hugging her tightly. "Ladies and gentlemen, I give you the Miller family." Ollie leaned over to kiss Jane again as their friends and family celebrated with them.

"Wait! You can't kiss yet. I got petals to throw when you two kiss. Right, Uncle Tubs?" Freya wriggled free, desperate to carry out her bridesmaid duties to the absolute letter. Jane and Ollie both knelt down in front of her, allowing her to tip her box of rose petals over their heads before she went running back to Toby proudly. He lifted her onto his knee and proudly high-fived the little bridesmaid congratulating her on a job well done.

"Well, Mrs Miller, how're you doing?" Jane's new husband whispered in her ear as everyone crowded around the newlyweds to take photos.

Jane's eyes sparkled in the last of the daylight. Her cheeks ached from grinning so much and the nervous butterflies she'd felt earlier had gone. In their place, a warm fuzzy feeling. "Just fine, Mr Miller, just perfect." The smile on Jane's face was evidence enough to prove she was indeed happy.

The light faded into the most gorgeous sunset Jane had ever seen. Beautiful oranges and purples stretched across the sky, lighting up the secluded bay. All the guests stood around eating and drinking under a canopied area, which was positioned a few feet away from where the ceremony had taken place. There was a local band playing in the restaurant, which adjoined to the villas the wedding party was staying in. It was far enough away not to dominate the evening, but still near enough to provide background music. Freya spent her time dancing with anyone who would entertain her as Jane and Ollie stood watching her.

Toby turned to the newlywed couple. "Here, I know you said no gifts, but I figured that didn't apply to me." He handed them a crisp, white A4 envelope.

Ollie took the envelope, his brow furrowed as he studied it curiously. "What's this? What did you buy, is it something ridiculous?" Ollie motioned for his new wife to open the envelope but Jane pushed it back towards him, insisting he do the honours. Jane eyed Toby and Jenna suspiciously, she and Ollie had turned down the offer of gifts from everyone, instead wanting them to simply enjoy the day with them. They didn't need anything, Ollie had made sure of that.

Ollie gasped as he stared open mouthed at what looked like some kind of official document he now held in his hand. "Bloody hell, man! How? I mean, jeez, what did you do to get these signed? We've been trying for ages but had no luck."

Okay, now he had Jane's full attention, just what

was inside that envelope? Ollie handed over the papers for Jane to read. Her eyes quickly scanned the documents. Unsure that they were actually what she thought they were.

In Jane's hands were the papers they'd had drawn up months ago for Ollie to adopt Freya, but Dave had been adamant he wasn't going to give up his parental rights. He wasn't interested in Freya anymore, the supervised visits had stopped long before Ollie and Jane had even moved in together. Dave had even stopped sending birthday and Christmas cards but he saw her as his last hold over Jane, he'd made that very obvious; the last weapon in his arsenal against her. By not signing the papers, he thought he still had some control over her life. Jane stared incredulously at Toby, she had no idea how he had managed this but she now held the signed and witnessed papers in her hand. It was real. They really *would* be a family now.

"They just need swearing by a judge when you two get home, but I've got all the details you need to sort it out when you get back. I've also talked to Freya too; she's cool with the whole new family thing you seem to having going on. I think she really likes you, Ol. God only knows why."

Ollie playfully punched Toby in the shoulder, causing him to step back and regain his balance. Ollie shook his head in disbelief. "How, though, I mean you didn't do anything stupid, did you, mate?" he asked.

Toby scrunched his nose. "Nah, of course not. These two are my family too you know. You're not the only one with connections; I can pull a few strings of my own, when I need to."

Jane presumed they'd never know *exactly* what it had taken to make Dave sign away his rights; that would niggle away at her in the future she knew but today was all about the positives. She had her family and friends, they enveloped her and Freya with all the love and security they could ever wish for. She'd tackle the truth out of Toby sometime in the future. He was useless at keeping secrets from her anyway.

Jane hugged her friend tightly. "Thank you!" was the only thing she could manage to say, her day was now complete. Freya would become a Miller too, as soon as they got back home. No longer would she worry about her daughter not having the same surname as her.

Toby hugged her back even tighter. "Don't thank me, Janey, just be happy. That's all the thanks I need. Oh, and you might want to check out the picture Freya drew for you guys. It's in the envelope too, she made me promise to give it to you."

Ollie searched inside the white envelope again, pulling out a small piece of paper with some colourful drawing on it. It was a picture of Jane in her wedding dress, standing in between Freya and Ollie. She'd had Toby help her write on it who the people were. Next to the drawing of Ollie, it simply said, 'Daddy Ollie'. Jane looked up in time to see the single tear run down his cheek as he took in the enormity of what he was looking at.

Toby pulled him into a man hug, patting him on the back to show he understood. "Just take care of them for me. They're kind of special."

Ollie nodded, running his hand across his cheek to clear the wetness away. "Goes without saying."

An hour later Jane stood on the deck of the villa again, only this time she wasn't alone, her new husband stood cradling her from behind as they sipped champagne. Everyone had drifted off to their own villas; Freya had finally agreed and gone with her grandparents for the evening, despite the epic tantrum she had thrown when she realised she wouldn't be staying with Toby and Jenna for the night. For one solitary minute, Jane thought Toby was going to give in and allow her to go with them; that was until he'd checked out the look of dismay on his girlfriend's face. He'd swiftly changed tack and helped convince Freya they could have breakfast together if she was good and went to bed.

Ollie cuddled up behind his new wife, his arms enveloped her waist as he held her close. "You look sad,

Jane. You can't be sad on our wedding day. What's wrong, babe?"

Jane stared out watching the rain hit the ocean, listening to it hitting the roof of the deck. A shiver ran through her body causing goose bumps to spring up across her flesh. "It's the rain, I hate rain. It's always a bad day when it rains. Do you think it's a bad omen?" Her thoughts drifted back to her past, a past where it had always been raining with no signs of any let up. A past where she'd struggled at the time to see a way out. Funny how the rain brought it all back to the forefront of her mind.

Ollie took the glass from Jane's hand, placing it on the table next to his. "Come here, I can fix this." He stated confidently. He was all about fixing whatever he needed to. He hadn't failed yet, and it was clear to Jane he had no intention of tonight being any different.

"Even you can't make the rain stop, Ollie. You're good but you can't perform miracles." Without speaking he gently pulled on her hand, leading her off the deck onto the wet sand. She laughed, wondering what on earth he had planned. "What are you doing? Are you mad? We'll get soaked, Ollie, let's go inside." Jane tried to make a move back onto the deck but he wouldn't let her. Instead he slipped his arm around her waist and pulled her close.

He leaned close and kissed her tenderly. "You

know what, Mrs Miller?" he whispered. "Sometimes you have to embrace it. I read a quote once on some social media site that said 'Life isn't about waiting for the storm to pass; it's about learning to dance in the rain'. And I don't know about you, wife, but boy do I wanna dance."

With that he began twirling Jane around slowly, swaying her to some imaginary music that played in his head, dipping her low, making her laugh out loud as it continued to rain down hard on them, gone were the gentle raindrops, they'd been replaced by huge, heavy ones now but neither of them cared.

With each spin and each drop of cleansing rain, Ollie was carefully erasing all of Jane's associated memories, replacing them with one fantastic new one that she would treasure forever.

Acknowledgements

First and foremost, the biggest thank you goes to my family for putting up with my absence while I sit and play with my imaginary friends and create new ones daily. I couldn't do this without their support.

My editor Lisa Hobman, for working your magic on this one and helping me produce something I'm proud of. I can't thank you enough for your patience and kind words. You rock, Lady!

My cover designer, JC Clarke, you are simply amazing! Thank you.

Lastly but most importantly, to everyone who has read any of my books, thank you for taking the chance and reading my words.

About the Author

Caroline lives in Leeds, West Yorkshire with her husband and two of her three children, her eldest having flown the nest. She started writing in 2012 and hasn't stopped since.
She is the author of The Risk Series and Blink which is a standalone contemporary romance.

You can keep up with Caroline and her releases on facebook: www.facebook.com/authorcarolineeaston.

Follow her on Twitter: @carolinelou70

Books By
caroline easton

The Risk Series

Taking a Risk

Worth the Risk

Risking it All

Standalone

Dancing in the Rain

Blink

Printed in Great Britain
by Amazon